For Stanzie, being herself is more dangerous than ever.

There's no place like home...or is there? When Stanzie is asked to investigate her birth pack--Mayflower–she isn't prepared for what she finds. No one respects the Alphas and the newest adult member of the pack is being encouraged to leave. Why?

To make matters worse, the men are dangerously intent on mating and shifting with her. How far will the pack she thought she knew go to get what they want? Without her bond-mate, Liam, Stanzie must face this alone and, barely ahead of the threat of violence, solve the mysteries, and fast.

Books by Amy Lee Burgess

The Wiolf Within Series
Beneath the Skin, Book One
Scratch the Surface, Book Two
Hidden In Plain Sight, Book Three
Inside Out, Book Four
About Face, Book Five
Across the Line, Book Six

Published by Kensington Publishing Corporation

Inside Out

The Wolf Within Series

Amy Lee Burgess

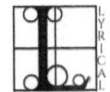

LYRICAL PRESS
Kensington Publishing Corp.
www.kensingtonbooks.com

This one is for Portia Scott Palko and her enthusiastic support of my writing over the years. The magic of friendship never ceases to amaze me.

Acknowledgements

Heartfelt thanks go out to Nerine Dorman for editing this one for me. Her eagle eye has saved me from trouble more times than I care to count. Kim Murphy also gets a shout out for being my awesome beta reader. And to everyone at Lyrical Press, especially Renee Rocco and her fabulous cover art skills.

Chapter 1

When I woke, I was in bed with two men. One of them, my Alpha Paddy O'Reilly, had his hand on my ass. The steady, inhale exhale of his breath was warm against the back of my neck.

The other man, Liam Murphy was my bond mate. Deeply asleep, he lay curled in a ball at the extreme edge of the king-sized mattress, his back to me. Still I'd managed to hook one ankle over his in my sleep. Awake, I'm sure I never would have done it because I was angry with him.

He hadn't been there for my tribunal. Though I'd begged him to stay with me, he'd gone to Virginia to search the Pack's archives for a case precedent which would have spared me from being put to death on a murder charge. However, I saved myself—or rather, my wolf had. She'd shown the Councilors on the tribunal the way to absolve me. In the end, I'd been commended for my service to the Great Pack—a twist I'd never expected even in my wildest imaginings. I'd been convinced I was doomed.

Thoughts of the tribunal and Murphy's absence made sleep impossible. After I lifted Paddy's hand off my ass, I wriggled from beneath the comforter and sheets, and slid down to the end of the bed.

My reflection in the mirror over the dresser frightened me a little. Damn I needed to wash my hair. Or at least brush it. I pushed blond snarls away from my face and stared at my eyes. Darker blue than normal. Definitely troubled.

"Bullshit," I muttered and stalked across the bland beige carpeting. I made a pit stop at my suitcase, which inconveniently blocked access to the bathroom. I threw the first things that came to hand—jeans, a t-shirt, and underwear—over my shoulder. Then I snatched up my toiletries and makeup bag, and took a long, hot shower.

The scent of hotel body wash and shampoo clung to my skin when I emerged forty minutes later.

Paddy O'Reilly, leader of my pack, Mac Tire, hung up the phone on the nightstand and turned to give me a cheerful smile. His curly black hair never looked neat, but the extreme state of bed head he boasted this morning was truly phenomenal. Yet, he still managed to look appealing. How did men do things like that? It wasn't fair.

"Room service is on the way. Let them in if I'm still in the shower, okay?" The Irish lilt to his voice reminded me of Murphy's. By association, my gaze slid to the figure still huddled beneath the comforter. He hadn't shifted position and, while he wasn't exactly snoring, he breathed loudly.

Paddy followed my gaze and grinned. "Dead to the world, he is. Be that way for several hours by my estimation. Guess we won't be heading back to Boston today, will we?"

I scowled. "We could wake his ass up."

Paddy gave my wet hair a friendly tousle on his way past to the bathroom. "Nah. He needs his sleep, Stanzie. He hasn't done anything but grab cat naps here and there for the past four days. Boston will still be there tomorrow and the day after that too, I suspect."

But I wanted to leave Connecticut *now*. I'd wanted to leave yesterday when the tribunal cleared me.

The tribunal had really hung me out to dry emotionally. I'd had some awesomely terrible experiences over the past three years, but that had been one of the worst of my whole life. Since I'd turned thirty, my life had blown up and everything I'd thought I'd have until I grew old and died had been systematically yanked away from me until I clutched at what was left with increasing desperation.

I tried to live on the bright side, only it was getting harder and harder to find anything but darkness.

Liam Murphy was one of the brightest things that had happened since my first bond mates had died in a car crash the night of my thirtieth birthday. Six months ago, under strange and dramatic circumstances, we'd bonded. Somewhere along the line, I'd fallen in love with him. He had no clue whatsoever that I loved him.

I knew and accepted, sort of, that he'd never truly love me as he'd loved his dead bond mate, Sorcha, but I had thought we were great friends and even better bond mates. Now my faith had been seriously shaken. Something in me had broken when he'd left me to face the tribunal alone. Other Advisors had also searched the archives for a precedent to clear me. He could have let them do it and stayed with me, and I tried to understand his reasons, but it was so hard.

Murphy had plead exhaustion and fallen into a deep sleep the minute we'd walked into Paddy's downtown Hartford hotel room last night, but usually he did not curl into a fetal ball at the extreme edge of the mattress to avoid me. Normally he met my eyes when he talked to me.

My life was once again a shit mess. The first step to make it less shitty would be to leave Connecticut behind, but Murphy had to sleep.

I had very little sympathy. He could sleep when we got to Boston. With a rattling briskness, I whipped aside the floor length curtains across the hotel windows. Hideous late-morning sunlight jabbed my eyeballs and I muffled a curse. Fucking sun. What was I? A vampire?

Meanwhile Murphy hadn't moved a muscle. Oblivious.

I shaded my poor eyes with one hand and forced myself to stare out the window. The hotel overlooked the Connecticut River, but not from our room. We had a view of a glass-and-steel office building which accounted for the truly appalling glare, and three stories below, a sidewalk where several young saplings were trained against sticks and surrounded with wire fencing for protection.

The hotel boasted the largest ballroom in the city and I'd played my harp there several times for wedding receptions when I'd belonged to the Riverglow pack. If I closed my eyes, I could conjure up the peach-and-cream floral pattern of the carpeting and the phantom scent of baked stuffed shrimp and prime rib. I hadn't played a harp in nearly three years and it was more than that since I'd played professionally. Did I still remember how?

I let the apricot-colored curtains fall from my hand and turned to the king-sized bed. Murphy was still scrunched up beneath the covers. Just his blondish brown hair protruded. And one bare arm.

From the bathroom Paddy burst into an Irish folk song. I understood one word in five. Maybe. He had a pleasing baritone that shook the shower gel off the side of the tub by the sound of it. Or maybe the container slipped through his fingers. My enhanced hearing made it sound like he showered with the bathroom door wide open. No, wait, the bathroom door *was* wide open.

I almost tripped over the dark peach footstool that matched the armchair by the windows. Everything in the room was peach, apricot, cream, or pale blue. Except for the wallpaper. That had wide yellow stripes on a cream background. Or maybe vice versa, I couldn't decide.

On my way to shut the damn bathroom door, someone knocked on the front door. Room service.

Great. My hair still hung in wet strings around my face. I had no idea where the hair dryer was, though I suspected it was in the bathroom where Paddy currently shook the walls with his voice.

I cast a look at Murphy curled in the bed. Not a twitch of movement. With a sigh, I opened the door.

The bellboy wheeled in a cart. He was maybe eighteen. He looked at my wet hair and Murphy's bare arm against the king-sized mattress. Paddy's exuberant singing vibrated the shower curtain which was visible through the open bathroom door.

"Niiice." He gave me a lewd smile and made a production of removing the silver covers off the plates. Appetizing smells wafted into the air— eggs, bacon, butter, toast.

I fumbled a five dollar bill from my pocket and shoved it into his hand. He continued to gaze at me lasciviously. I could only imagine the tales he'd spin for the hotel staff when he left the room.

I herded him to the door and, after I locked it, I leaned my forehead against it and counted to ten, which didn't help matters.

Paddy stopped singing and shut off the water. When I heard him enter the bedroom, I turned around. "We're checking out."

Paddy elevated an eyebrow. Just one. I'd only ever seen Mister Spock on *Star Trek* pull that off. Paddy had one blue eye and one brown eye. The raised brow was above the blue eye.

Black curls were plastered down onto his skull and he wore nothing but a towel wrapped around his waist. The man's chest hair was marginally less curly than the stuff on his head. His bond pendant dangled from a gold link chain around his throat. I couldn't see which two birthstones made up the pendant because they were buried in the chest hair.

"In approximately fifty-five seconds, the entire staff of this hotel will think we spent last night in a torrid threesome."

"So?" He had another towel in his hands which he used to scrub at his hair. Curls sprang back into shape.

"So I don't care to be the object of all their lewd speculations. Plus, I hate it here." I stalked over to the room service cart and plucked up a crisp piece of bacon which I devoured in two bites.

Paddy looked around the room. "It's not the grandest hotel room in the world, but it's not hideous. For three hundred dollars a night, it better not be."

"Here as in Hartford, Connecticut, not this hotel in particular. Although now that you mention it, Paddy, this peach-and-cream color scheme gives me headache."

Perhaps in response to my rant, he nonchalantly dropped the towel around his waist and headed for the dresser.

I rolled my eyes. "Can you put on some pants, damn it? I'm trying to have a conversation about how indignant I am at the hotel staff's delusions and you're walking around without your pants. Or anything else."

He had a nice ass. Not as nice as Murphy's, but still nice.

"If you hold on for about twenty seconds I will have pants. I promise." Paddy cast me an amused look and opened one of the dresser drawers. "What do you care what Others think? They don't understand. You, Liam and I are pack mates. Pack mates frequently sleep in the same bed together. As many as the bed will hold sometimes. With or without sex involved."

I curled my lip at him. Yes, he had a point. When I'd been a member of Riverglow we'd go back to Callie, Peter and Vaughn's house after every hunt and pile in an exhausted heap on Callie's bed. No carnal thoughts in any of our heads, just exhausted sleep together.

We'd wake in an affectionate tangle half on top of each other. If I'd opened my eyes first and was on the bottom of the pile, it had sometimes taken me five minutes to extricate myself.

That seemed so long ago. Maybe I had forgotten some things about belonging to a pack.

I picked up the carafe of orange juice and took a slug. I couldn't be bothered with a glass.

"Hey, save some for me. That was supposed to be for all of us!" Paddy hastily withdrew a pair of black boxer briefs from the drawer and pulled them on.

"He who hath not pants, getteth not the orange juice," I declared and swallowed half the contents of the carafe in one long gulp.

Paddy balanced on one leg like a hairy stork and when he laughed, he had to grab the edge of the dresser so he wouldn't crash to the floor. The boxer briefs slipped down to his ankles. Truly a nice ass.

As Pack, we were not prudes and were used to group nudity. Group sex for that matter. But I still preferred to have most of my conversations with people who had their clothes on.

"I have pants, damn you, woman!" Paddy roared as I continued to suck down the orange juice.

Murphy unclosed one eye and peered blearily around the room until he found us.

"Liam, this woman is taking shocking advantage of her Alpha. My word should be law!"

Murphy struggled to focus. "Take care of Stanzie. Please, Paddy?" His fight to push aside the covers ceased as he fell back to the pillows and into sleep.

Offended, I set down the mostly empty juice carafe and stalked to the peach-colored chair by the window. I threw myself into it and drew my knees up to my chest as I stared out at the goddamn shiny glass building next door. I did not need to be taken care of. Who the hell was Murphy to delegate the assignment to Paddy as if I were some sort of weak little girl?

Paddy finished dressing—he put on a pair of dark brown corduroys over the boxer briefs, but nothing else, and fixed himself a plate of breakfast.

As he scooped eggs and bacon into his mouth, he watched me, but I refused to be drawn.

After he set down his empty plate, he got one for me and padded over on bare feet to hand it to me.

"Not hungry." My stomach gurgled. Paddy elevated an eyebrow again, this time the one above his brown eye, and put the plate on the little side table by the chair.

He went back to the cart and took the plate which would have been Murphy's if he'd bothered to get up and balanced against the edge of the dresser before he dug in.

Murphy abruptly began to snore.

I pressed an apricot-colored pillow to my chest and resisted the urge to throw it at his head.

Paddy's chewing didn't help me either. Resentment, seething and malevolent, swirled around me in an almost visible mist. Paddy smelled it—he couldn't help it with his enhanced senses—but continued to eat until his plate was once again empty.

He regarded the orange juice carafe for a moment and chose coffee instead. My stomach gurgled again. Murphy rolled over and stopped snoring.

"Are you pissed off because we haven't had the torrid threesome the hotel staff is supposedly gossiping about?"

I aimed the apricot-colored pillow at the coffee mug in his hand and scored a direct hit. Hot coffee splashed along the bottom of the dresser. The mug hit the brass handle of one of the drawers and cracked in two.

"A simple 'no, Paddy, that's not the friggin' problem, you idjit' would have sufficed." Paddy surveyed the damage with a rueful shake of his head. He found another mug and, before he poured more coffee, cast a wary look to make sure I had no more ammunition.

"Eating something might improve that temper of yours," he remarked and ducked to protect his coffee when I winged my fork at him.

"I don't want to spend the whole damn day in this cramped hotel room listening to him snore and you chew, Paddy." The smell of breakfast drove me crazy but I did not give in and grab up a handful with my fingers. Not even the bacon.

"So, who's stopping you?" He sounded impatient but not mad. Yet.

That response took me aback for a moment. He had a point. I was no longer a "guest" of the Councils, unable to leave the premises without an escort and permission. House arrest was over. I was a free woman.

Still suspicious, I said, "I can go out? Like leave the hotel?"

"The world's your oyster, woman. Well, within reason. I would like to take you out to dinner tonight so you'd need to be back here around six." He grabbed his watch from the dresser top. "That gives you nearly seven hours. That enough time for you?"

I didn't need another invitation. I leaped to my feet and dashed to the overnight case which held my shoes. All seven pairs. Before I'd even unzipped it, I started to fret. Did I have a pair with me I wanted to wear? I'd worn the ballerina flats yesterday and my Louboutin pumps didn't go with jeans, plus Murphy had given them to me and I didn't want to wear anything from him. That only left the nude pumps, knee-high brown boots, an impractical pair of red stilettos—what the hell had I been thinking when I'd packed? Sexy red stilettos at a tribunal?—my navy blue Chucks and the loafers I'd worn in the car on the way to the safe house from Vermont. Bleh. No fucking way. They still had mud on the insides from Grandmother Emma's dirt driveway.

I tossed them toward the trash can by the dresser. One of them actually made it in. Paddy ducked again until he realized I wasn't aiming for him.

Once the Chucks were tied, I stood and craned my neck around in search of a damn room card and my purse.

"I only have the one card." Paddy knew what I looked for which was somewhat amazing for a man. "Let me keep it in case I want to go out. You can knock on the door and Sir Sleeps-a-lot can let you in if you get back before me."

I opened my mouth to argue but he shook his head.

"Alpha," he reminded me and tensed, as if he expected me to throw something at him again.

I had the door half open when he called my name. I turned back and he tossed me something that jangled. I caught whatever it was automatically and stared down with dismay. A set of car keys rested in my palm. I didn't drive cars. Not since the night I'd crashed my birthday present Mustang and my bond mates, Grey and Elena, had been killed.

Paddy knew damn well I didn't drive. He had to. Murphy told him everything. I'd spent half the ride to the hotel yesterday white knuckled with fear because Murphy had been too tired to take the wheel and I hadn't known or trusted Paddy's driving. The bastard wasn't used to driving on the right side of the road, as he came from Ireland, and that had only added to my extreme anxiety. I had never been so glad to get anywhere in my life as when we'd arrived at the hotel.

Paddy had wanted me to help with the luggage and stay in the car as he parked, but the very idea of a parking lot, and an underground one at that, had proved too much. I'd shrilly demanded to be let out by the hotel entrance and I'd waited in the lobby. Murphy, exhausted as he'd been, had been forced to help with the luggage. He hadn't complained because he knew why I was scared.

In fact he'd looked absolutely guilt-stricken in the harsh lights of the elevator as we'd ridden to the third floor. He'd forgotten I would be scared to drive with Paddy. It was an indication of his level of fatigue, but at the time it had seemed yet another betrayal.

"You're fucking with me, aren't you?" I glared at Paddy and my fist closed over the keys so tightly I felt the edge of one of them dig into the flesh of my palm. It hurt.

"Maybe a little," he admitted and ducked when I threw the keys at his face. He knocked them away and they fell with a jangle to the carpet. When he looked at me, I knew I'd finally goaded him into anger.

"Throw one more thing at me, Constance Newcastle, and you'll be one sorry woman."

"Gonna beat me?" I mocked. He lunged at me and before I could escape out the door, he'd slammed it and had me pinned. I jutted my chin and braced myself for the blow, but it never came.

"I don't hit women." From his scowl, I guessed Paddy was highly insulted that I'd even entertained that notion. His mouth was approximately two inches from mine and the entire length of his body was pressed— none too gently—against mine. In fact, I found it a little hard to breathe. One of his hands was pressed flat against the door near my head, the other clamped firmly to my shoulder. A knee rested against my locked-together legs.

He elevated one of his brows again. "I do, however, kiss them. You are kinda turning me on here, woman." He dipped his mouth closer to mine and laughed uproariously when I turned my face and his lips landed on my cheek instead.

"Be a pity to make the entire staff of this fine hotel into liars, wouldn't it?"

"A threesome generally takes three people," I reminded him.

"So we'll wake Liam." Paddy moved his mouth to my ear and nibbled at my earlobe.

"Padraic O'Reilly, you let go of me," I demanded, but his breath in my ear did send a tingle down my spine. A small one, but a tingle nonetheless. Damn him.

"He did tell me to take care of you, Stanzie. I'd just be doing what he asked me. You want to make him happy now, don'tcha?" Paddy moved the hand on my shoulder south and I twisted away from his fingers.

"I don't..." I gasped when his knee nudged my legs apart. "...think this is quite what he had in mind, Paddy!"

"I've known him his whole life. You just met him six months ago. I think I might have a wee bit better understanding of how to interpret his words." Paddy nuzzled my exposed neck. "You smell fantastic, Stanzie. No perfume. Why do Pack women insist on wearing perfume and covering up their natural, gorgeous scents? Every Pack woman smells the same, yet different. You're nearly irresistible, you know that?"

"That's *why* we wear perfume. So big goons like you don't mack on us like we were catnip." I gave him a shove, but it didn't do any good.

"Every day for three days I sat next to you at that damned conference table smelling this scent and thinking what a good thing it was I was sitting down and the table was there." Paddy traced a circle on my neck with his tongue then sucked at the center of it.

"I'm going to tell Fiona on you!" Fiona Carmichael was his bond mate. And Murphy's twin sister.

"Fiona knows what Pack women's scents do to me." Paddy was supremely unconcerned. He moved his hand south again and this time found his target and gave it a gentle squeeze. "Oddly enough, she has the identical problem, only with the scents of male Pack members. Funny, isn't it?"

"Hilarious," I muttered.

"Wouldn't you rather sleep with me than have me drive you around the city?" He was back to my ear again and his tongue invaded with such skill my knees went weak.

"I'm never getting into a car with you behind the wheel again, Paddy."

"So is that a yes to sleeping with me? The bed's king-sized so Liam won't fall off. Probably." Paddy drew his nails up the side of my arm hard enough to leave red marks, but they didn't last.

"No. I'll walk or take the bus. But I seriously need you to let go of me so I can unlock the damn door."

He smiled at me before he relented and took a step backward. An entire foot of space now separated us. His playfully lustful expression was replaced by genuine affection. Paddy liked me. I had the sneaking suspicion I liked him too. I hadn't been close to my Alpha in a long time and for some reason the fact he liked me made me want to cry.

I don't know what he saw on my face, but he said, "Can't I come with you? Walking? I've never taken the bus in America yet, that could be fun."

I told myself he was just being kind and not protective. I could handle being alone. But it would be nice if I had some company.

"If you want to walk with me, you need a shirt. And shoes."

Paddy chuckled, but he did get dressed.

Chapter 2

I'd been under Pack house arrest for less than a week, so I couldn't understand the serious sense of liberation and outright joy I felt as Paddy and I walked the sidewalks of downtown Hartford.

At first we stayed near the river, but then we ventured away, lured by the promising scents of coffee and food at lunchtime as workers escaped their urban office buildings and filled the streets with their small talk, cologne and jostling elbows.

Paddy and I bought corned beef sandwiches on rye at a small deli. He took one bite of his dill pickle and grimaced, so I snatched it away and ate it before he could toss it into the trash. We sat at a small, rickety table set out on the sidewalk. The table even boasted an umbrella with most of the fringe still intact.

We ate quickly, mindful of the lunch crowd which turned tables into highly desired objects, and continued our stroll.

When we found ourselves outside a small, upscale shoe store with a wicked pair of Jimmy Choo pumps in the window, I couldn't resist.

Paddy stoically endured the half hour it took me to try on six different pairs of shoes. He checked for messages on his cellphone and grew increasingly impatient each time he saw the sales clerk head for the store room for yet another pair of shoes.

I admit the more agitated he became, the more interest I suddenly developed in a new pair. I had fun. Not as much fun as I had when I shoe shopped with Murphy because he liked it and gave me honest opinions when I paraded around the store in a pair of potential new shoes, but I enjoyed myself.

I had narrowed down my choices between a pair of Stuart Weitzman ivory crochet espadrilles and a pair of Vera Wang Lavender leopard print ballet flats when Paddy's phone rang. He'd been in the middle of another hopeless search for new text messages, and the noise startled him so he nearly dropped the damn thing. He caught it before it escaped and, with a grateful smile, pressed talk.

I didn't pay attention to the call because I had a serious decision to make. Just as I was about to definitely settle on the espadrilles—perfect for summer even if they were twice as expensive as the ballet flats—Paddy snapped his phone shut.

"Stanzie, we need to go." Something in his voice was off and all thoughts of shoes fled my mind.

With a mumbled apology to the sales clerk, I hastily retied my Chucks and followed Paddy out to the sidewalk.

A cab idled at the curb and Paddy hailed it. Some people have taxi magic, others, like me, don't.

"What's wrong?" I asked as the cab pulled into midday traffic and headed for the river.

Beside me, Paddy looked extremely tense. "I'd rather wait and explain at the hotel. Liam needs to hear this too and I don't want to do it twice."

That made sense, but it also made for an uncomfortably silent ride. Luckily, it was a short one.

* * * *

Murphy was still in bed when Paddy and I entered the hotel room, but he was awake. He turned his face toward the door as we walked in. He'd obviously heard us in the hall. Although he didn't bother to hide his tired expression, he appeared a lot more rested than he had the day before.

One look at Paddy's grim face and Murphy knew something was wrong. He sat up in bed, the covers pooled around his waist. He was naked—Murphy preferred to sleep naked unless it was freezing cold outside—but he was completely unselfconscious about it.

So was Paddy. He moved to the edge of the bed and had me sit by Murphy. I'd had some time to think about it in the cab ride and figured I knew what Paddy had to say.

Councilor Jason Allerton's bond mate had died. Allerton had left her on her deathbed to come to the last day of the tribunal and he'd told me it was simply a matter of days, maybe hours, before she passed away.

"I've afraid I've got some bad news." Paddy's voice was hushed as he prepared us for the blow. I braced myself and felt Murphy's breath on the back of my neck. It was unexpectedly comforting.

"Bethany Dillon died this morning," Paddy told us and even though I was prepared to hear about death, it was not hers I'd expected.

* * * *

Reflexively, I spit out a mouthful of something foul. For a moment I am dazed, not knowing what I look at but then it comes to me. Shredded skin. I am staring at shredded skin.

Vomit chokes my throat then sprays in liquid chunks against the dirt wall. It smells of blood and bacon and I puke again. When I wipe my mouth with the back of my hand, it comes away bloody but I am not hurt. It is not my blood.

Bethany is very quiet—I recall she is there and after that I remember where we are. I can hear her hammering heart almost as loudly as I can hear my own.

The stink of blood and terror is overpowering, but underneath it all lurks something worse. Death.

I am in a corner behind the metal hospital gurney. I use it as a support so I can stand because my legs are weak and unresponsive.

A figure sprawls in the dirt by the ladder. A man's body dressed in jeans and a t-shirt that is now more red than white. Face up with throat torn away in ragged chunks. Sightless eyes stare up at absolutely nothing. A mouth contorts in a silent scream of both terror and rage. Nate is dead and my wolf has killed him.

I clap a hand to my mouth not sure if I am going to puke, laugh or scream. If not for the gurney, I would collapse to the ground.

I told you not to kill him. *Inside my head my voice is mournful. Wolf-on-human violence could have been excused in this situation, but there is no defense for deliberate murder. My wolf hadn't even hesitated. I remember everything with a vivid suddenness that makes me cry out, my voice muffled by my hand.*

He deserved it. He fucking deserved it. *My voice is loud in my ears even though I don't speak aloud. Loud as if to drown out the very treachery of the thought itself. He. Deserved. It.*

"Stuh—Stanzie?" *Bethany sounds very young and scared, but also hopeful. If she can see Nate's ravaged body, it doesn't freak her out the way it does me.* "You shifted back. Can you get me free? Please?"

For the first time I can see her. When I do, I start to cry. Her body is a mass of bruises and burn marks. The wrist and ankle restraints have chafed so badly she's bled and her wounds are infected. I can both smell that and see the swollen red streaks that ooze a puslike liquid. Her hair might have been blond, but now it is a matted, greasy mop of indeterminate brown. Blue, feverish eyes lock to mine pleadingly.

"Hang on," I force myself to say past tears that clog my throat. There is no time for crying. I have to look for the keys in Nate's pockets. That means I have to go near him and face what I've done to him up close.

* * * *

Someone made a sound like an injured animal and a split second after I heard it, I realized it had been me.

Murphy leaned his forehead against the back of my skull. The spot where I'd hit it when Nate had knocked me into the woodpile in the shed was still sore. Every morning for a week, I'd woken with the sick residue of a headache. Murphy avoided the sore spot with his forehead, but his lips were a millimeter from it. I wondered if he knew it was there. If he *remembered* it was there. He'd found it the night I'd gotten it, but he'd been gone for the next three days so maybe he'd forgotten.

"How?" I didn't even recognize my own voice, twisted as it was with anguish and bewildered anger. We'd gotten her out of that root cellar alive. How could she be dead now?

"Infection," Paddy watched me closely. "She had a miscarriage while she was...in the root cellar and although they did a D-and-C, it was too late. Infection had already set in."

"From the beer bottle. From being raped by a beer bottle," I snarled. Paddy winced, his face pale. I sucked in my breath as the whole world narrowed to a small pinhole while black spots performed a macabre dance across the tiny expanse that was left.

I wasn't even aware I'd gotten up until I was halfway across the room. I had nowhere to go and no idea what to do, so I stopped, my shoulders hunched.

"He won," I whispered. "That bastard won."

"No!" Paddy's eyes blazed as he turned to stare at me. "He did not win."

"She's dead, Paddy."

"She died in the company of her family, her pack," he argued. "I'm not telling you she wasn't in pain or scared, but she wasn't in that fucking root cellar with a madman's laughter the last thing she heard. You did that for her and nobody else."

"But she's still dead." I wasn't comforted at all. Every time I closed my eyes I could see her bruised and battered face, and the pain and terror stamped across it.

"I want my mom," she'd told me and Vaughn when it was all over as we tried to get the damn wrist and ankle shackles off of her. "I want my mom."

My own mother's face flashed before my eyes and I saw her walk behind my father across the conference room floor after he'd renounced me as their daughter in front of the tribunal. She hadn't looked back.

I burst into tears.

Both Murphy and Paddy moved toward me, but it was Paddy I went to. He'd been there in the conference room when I'd had to recount the hellish hours I'd spent chained up with Bethany in Grandmother Emma's root cellar. He'd been there when my parents had ripped me to shreds in front of the New England Regional Council and three members of the Great Council.

He enfolded me in his arms and rocked me while he crooned something comforting in my ear. He smoothed my hair, careful to avoid the sore spot. He remembered it was there.

* * * *

Paddy rummaged in the mini fridge while I sat on the peach-colored chair and blew my nose into a tissue he'd pressed into my hand as he'd settled me gently. Beyond in the bathroom, the sound of running water as Murphy showered, provided a strange counterpoint to the soft jingle of small glass bottles.

"Gin, vodka or tequila?" Paddy held three nipper bottles in front of me and I shuddered.

"Is there orange juice? If there is, I'll take the vodka. Isn't there any wine?"

"Not strong enough." He returned to the fridge and rummaged around for a can of juice.

I cast the used tissue toward the wastepaper basket near the desk and missed spectacularly. My nose still ran, so I snatched another tissue from the box on the end table and blew.

Late afternoon sunlight slanted through the vertical blinds drawn across the window and fell in stripes across the bed. I could see the indentation of Murphy's head in the pillow. His socks were on the floor beside his jeans and one of his Timberland boots. The other one was probably under the bed with his shirt and underwear.

The crack the orange juice can made as Paddy opened it competed with the sound of the shower for a moment. Even from half a room away I could smell the vodka.

"Is there ice?" I wondered and Paddy swore good-naturedly before he grabbed the ice bucket on the dresser and headed for the door.

"Be right back," he promised and was gone.

The water shut off and the shower curtain rings chattered together as Murphy drew the curtain back. A moment later, the buzz of his electric razor filled the air. I blew my nose for the third time and leaned back against the chair, overwhelmed by a sudden dispirited lassitude that sucked all the vitality out of my bones and left me bereft and powerless.

I was crying again when Murphy walked into the room with a towel wrapped around his waist. His hair was wet but combed and the zig-zag pucker of the bullet scar on his right forearm was a vivid reminder Murphy'd come by that wound while protecting me. He'd covered me and exposed himself, and now he'd always have the scar to prove it.

He saw my tears right away but didn't say anything. Instead he found a clean pair of briefs from his leather overnight case then pulled on his jeans.

The muscles of his back and neck were so tense they vibrated. He pulled a fresh tissue from the box and handed it to me. When I took it, our fingers brushed.

"I'm sorry, honey." His voice was a low rasp. He sounded exhausted still, and his eyes were bloodshot.

"Gin or tequila?" I asked him and he blinked at me. I gestured toward the mini fridge.

"Paddy's making drinks. I called the vodka and that leaves gin or tequila."

He grimaced. "What happened to beer?"

"Not strong enough," Paddy said as he came through the door, a bucket of ice in hand.

"Gin," Murphy said with the air of someone forced to do something totally against his principles.

"Please don't tell me you want something exotic to go with it and make me go out and search again." Paddy rolled his eyes.

"Ice is hardly exotic. And it's not like you had to go to the Arctic to hand chip it." I pointed out.

"You ever try finding ice machines in hotels?" Paddy asked me as he slipped three or four ice cubes into my drink.

"Is there tonic water?" Murphy knelt by the mini fridge to look.

"For about six dollars there might be a wee little mouthful."

Murphy gave him a look. "I'll pay."

"Like hell, Liam Murphy."

"You rich, Paddy?" I asked as I took a sip of the drink. It was strong but the can of orange juice was too far away to reach.

"I'm Alpha of Mac Tire," he told me as if that explained everything.

"While he's Alpha, he's got access to the pack funds. They're..." Murphy searched for a suitable word. "...considerable."

"But when you're not Alpha?"

"Ah, then I'll have to subsist on my bond mate's generosity." Paddy's sigh was mournful. "'Tis a terrible thing to have a bond mate with more money than you."

Despite myself I laughed. In our duo, I was the one with the bond mate who had more money.

Paddy looked enormously pleased with himself because he'd made me laugh.

"You get the tequila," Murphy reminded him as he poured a can of tonic water into his gin.

"I'm Alpha and I have to drink the tequila. What the hell is wrong with this picture?" Paddy said. He unscrewed the cap of the nipper bottle and held it aloft.

His face became serious. "To a brave girl who suffered more than she should have at the hands of a perverted and evil man. May she find herself in a better place surrounded by family and pack that passed before her." He downed the contents of the bottle in two swallows.

Tears burned in my eyes again as I gulped at my screwdriver. Murphy's face was solemn and shadowed and he clenched his glass tightly as he drank.

"The funeral's tomorrow. They've asked us to go." Paddy tossed the empty tequila bottle at the waste basket and scored.

I didn't say anything. The cold glass in my hand became the center of my universe for a few seconds until Murphy said, "You don't have to go, Stanzie."

"Oh, yeah," I said. "I swoop in and rescue her and then don't bother to show up at her funeral because she had the temerity to die on me. That's great."

"You don't have to go." Ice cubes shifted in his glass as he drained the rest of his drink and set it aside.

"You think I'm such a coward, don't you?" I was angry and full of grief, and there was nothing to pin a target to except the first person who spoke. The same person who had conveniently skipped out on my tribunal and consequently had no idea what was going on in my head—he only thought he did, which was doubly infuriating.

"I think Maplefair has a lot of bloody nerve asking you back there after what you went through. That doesn't mean you're a coward if you don't want to go." Murphy found a navy blue t-shirt and put it on with angry, economical moves.

"What I went through was bullshit compared to what Bethany did." I wanted to throw the glass at his face but didn't mostly because I was aware of Paddy as he watched us.

"Don't underestimate the effects of what you went through, Constance. She may have been down there longer and tortured, but your wolf tore Nate's throat out. That is not something you get over in a matter of a few days."

"Oh, thank you for pointing out how fucked up I'm supposed to be over this, Murphy. Jesus, I wonder what I would do if you weren't around to tell me these things? Oh, yeah. I'd do just fine on my own. Like I did for the whole tribunal."

"Are you going to hold it over my frigging head for the rest of our lives that I wasn't there for that goddamn tribunal?" Murphy's eyes gleamed with a dangerous fury.

"Nice. Now you're angry at me. *You* are angry at *me*. You can turn it around and play the martyr all you like, but the truth is you know you were wrong and not admitting it is not going to change anything."

"I was not wrong." Murphy stormed over to his boots and stuffed his feet into them without benefit of socks. "You're too damn stubborn to acknowledge that I was trying to help you."

"Save me, you mean." My voice was savage. Paddy's gaze went back and forth between us as if he watched a brutally competitive tennis match.

"What is the fucking difference?" Murphy demanded.

"That's the biggest problem. You don't know and you can't tell the difference or see how insulting it is that you think I'm so fucking weak that I need you to save me because I'm not capable of doing it on my own. Go to hell, Liam Murphy!"

"You were on trial for your life!" Murphy's voice shook he was so angry. "You could have been put to death. Can you set your damn ego aside for one minute and see it from my perspective? I had to do everything I could and finding that damned precedent was the one thing I knew for sure would save your life. It had nothing to do with whether I thought you incapable of saving yourself. You couldn't search for the precedent, but I could. That's why I did it.

"If saving your life is a crime, then I confess. I'm guilty as hell of at least trying my damndest to do it. Just because it ended up the tribunal set its own precedent, doesn't invalidate my decision to search for one that already existed.

"I'd do the same thing over again, you know that? The same fucking thing."

He glared at me, his mouth tense and tight before he slammed out the door.

Paddy watched it for a moment and abruptly headed across the room. His hand on the knob, he turned back. "Stay here." The door banged behind him.

My hand shook as I set aside my half-drunk screwdriver, and curled up in the chair.

* * * *

Hours later Murphy and Paddy returned to the room. They smelled of wind and beer, as if they'd gone for a long walk after a visit to a bar. They were not in the slightest bit intoxicated, and Murphy's anger had burned out. Paddy took one look at me, swore under his breath, and went into the bathroom. Water began to gush from the shower.

I hadn't moved in the chair since they'd left. My legs, drawn up beneath me, had long since lost all feeling. My head hurt both because of the sore spot on the back of my skull and no dinner. Half a vodka and orange juice had not helped.

If my legs hadn't been numb, I would have crawled into bed long ago but I was afraid to get up because I thought I would fall. So I sat with my head against the back of the chair, eyes open but not focused on anything in particular.

"Stanzie?" Murphy kept his voice low when he talked to me and came to stand close by the chair. If I wanted to see his face I had to turn my head. But I kept it still. He knew I heard him though, my body betrayed me as it always did when he was near.

"It's late, honey. You want to go to bed? We'll need to get up early tomorrow to drive to Vermont."

"Did you eat anything?" My voice was hoarse, as if I'd shouted for hours on end when all I'd done was kept silent.

"We ate at a sports bar a few blocks from here. You hungry? I could order you something from room service if you like." He sat on the foot stool and reached out a hand to touch me, but let it fall short of actual contact.

He said, "I should have been there with you, but I didn't want to lose you and I had to do all I could."

"I had people," I said. "Paddy and Vaughn and Jossie. Kathy Manning."

"But you wanted me," he said. "I let you down."

"I am scared to go to Maplefair," I admitted painfully. "I am a coward."

"No, you are not. You are one of the bravest people I know. If you had a fan club, I'd be the president."

I opened my eyes and he had the same look of infatuation on his face he'd had a lot lately when he looked at me. I didn't understand it. It couldn't be infatuation because he loved Sorcha. He was fond of me, devoted even, but he would never love me the way I loved him. Every time he stared at me that way I wanted to cry because it was so hard to know all I'd ever be to him was a dear friend and companion. Someone to take care of and to save and keep him from mourning Sorcha's loss.

Chapter 3

I was restless. Paddy's profile was clear from my vantage point in the backseat of the Prelude as he slouched in the front passenger bucket. At some point, he must have given Murphy the Mac Tire pack ring, because it gleamed on the middle finger of Murphy's right hand which I could plainly see as he gripped the steering wheel.

We were all dressed in funereal black, and Paddy had managed to calm his wildly curly hair somehow.

Each passing mile on the highway brought us inexorably closer to Vermont—to Maplefair's territory in Easton.

Part of my restlessness could be traced to that fact, but a lot of it was simply being confined in the cage of the car.

Murphy, exquisitely attuned to my rising level of agitation as he always was when we drove together, cast me a sympathetic look in the rear-view mirror.

"There's a rest stop two miles ahead," he told me. "Just over the border."

I gulped. The Vermont border. After we crossed, it was only another hour or so until our destination.

Paddy checked his watch, a subtle reminder that we were due in Easton by noon, and it was already edging past eleven.

Aside from a slight tightening of his mouth, Murphy ignored him and switched lanes to position us for the exit. Paddy sighed and slouched further into his seat.

He'd spent the past three hours in rapt observation of the New England scenery. Not that he'd gotten much from the highway. It must have been sufficiently different from Ireland to interest him because he'd seemed mesmerized. He'd slurped Dunkin' Donuts coffee and cursed when powdered sugar from his jelly doughnut had sprinkled across his black dress pants but, aside from that, had kept mostly quiet.

Murphy had concentrated on driving—probably in an effort to keep my agitation at a minimum. I'd sat in the backseat and munched glazed doughnut holes and sipped French vanilla-flavored coffee. My head hurt—a stress headache combined with the knock on the head I'd received nearly a week ago. Today was Tuesday. Tomorrow would make one week since I'd woken in Grandmother Emma's root cellar chained to a metal morgue gurney, with Bethany Dillon chained to her own gurney a feet away.

Bethany. Her name swept a rush of guilt and hopelessness through me and I sighed.

"Almost there, honey," Murphy said from the front seat. He was right. The car was on the off-ramp and, a moment later, we pulled up in front of a low brick building which housed public restrooms and a small vestibule filled with racks of brochures printed by the Vermont State Department of Tourism. The door to the vestibule was chained and bolted shut, but the restrooms were open.

The moment the car stopped, I was out the back door and onto the asphalt pavement. A caressing May breeze lifted the strands of hair around my face and blew away some of the restless tension that twisted my muscles painfully. I couldn't bear the thought of spending even one second of the precious few minutes we'd linger here in the cramped confines of the ladies' restroom and instead began to pace so I could feel the wind against my skin.

I was still alive. Alive and free.

Paddy leaned against the car and consulted his cellphone for messages. I'm pretty sure he didn't expect to find any, but the rest stop's scenery did not seem to enthrall him as much as the highway's.

Murphy watched me pace for a moment then, with a resolute shift of his shoulders, he joined me.

He made sure not to touch me—of course he wouldn't—but he was near enough that I was comforted. I wanted to touch him but I didn't. My emotions were shredded.

Fear, bottomless and dreadful, whipped through my body and snagged in my brain where it turned my thoughts into a whirling mass of fleeting impressions—the cold of the gurney against my bare skin—the stink of Bethany's fear and unwashed, infected body. Nate's laughter in the wood shed as I swung the wrench ineffectually at his head.

Then the tribunal. The relentless damnation of my poor, damaged wolf.

"God, I wish I were anywhere else but here," I whispered. Murphy gave me a sympathetic smile.

"Not too late to turn the car around and go back to Boston." He was so close I smelled his cologne, but so far away he might have been on the moon.

I wrapped my arms around myself and walked toward a chain link fence that separated the rest stop from a small stretch of pine trees. The crisp scent of evergreen was pungent in my nose and I drew deep breaths in an attempt to cleanse myself. My head hurt again and, when I touched the sort spot at the base of my skull, I winced.

Murphy waited patiently but, after a moment, Paddy stalked over and assessed the situation.

"She wouldn't suffer half so much if she had the pack bond to fall back on." Paddy glared at Murphy as if to accuse him of something. Murphy's jaw tightened but he didn't say anything.

"Pack bond?" With reluctance, I turned away from the pine trees. My fingers were hooked in the spaces between the chain links so hard the wire left indentations. My brain was less fuzzy and the awful memories had retreated. For the moment, anyway.

"That's right, you've been in small packs all your life," Murphy murmured. The May sunshine illuminated his brown hair and brought out the gold highlights.

"Sure and you've heard of it, though." Paddy was astonished and almost angry. His different-colored eyes bored into my face as if he could find the knowledge buried in my brain somewhere if he only probed hard enough.

"You need at least forty people in a pack to do it, otherwise the Alphas have too much control." Murphy spoke again as Paddy stared at me.

"I know what it is," I told them both. Did they think I was an idiot— ignorant of the Pack's history? "I just didn't think any pack did that anymore."

The pack bond was mind control pure and simple. Blood from both Alphas was mixed with an herbal concoction then consumed by each pack member. Through the Alphas, the pack as a whole was connected. The Alphas could exert subtle control over individual pack members. I hesitated to call it magic, it was more instinct—an innate ability unique to the Pack akin to the fusion that occurred during group sex before a hunt.

Generally it was used to bring harmony into a large, diverse and potentially dangerous group. It also sped up the healing process in injured pack members. Pack healed more rapidly than Others, but with a pack bond the healing was supposedly even more accelerated.

Amy Lee Burgess

"We have the Councils to oversee us now," I argued, although neither man with me said a word. "We don't need some barbaric method of mind control from the Dark Ages."

Paddy began to quietly fume.

"Nobody uses it to control and dominate anymore," Murphy said hastily. "It's meant to help, Stanzie. When someone in the pack is hurt—physically or mentally—the Alphas can use the pack bond to speed up healing. That's all. No Alpha in Mac Tire has abused that sacred trust in centuries. In big packs like Mac Tire, we have to have it to keep the peace."

"Then you do use it to dominate and control," I said. "I'm not going to do it."

"Friggin' Americans. One by one you bloody idiots have discarded the old ways until the Pack is a fucking shadow of what it used to be." For some reason Paddy was really angry. The scent of his fury coated my tongue and clogged my sinuses. Alphas were intimidating as hell when they really got pissed.

His words sent a paralyzing shot of ice through my veins. Paddy. Defending the old ways? Could his anger have made an idiot of his tongue? Or did he think Murphy and I weren't aware of the conspiracy within the Pack?

"In Europe packs less than forty are almost never allowed to form and if accident reduces the numbers somehow, two packs are blended together. How can you have a proper pack with only seven or eight frigging people? It doesn't work. You bounce the Alpha status between yourselves like a bloody rubber ball and nobody respects anybody. You have to work to be Alpha of Mac Tire and other packs in Europe. You have to fight and prove yourself. You don't just get handed the baton because there's only the seven of you."

"Alpha pairs are mainly for procreation," I responded before I saw Murphy's warning shake of the head. I ignored him. I wouldn't have shut up anyway.

Paddy's withering glare made me stiffen.

"Now there speaks a truly ignorant American." He raked a hand through his curly hair and grimaced when his fingers got stuck. "Oh for fuck's sake. Can we please get on our way? We're going to hold up the entire friggin' funeral debating pack culture. And you'd lose, Constance Newcastle, because you haven't got a friggin' leg to stand on."

Without waiting for us, he stomped back to the car.

"Do you think—" I began in a scared voice.

"No," Murphy said sharply.

"Just because he's your friend doesn't mean he can't be a part of it, Murphy."

"He's not just a friend. He's bonded to my twin sister. And he's my Alpha." Murphy's expression made it clear he was finished with the conversation. "Let's go." He stalked toward the parking lot and I was forced to follow, although I was far from done with the subject.

Paddy waited in the car which smelled like coffee, doughnuts and his anger. I buckled my seatbelt and avoided his eyes. Murphy slid behind the wheel and started the engine.

"I'm sorry I lost my temper," said Paddy after we'd merged onto the highway. "Now's not the time to discuss it, but the pack bond is a fact of life for members of Mac Tire.

"Later," he insisted when Murphy opened his mouth to say something.

I didn't bother to argue but there was no way in hell I was taking a pack bond. We did not live in the Dark Ages anymore, no matter what some people wanted to believe.

* * * *

My body understood where we were before my brain did. The moment we crossed the border into the small town of Easton, Vermont—Maplefair territory—I broke into a cold sweat.

Murphy's GPS device directed him to turn right and when he did, I realized we were on the pack's road and in less than two miles we'd pass a small blue mailbox and a dirt driveway that led straight to hell. And it was on my side of the damn car.

"Fuck." I spoke the word aloud before I could call it back.

"What's wrong?" Paddy had never been here before so he didn't have a clue, but I could tell by the sudden tenseness of Murphy's shoulders that he got the picture.

"I'll turn around," he told me.

"No. No, just drive fast. I'll close my eyes."

I'm not a coward, I told myself, even though I was pretty sure I was.

With my eyes shut, I felt the car accelerate then, a moment later Murphy said, "It's okay. We're nearly there, Stanzie."

"Where is there?" I asked. My black blouse clung to my ribcage like a sodden second skin. The car's interior was flooded with the unattractive sour scent of my fear.

Paddy was half turned in the passenger bucket so he could keep me in sight. Pack don't like to turn their backs on people who smell of terror. They were too unpredictable. Even in human form.

"The forest," Murphy answered. Up ahead I saw the maple trees thin out to reveal a small dirt lot crammed with cars. Most of Maplefair could have made it here on foot from their houses. The cars belonged to people from other packs. Bethany's funeral would be a big one.

Murphy parked between a light blue Toyota Camry and a forest green Jaguar that looked all too familiar—Kathy Manning's car.

Terror had left my legs weak and rubbery. I had no idea if I would be able to walk.

"Jesus Christ, I'm more scared now than I was when I woke up chained to that fucking gurney. What in the hell is wrong with me?" I pressed my clammy forehead to the window and wished I could bash through the glass with my stupid skull.

"You've had time to think about it," Murphy told me. "But Nate Carver is dead, Stanzie. Your wolf killed him. He can't harm you or anyone else anymore."

Simple statement. Obvious. Nothing I didn't already know. But it helped.

I closed my fingers around the door handle and pulled.

The parking lot smelled of dirt, oil, metal and trees. I stood in the dappled sunlight flanked by Murphy and Paddy. Several other people gathered nearby. I recognized members of Maplefair, Snowmoon, Nightclaw, Darkhunt, Wolfsong, Liberty and Riverglow—all New England packs.

Snowmoon was a Vermont-based pack like Maplefair. Darkhunt was Rhode Island—Kathy Manning's pack. Wolfsong was the premiere pack from Maine, Liberty was the New Hampshire pack, Nightclaw and Riverglow, of course, were from Connecticut. There was no sign of anyone from the Massachusetts pack, Mayflower. My birth pack. I would have been shocked if there had been. Mayflower was the oldest pack in New England, but notoriously private. They rarely attended Regional Gatherings and never outside funerals.

When people recognized me, they offered me strange smiles. They had no clue what to say to me. *Congratulations on killing the bastard? So glad the tribunal didn't put you to death? Guess your defective wolf came in handy after all?* It was better to say nothing.

Councilor Kathy Manning was the only one who came over to me and shocked the hell out of me with a fierce embrace. She smelled of floral perfume and the gold highlights in her pixie-short brown hair gleamed in the sunlight.

"No one knows what to say to you," she said in a voice loud enough that it carried.

Beside me, Murphy made a strangled noise that sounded more like laughter than a cough. He and Kathy had never quite figured out whether they liked one another.

"Maybe people are overwhelmed by all the Councilors," Rosemary Young, of the Great Council, remarked as she sauntered over. "People do tend to become tongue tied the more there are of us in one place."

Where ten seconds ago there had been empty space, now five Councilors stood ranged around me. In addition to Kathy and Rosemary, now there were also Councilors Hill, Perkins and Allerton. Save for Allerton and Young, they were all from the New England Regional Council. Allerton and Young, of course, represented the Great Pack itself.

Allerton put a proprietary hand on my shoulder. As usual, he wore a tailored designer suit. Today it was black pinstripe. His aristocratically handsome face was somber. Although Kathy was his mistress, in public they maintained a formal distance, but I'd seen the quick flash of affection in Allerton's blue eyes when he'd looked at her as he'd made his way over to us.

Power thrummed around us all.

A robin called from the branches of one of the maple trees and another answered from a few trees away.

Tires crunched on the dirt parking lot and, if it had been silent before, it suddenly became hushed. The car was an older SUV driven by my friend and former pack mate, Vaughn Pelletier. Jossie Wilbanks, Nate Carver's ex-bond mate and current Alpha of Maplefair, sat beside him in the passenger bucket. The SUV stopped just short of where we were all gathered and the back door slid open.

Gina Dillon and Ron Bradley, Bethany's parents, stumbled out, followed by Cody Brown, his parents and his twin brother, Kyle. Cody had been Bethany's boyfriend. He was devastated. The sleeves of his suit jacket were too short—he'd obviously grown a couple of inches since it had been purchased—but the waist band of the matching trousers was loose.

The grief that poured out of him combined with that of Bethany's parents and nearly drove me to my knees. If not for the steady pressure of Allerton's hand on my shoulder, I would have crashed through the underbrush and run away.

Gina Dillon held a small white urn in her shaky hands. She'd cried so much over the past day and a half that her eyes were puffy and so

Amy Lee Burgess

bloodshot I couldn't tell the color of her irises. She wore a plain black dress and sensible flats. We had to hike through the forest, after all. None of the women wore pumps, although most wore skirts or dresses. Boots were the most popular footwear choice for men and women alike.

Ron Bradley kept an arm around his bond mate's shoulders. His eyes were red-rimmed and puffy from crying.

Jossie had her hair piled on top of her head and it made her look almost regal. Her face was dreadfully pale and she wore no makeup. Dressed in an old black sheath dress that was five years out of style, she carried if off as if it were the latest fashion.

Vaughn stood beside her as she looked at all of us.

"I think we can start now," she said. She and Vaughn would become bond mates today after the funeral. Together, they would continue as Alphas of Maplefair. The entire pack was behind this mating and Jossie's continued Alpha status. No one blamed her for Nate's criminal actions.

As Alpha, she led the way, followed closely by Vaughn then Gina, Ron, Cody, Kyle and their parents. After that, the Councilors were given the opportunity to follow. Paddy, as an Alpha, had the right to fall in behind them.

Since this was a larger gathering made up of members of several different packs, it was more formal than if it had just been Maplefair.

Murphy and I went behind Paddy, and the others sorted out their ranks and made a single line behind us.

No one spoke as we walked the forest trail. Sticks and leaves crunched underfoot, and a curious robin kept pace with us for nearly a mile. He flitted from tree to tree and cocked his head so he could fix us with his bright black eyes. Most birds were afraid of us, but this one's curiosity got the better of him.

So I wouldn't have to think, I watched him and silently begged him not to abandon us and fly off. As long as he kept pace with us, I could focus on him and not the grief that surrounded us like a shimmering miasma or the muted sobs of Bethany's mother as she carried her daughter's ashes through the woods.

The thirty-five minutes it took to scatter Bethany's ashes were among the worst in my life. Too many of us stood in the traditional circle to each take a turn to say something and toss a handful of ashes, so only her parents, Jossie and Cody stepped inside the ring to the center where the urn was placed.

I kept my gaze fixed to the tips of my black boots so there was no chance I would be offered a chance to speak. My throat was so tight I could barely suck down enough air to keep upright, so there was no way I could have said anything.

Besides, I was not handling things very well. I'd thought I'd felt guilty for tearing Nate's throat out against Pack rules, but it was nothing to the total annihilation I experienced when confronted by the sight of Bethany's urn and the knowledge that I hadn't saved her after all.

If I'd been a day earlier in figuring things out would that have made the difference?

Women of the Pack could bring only one pregnancy to full term. The process of the birth rendered us barren. We could have multiple miscarriages, but once we carried to term, that was it.

Children were cherished, precious resources. Beloved by the entire pack when they were little and guided to adulthood with affection by all the adults.

Twins were more common, but Bethany, like me, had been a single child.

Gina and Ron had no remaining child to comfort them. They were alone now and their most valued contribution to the Pack was gone in so many scattered ashes.

Gina broke down in the middle of the circle and had to be led away by Rosemary Young so Ron could take her place. He managed to get through what he wanted to say, but to me it was so much lip movement. The blood pounded in my ears far too loudly for me to hear anything.

Grief infected the mourners in the circle. Tears poured down male and female faces regardless of pack affiliation. The women from Nightclaw sobbed just as hard as the women from Maplefair.

Jossie went last and, when she had solemnly scattered the last of the urn's contents and placed it upside down on the ground, she unselfconsciously stripped off her modest dress and Wal-Mart cotton underwear so she could drop on all fours and shift.

Five minutes after Jossie had shed her clothes, more than half the mourners were in wolf form. Grey wolves, red wolves, black wolves, all shades between and one, gorgeous pure white wolf—Kathy Manning.

As one they sat back on their haunches, tipped their heads back and filled the forest clearing with eerie, ululating wolf song.

Those in human form threw back their heads and joined in. Most of them could mimic the real wolf song to near perfection. Paddy's voice rose above them all—strong and wild. Murphy's howl was not as loud but indistinguishable from the sound that issued from the dark gray wolf which sat beside him.

I could not join in. Even if I'd wanted to try, my throat was clogged with grief and guilt.

I stumbled away from the circle and started back down the trail to the dirt lot. The pure white wolf kept pace with me and when we'd left the tragic wolf song behind, I said, "Kathy, you realize your clothes are back there, right? Are you going to the after gathering nude? Is this your newest fashion statement? I think I have a spare pair of heels in the trunk if you want."

The wolf sneezed and bumped the back of my knee with her head. I kept walking.

She bounded ahead of me a few paces, whirled, and then went down on her front paws, butt in the air. Her tail wagged furiously. Was she a dog or a wolf?

"You want to play?" I shook my head. "This is a funeral. Wolves are so dumb sometimes. You're twenty yards away from the circle and you've already forgotten why you were there, haven't you?"

The wolf yipped and tossed her head.

"That would be my wolf anyway. Who knows what you're thinking."

The wolf pounced on me so that she managed to wrap her paws around my neck as if she hugged me. She exhaled slobbery wolf breath in my face and swiped her moist tongue across my nose and mouth.

"Disgusting." I gave her furry chest a push, but she was a solid block of muscle. When she gave my ear a lick with her tongue, I couldn't help but smile. Damn wolf.

"I am not going to play," I told her firmly. Another push, but she would not budge, so I started to walk and she was forced to hop backward on her hind legs. Wolves are not made for maneuvers like that, so she retaliated with a mock growl and another slobbery lick.

My push had more force this time because she got down. She blocked the path with her body, but I stepped around her and kept going.

She whined and I hesitated, but then started forward again. Another whine, this time punctuated by a high-pitched yelp.

I stared at her. She wanted to play. A girl's ashes were scattered on the forest floor a few yards away and this silly wolf wanted to play. I shook my head.

She whined again, tail tucked between her legs, downcast and bereft. I had a fleeting image of my own wolf as she cringed and cowered before the wolves of the tribunal. More images of her as she ran with Grey, Elena and Vaughn's wolves in the days when she did want to play.

Why did Kathy's wolf get to play and mine didn't? Why did she get to forget that three minutes earlier she'd been a mourner at a teen's funeral while I could never escape? Would my wolf ever have the capacity to understand someone else's grief or joy? Would she ever be able to walk by the side of someone in human form and try to comfort them? No. No, she wouldn't.

Kathy's wolf crept toward me, eyes hopeful.

A stick cracked and Murphy and Paddy appeared out of the shade.

The white wolf whined softly.

"She's worried about you," said Murphy. Kathy's wolf trotted to his side and sat. Almost absently he reached down to put a hand on her head and she leaned into him trustingly.

"'Tis rude to leave the circle when the wolves sing," Paddy told me, as if I were some clueless idiot. "It's disrespectful of the dead, Constance."

"It was hard enough to be there in the first place. But the wolves made it worse. You don't understand, Paddy, your wolf is normal."

Murphy flinched.

Paddy looked up into the canopy of the trees overhead as if for inspiration or perhaps some small measure of patience. "You're so goddamn stubborn, Stanzie."

Chapter 4

"Let the feckin' thing alone," Murphy snapped on the drive back to Boston. Paddy snatched his hand away from the radio dial and muttered something acidic beneath his breath. The tension in the car ratcheted up.

"Stanzie, there's a rest area ahead. Do you want to stop?" Murphy asked and Paddy blew out his breath.

"Damn it, man, it's already frigging midnight. We've stopped twice already. We might as bloody well sleep in the frigging car at this point."

"It's all right. We don't need to stop." I kept my eyes closed. I'd tried to pretend I was asleep but Murphy knew damn well I never slept in a moving car.

"Don't you let Paddy keep you from stopping if you want to." Murphy cast a malevolent look at Paddy, who glared back.

"I'm not keeping you from stopping. I'm just trying to point out it's getting late and we're all knackered. The sooner we get home, the sooner we can go to bed. That's all I'm trying to say."

They exchanged another antagonistic glare and I almost said I did want to stop. Anything to get a break from their bickering. What the hell was with them? They'd been tense all afternoon after Bethany's funeral. Jossie and Vaughn had gathered the pack together at the farm house for a backyard picnic. Murphy and Paddy had spent the majority of it avoiding each other. Paddy had been my constant shadow and had never left my side. At first I'd thought Murphy had been avoiding *me*, but as we drove back to Boston, I'd become more and more suspicious it was Paddy, not me, Murphy hadn't wanted to be around.

We arrived at the condo close to one in the morning and crept up the stairs into the living room. I went straight for the bedroom, and Murphy and Paddy followed me.

We slept three in the bed again even though there was a spare room. Paddy didn't hesitate to strip off his clothes down to his boxer briefs and crawl beneath the covers. Murphy's mouth tightened but he didn't protest. He shed all his clothes while I put on a nightgown.

The bed in the hotel had been a king and my bed was only a queen, so there was no way to avoid contact. I turned my back to Murphy so he could put his arm around my waist the way he always did when we slept together, but he rolled over and hugged the very edge of the mattress. His legs brushed mine, but only because the bed was too small for three. He'd done the same thing the night before. This stung.

I put one hand on Paddy's chest so I could feel the steady thump of his heartbeat. At first it was rapid and angry, but my touch gradually calmed it to a normal rate.

Contact dissolved my tension and I fell asleep soon after.

* * * *

I woke to the enticing aroma of bacon and eggs, and drifted in a daze to the kitchen. Paddy and Murphy sat stiffly at the table drinking coffee. Full plates steamed in front of them. One waited for me at my usual place.

My morning greeting was received with half-hearted smiles. Both men hid behind their coffee mugs. They must still be pissed with each other for whatever obscure reason. However, I didn't intend to miss a home-cooked breakfast and took a seat.

Paddy watched me pour ketchup on my eggs as if I were performing some sort of strange ritual.

"Want some?" I held the bottle out to him just to watch him shudder.

"I've booked seats on the four-thirty flight to Dublin," he blurted.

Murphy stared at his plate as he sopped up egg yolk with a piece of buttered rye toast.

"Four-thirty as in today?" I consulted the clock on the kitchen wall above the sink. Unbelievable. "Six hours from now?"

"I'm all packed. I'll do the breakfast dishes." Paddy sprang from his chair and began to pile the dishes on top of each other. I had only managed half a slice of bacon, but Paddy whisked my plate away as if it had been empty.

I rubbed my eyes. Somewhere I'd missed something. Maybe I was still dreaming?

"I'd better go pack," I said. Paddy clattered the dished into the sink and I winced. If half hadn't broken, we'd be lucky.

Murphy continued to push his toast through the egg yolk. He needed to shave and shower. His hair was tousled and he wore a pair of sweat pants and a Faneuil Hall t-shirt. Bare feet. His Mac Tire pack ring glittered in the late morning sunshine that streamed through the kitchen window.

Paddy's mop of black curls made me think of Medusa's serpents tangled and twisted. Any second I expected them to hiss at me and tell me to move my ass. He was still in just his boxer briefs and I couldn't decide if I thought it was sexy or rude to eat breakfast half-naked at my kitchen table. He needed to shave too.

Twenty minutes later, I stood in the doorway of the walk-in closet and helplessly surveyed the shoe racks against the walls. How the hell was I going to pack all my shoes and my clothes in three suitcases?

Murphy stood in the doorway and watched me.

"I thought we'd have time to go through my stuff and get this place together before we left. There's wash to be done and we need to clean out the fridge and the cupboards. Why do we have to leave today, Murphy?"

I turned around and stopped talking. Murphy was showered and dressed, but he still needed to shave. His expression scared me. I'd never seen him look so awful.

"Are you all right?" I went toward him, but he backed away, so I stopped.

"Honey, come sit down." His voice matched his face. Fear clouded my mind and sped up my heart. More bad news? What the hell could be left to go wrong?

I sat on the edge of the bare mattress. The sheets and comforter lay in a tangle on the hardwood floor.

Murphy sat too, but maintained a distance between us so we didn't touch. My heart beat turned erratic as if it already knew what Murphy had to tell me even if my brain did not.

"I know you gave me until August, but I think we both know that a couple of months isn't going to change anything."

Gave him until August? At first I had no idea what the hell he was talking about, but then my stomach clenched. Good thing I hadn't eaten breakfast or I would have puked.

"You're not happy. I'm not happy," he continued, but he wouldn't look at me, damn him. He wouldn't look me in the face. "You're not coming to Dublin. Paddy and I are leaving."

Paralyzed by massive shock, I sat there like a fucking statue and said nothing as my whole life crumbled beneath me.

Not happy? What the fuck was I supposed to be? Jumping around for freaking joy after my wolf had torn out somebody's throat and I'd faced a tribunal? Bethany had died anyway and Murphy hadn't been there when I'd desperately wanted him?

No, I wasn't fucking happy, but I never wanted this. I'd told him I didn't know if we were okay, but I'd also told him I needed time to think, to get things straight.

"Is this cause I won't talk to you about things?" I whispered. "Because I..."

"I'm sorry, Stanzie. It was a long shot, it would've worked. We knew that when we went into it."

Had we? I'd gone into it because he'd convinced me to do it. In Houston after he'd been poisoned and nearly died, I'd tried to leave because the conspiracy had been uncovered and I was no longer in any danger of being blamed for Rudi's death. But he'd been the one to ask me to please stay until August, to give him a chance until then.

It was only first week of May. And, despite everything that had happened, I loved him. I just needed to think. Horror and shame engulfed me. Maybe he'd finally realized I wouldn't fit in with Mac Tire and I was too different. My wolf was fucked up and so was I. Maybe he'd decided that while he could handle this when we were two people on our own, once we tried to blend into a pack, it wouldn't work. But I wanted it to work. I wanted to at least try.

He doesn't want you, Stanzie, I told myself before I begged him.

Paddy appeared in the doorway, his face somber.

I looked at him. Four days earlier after my father had renounced me as his daughter, Paddy had taken me aside to tell me that I did have family. Him. Murphy. Mac Tire. A lie? Had it been a lie?

"So he's told you, has he?" Paddy's mouth was small and tight. "Got anything to say for yourself, woman?"

It was a challenge, but I didn't know how to respond or why he'd issued it in the first place. Anything to say for myself? Did he think this was my idea? My fault?

I hung my head.

Murphy's suitcases were already packed and set by the bedroom door. I'd been the last one up this morning and he and Paddy had used the time to get him packed. Then they'd made me a hearty breakfast before they broke my heart. They'd *planned* this. I remembered all the strange looks and tension that had passed between them yesterday and how they'd disappeared for hours together the night before.

This wasn't spur-of-the-moment.

For a bad moment, I was back in the same headspace as I'd been after Grey and Elena's funeral and I'd moved here to Boston. Those first awful weeks alone in exile when I'd bitterly wished I'd died with them in the car crash because it hurt too much to be alive without them.

"I'm going to call Vaughn and have him come here," Murphy said.

"No!" My voice was sharp. I'd lost track of time and at least one minute had passed where I hadn't spoken or moved.

Murphy's face was drawn and haunted, and Paddy looked just plain miserable. Nervous tension spiked the air and made it hard for me to breathe. Silver spots danced before my eyes as my whole life collapsed into futility. What had I done wrong? I wished I'd never let him know how angry I'd been when he hadn't stayed with me for the tribunal. Maybe if I could explain to him that I didn't mean it, he wouldn't leave me.

The words wouldn't come. They stuck in my throat like burning spikes. Who was I to beg him? Fucked-up wolf, fucked-up human. Who could blame him for not wanting to bother anymore? I loved him so much, but he didn't love me. That's what I had to remember.

When I could speak I said, "I'll call him after you're gone." The digital clock on the nightstand read twelve-thirty. "You'd better go so you have plenty of time to check in at the airport."

Paddy lunged at Murphy's suitcases. He couldn't wait to be gone. I hated him in that moment. I hated him so much, the fucking lying sonofabitch. Family. Right.

Murphy got up and walked for the door.

After six months and everything we'd been through together, he was just going to fade out without even a backward look. I tried to hate him, and for a moment I did. But I couldn't sustain it.

Murphy hesitated at the door, but didn't turn around. "It's better this way. You'll see. Take care, Stanzie."

He waited for me to say something, but I was damned if I would. I'd just beg and make a fool of myself.

I held my breath. Thirty seconds later the front door banged and they were gone out of my life.

Chapter 5

Six weeks and one day later, my cellphone chirped. Literally. I had the ring tone set to the sound of crickets.

I was six feet off the ground on a small step ladder with a paint roller in my hand. My cellphone was on the bookcase across the room.

At the first chirp I jerked and nearly fell off the ladder, but when I processed that it was crickets and not the bell tone. I recovered. Sagged even. Bell was the ring tone I used for Murphy's incoming calls. Not that there'd been any.

I'd wanted to call him, but I hadn't. I heard his voice in my head *"It's better this way."* And *"I'm not happy"* and when I did, I put the phone down and walked away.

I heard Paddy ask me if I had something to say for myself and Paul renounce me as his daughter.

It wasn't better for me this way, but it was for Murphy and every time I wanted to call him, I reminded myself of this fact and, so far, I'd managed not to make the call.

Sometimes in the middle of the night, after one of my nightmares, I scrambled for the phone on my nightstand and stopped myself from calling him by the sheerest thread of self preservation. It would be emotional suicide to call after a nightmare. I'd cry and I'd beg and he'd be kind, but firm and reject me all over again. I'd stopped leaving my phone on the nightstand and instead kept it hidden in my purse at night. I unplugged the landline on the desk. It wasn't likely he'd call me in the middle of the night anyway. Not that he was ever going to call me.

The first week after he'd left, I'd spent cleaning. Walls had been scrubbed, windows had been shined, and furniture had been polished. The week after that I purged.

I found Murphy's Faneuil Hall t-shirt under the bed where he'd tossed it on the way to the shower that last day. The sweat pants were gone, but the t-shirt had been left behind. I'd worn it to bed for six nights without washing it until his smell had been completely erased by mine.

I still wore it every night, but at least now I washed it.

As I'd cleaned and purged, I'd run across several painful things. A bottle of half-drunk Jameson's that he'd bought at the corner package store. A book he'd been reading, face down on the nightstand between pages seventy-two and seventy-three. His shampoo in the shower stall.

I'd put all of it in a box in my closet unable to throw any of it away.

The third week I'd started painting. First the kitchen in a light blue edged with cream. Then the living room in an earthy cinnamon red. The hallway in the same cream as the edging in the kitchen. Sage green for the bathroom.

When the phone chirped I was in the guest bedroom, which I'd converted back into a little office. All traces of Vaughn were gone as well. He'd called me three times since Bethany's funeral and I'd managed to sound cheerful and normal, even while it killed me. He had no clue I'd been dumped, so he thought Murphy and I were still in Boston together packing the condo up for our move to Dublin. For the most part, he preferred not to talk about Murphy because he was still mad at him, and that worked in my favor. He wanted me to visit and I put him off, but I knew I couldn't do that forever. The last time he'd called, he'd asked when we were going to Dublin and I'd pretended something was boiling over on the stove and cut the call short.

I wouldn't be able to fool him for much longer but I didn't need to. After the office was painted, I only had the bedroom left and, once the bedroom was done, I would stop obsessing and face up to everything. But only after the paint dried in the bedroom.

The color I'd chosen for the office—a pale peach that verged on tangerine—had seemed much prettier in the can. I didn't know if I could face four walls of the stuff and had begun to think about cream for the remaining two walls. Or possibly a complete do-over with a different color. But I wasn't sure yet. Maybe the peach would grow on me if I gave it a chance.

I took my time to descend the ladder because I didn't want to talk to anybody, except Murphy, but managed to answer the phone just before it rolled to voice mail.

"Constance." Jason Allerton knew everything. I could tell just by the way he said my name. Fuck.

I sank onto the plastic-shrouded futon and realized I still had the damn paint roller in my hand.

"Hello, Jason."

"I just heard." He sounded accusatory and I bit my lip. Jealousy swarmed around my head like a hive of killer bees. He had talked to Murphy. Heard his voice. All I had was memory. "Are you in Vermont?"

"Boston." I gulped.

"Why not Vermont?" Allerton was angry with me and self-pitying tears glazed my eyes. The man hadn't bothered to check in with me for six weeks and now he was giving me the third degree?

"Why would I be in Vermont?"

He heard the catch in my voice and hesitated so he could choose his words carefully. "Because it would nice if you were with friends at a time like this."

"I'm fine." My throat began to close up again and I willed my air passages to stay open. I needed to tell somebody the truth. It festered inside me.

Allerton sighed in my ear. "I should have called you sooner. My bond mate passed away three weeks ago and I have been distracted."

I felt like total and complete shit now. Tears spilled down my cheeks and I dashed them away. I forgot about the paint roller and got a smear of peach paint across my cheek. Luckily I didn't get any in my damn eyes.

"I'm so sorry."

"It was a blessing. She was suffering." He clearly didn't want to talk about it. He sighed again. "I have a bit of a problem now because if you don't bond with somebody soon after your birthday, you won't be able to act as my Advisor any longer."

"You still...I mean after my wolf and..." I floundered.

"I still want you to be my Advisor."

"But you..." I faltered as I tried to tread carefully.

"I need a bond mate too?" He finished for me. "Yes, I know. I have three months to find someone suitable before I'm asked to leave the Great Council. Rest assured, I will not be leaving the Council. There's too much to be done to allow myself to slip into self-pity."

"Kathy Manning loves you," I whispered. I hardly dared to believe I had the guts.

There was a strangled noise from the other end of the phone. Was he crying or laughing?

"Kathy's got a bond mate and a position on the Regional Council. She endeavors to one day join the Great Council. As a former mistress, particularly because I'd have nothing to do with her appointment, she stands a chance. As my bond mate she would be ineligible. Kathy

Manning is not one of my options, but thank you." I couldn't tell if he was being sarcastic or not. Maybe it was a sore spot. Maybe he'd asked her and she'd turned him down.

"Former?" I never could guard my tongue.

"I can hardly justify a mistress if I have a bond mate that actually speaks to me and tolerates my presence, can I?" She'd definitely turned him down. Constance Newcastle chokes on her own foot. I caught a glimpse into the tortured ties that had bound him to his dead bond mate and wondered if he'd ever forgive me for that.

"But she makes you butterscotch squares." Apparently my mouth had room for one more foot.

Allerton laughed. Somehow I'd amused rather than enraged him.

"All you need to know is that I'm not leaving the Council, so shall we put this conversation to rest?"

I went silent as a mouse who feels the shadow of a hawk overhead.

"I discussed a job with Liam. I'd meant it for the both of you, obviously, but now it will have to be just you."

I winced but didn't say anything, so after a moment he went on. "Stanzie, this one will be particularly difficult. I understand this better than you know. I'm compelled to ask you because the Alpha requested you specifically. She bypassed the Regional Council because she knew you were my Advisor. And, while I do not generally offer my Advisors the choice of opting out of an assignment, under the circumstances, the numerous circumstances, you are not to feel obligated. Is that understood?"

This did not sound good at all. A cold chill slipped down my spine and, for a moment, I wanted to press end on my phone and go hide beneath my bed. I wasn't ready for this shit.

"Why would an Alpha ask for me?" Once again I could not keep my mouth shut.

I didn't know any female Alphas well enough for them to ask for me personally except for Jossie. "Is something else wrong in Maplefair?" My stomach clenched.

"Not Maplefair, Constance. Mayflower."

My birth pack.

Chapter 6

"Mayflower." My voice was mostly flat, but there was a tinge of horror buried in it. My mind reeled. Paul and Lauren had renounced me. I had no standing in Mayflower. I realized I had no idea who was Alpha and maybe that should be my next question.

"Faith Newcastle and Scott Charest are Alphas," Allerton replied after I asked.

Faith. My cousin on Lauren's side. Mayflower was not Lauren's birth pack. She'd come from Aspenmoon in upper state New York. When she'd bonded with Paul, her twin sister, Lily, and her pack mate, Todd Marshall, had come to Mayflower with her. Lauren and Lily had been inseparable until Lily's death from complications after the birth of her daughter Faith.

I'd been five years old at the time. I remembered sneaking into the room where Lily had labored. It had been a hard birth and nobody had noticed me. I'd hidden behind a chair and watched without comprehension of what was happening. I only heard my auntie scream and my mother sob. There had been a lot of blood in the bed then all the women in the room cried so hard I barely heard the thin wail of my newborn cousin.

Todd, Faith's father, bonded with the duo who took over as Alphas, and raised his daughter with love and affection. I'd always been jealous of Faith's relationship with her father. So different from mine. She'd never walked on eggshells the way I had. She never seemed to do anything wrong the way I always had.

From her toddlerhood, she'd adored me. She'd followed me around and, when I came into a room, her face had lit up and she'd abandon any toy or person she played with to get to me.

I had been equally smitten because she'd been a little doll of a child with pale blond hair and autumn brown eyes with the cutest rosebud mouth.

We'd grown less close as we'd matured and the five-year gap became wider. By the time I'd left Mayflower to bond with Grey, she'd been a coltish fifteen-year-old and we'd had virtually nothing in common anymore.

The passage of time seemed brutal suddenly. Wasn't it just yesterday she was three years old and I was eight and we'd had tea parties on Grandmother Elaine's front lawn with my dolls and her teddy bear?

"Paul renounced me," I blurted in an attempt to drive away useless memories of a time that would never come back.

Allerton snorted. It was an undignified sound and indicative of how at ease he felt with me. The formality of our association became less each time we interacted, and I wasn't sure how comfortable I was with that. I liked to think of Allerton as lofty and untouchable. Always in control. In charge. Vulnerability unnerved me.

"You are an Advisor to the Great Council. Whether your father likes it or not, you will have access to Mayflower or he'll answer first to me and then to the Council. I'm relatively sure he won't present a problem. A minor inconvenience perhaps, but only if you allow him that much. In your shoes I wouldn't take a thing from him. You don't have to."

I pictured Paul's sour lemon face when I arrived on Mayflower territory. It almost made the idea attractive.

"What's wrong with the pack?" No more serial killers. No more conspiracy death. No more danger and drama. My heart was broken in enough pieces already.

"That's the question," Allerton responded.

* * * *

Faith at twenty-seven was not the same as the Faith I remembered at fifteen. Back then she'd been all skinny legs and pink-streaked spiky hair, dressed in black with her nose in a book. Anti-social and rebellious.

The short spiky, pink-streaked hair was gone, replaced by a sleek shoulder-length layered fringe with choppy bangs. She had my mother's smile, which wasn't surprising since Lily and Lauren had been identical twins. Instead of hyacinth blue eyes, hers were autumn-leaf brown and widely spaced—a legacy from her father.

It was a gorgeous June afternoon and she sat at one of the tiny shaded tables outside the Starbucks on the corner of Cambridge Street, an untouched bottle of water on the table before her. She played with the straps of her white purse—a counterclockwise twist and unwind followed by a clockwise twist and unwind. Silver hoops dangled from her ears and matched the bangle bracelets laddered up her bare left arm. The short sun dress she wore was multi-colored with wide swirls of black. Her flat sandals were black and studded with silver rings and beads. I'd seen the same pair for twenty bucks at Target the last time I'd shopped there for throw pillows to match the cinnamon red of my living room walls. I'd seen the dress too—twenty-nine ninety-five.

I'd been spoiled by Murphy's money and by my own—earned as an Advisor to Councilor Allerton. I used to buy Target shoes and clothes, but I was more upscale now. Department stores for clothes and trendy shoe stores for designer name shoes. I despised myself for a moment and wondered if I'd forgotten my roots.

Before I'd left the condo, I'd slipped my bond pendant around my neck and called myself a fraud as I did it. I hadn't worn it for five weeks, but I had to if I wanted to avoid questions from Faith. I drew the line at the pack ring, though. Paddy O'Reilly was a fucking liar and I was damned if I'd wear his ring, even though I technically was still a pack member.

I couldn't think what to say when she abandoned her purse straps and looked at me without a smile. The naked worry on her face scared me so I murmured an awkward hello, pointed at the store and dodged inside for an iced chai latte—anything to buy me a few moments to sort myself out.

Mayflower. Just the name conjured up a thousand, jumbled memories, and most of them weren't good.

My mouth tasted sour, so I sucked a mouthful of chai latte through the straw as I walked back to Faith's table. Faith had still not touched her water, but she'd set her purse aside and now played with the bangle bracelets on her wrist. She didn't look up when I pulled out the wrought iron chair opposite her and took a seat.

"Nice shoes," she said. I followed her gaze beneath the table to the black tar sidewalk and my feet.

My sandals were flat as well—tan leather gladiator style. Cocobelle Safari. A hundred and fifty bucks. Sometimes I got tired of the paint fumes in my condo and went shoe shopping. Of course each time I walked out of a store with a new pair of shoes for my ever-expanding collection, I thought of Allerton and his comment at the Paris Great Gathering. He believed I bought shoes to fill the hole inside me. Lately, I conceded he might have had a point.

Sometimes it seemed the more my shoe collection expanded, the bigger the hole inside me became. Not smaller. But that didn't stop the mindless acquisition. I could only take so much redecorating and I had to keep busy and on the move. Otherwise I would curl up in a defeated ball and cry. Screw that.

"Why Boston?" Faith reached out for her water but didn't take a sip. Her brown eyes were inquisitive. "After you were exiled you could have gone anywhere in the whole world. Why Boston? Why so close to Mayflower? None of us ever acknowledged you were here. Didn't that hurt?"

"Why Starbucks? Why wouldn't you come to meet me at the condo?" I countered.

A small smile quirked the corner of her mouth and I was reminded of my mother. Lauren had the same smile when she thought something was funny. For Lauren, this specific smile made a rare appearance.

"I asked first, Stanzie."

Faith had dubbed me Stanzie. She couldn't wrap her tongue around Constance when she was little and somehow she'd come up with Stanzie. Soon everyone in the pack had called me that and it had stuck. I'd made sure of it because I'd never liked Constance. The name was too formal and old-fashioned.

My father, of course, had despised the nickname. He'd taken it as a personal insult because he'd chosen my name. Supposedly, there had been a girl named Constance on the Mayflower when it had arrived in Plymouth Harbor one cold November day in 1620. Constance had had a twin brother, a father and a mother. They, and another young couple aboard, had had an inside secret. They weren't Others—they were Pack.

Paul had spun stories for me about this Mayflower Constance when I was a little girl—about her voyage and her family and what it was like to be in a pack in Colonial Massachusetts. Whenever I was bad, he would throw this Mayflower Constance in my face and tell me how she would never have cried like a baby or begged for such an expensive toy or talked back to her father the way I did. By the time I was seven, I hated the Mayflower Constance with a passion. She was the main reason I insisted on being called Stanzie. The Mayflower Constance would never have shortened her name and would have been horrified by anyone who'd tried to give her a nickname.

I played with my straw for a moment and Faith waited, her eyes thoughtful and wary.

"Every summer the mothers would take all of us kids to Faneuil Hall for a daytrip. We'd eat lunch at Quincy Market and walk through the stalls and vendors. We'd go outside and eat under the sun. Take walks to Paul Revere's house and the Old North Church. Go sprawl on blankets by the river. I'd fall asleep in Lauren's lap."

A reminiscent smile tugged at Faith's mouth.

"Boston was always a magical place for me. Full of potential and mystery. Joy. Plus it was one place that I'd never shared with Grey and Elena, so there were no memories here with them."

Faith's smile faltered and she stared at the sweating bottle of water on the table for a moment.

"I'm pregnant," she announced, but it didn't seem as though she expected grins and congratulations. "So maybe this is all in my head. Paranoia caused by raging pregnant-woman hormones, but I don't think so. I didn't want anyone to think I'd come here deliberately to see you. If someone from Mayflower spied us together, I could always say I saw you sitting here on the corner and had to stop. But if I went to your condo, they'd know I sought you out deliberately."

It was a two-hour drive from Willoughby, the small town where Mayflower made its home. Willoughby backed up to the Wendell State Forest where the pack ran. When the pack had first formed, it had been much closer to Boston but as the land had been built up and cities and towns founded, the pack had moved toward the state forest.

"What are you afraid of?" I leaned across the tiny table and put my hand on her arm. Her skin was slightly clammy with perspiration, but it was her pulse rate I wanted to feel. It raced.

"I don't know," she confessed in a low, confused voice. She began to pick at the label on the water bottle and tore small strips of paper away which she rolled into little balls with her thumb and forefinger then deposited on the table.

She stared straight into my eyes. "What did Councilor Allerton tell you?"

"Not much. He wanted you to tell me. I had the feeling he wasn't quite sure himself what the problem was, only that he believed you needed help."

"And that's what the Great Council is for, right? Help?" Faith didn't sound convinced.

"Among other things," I agreed.

"Like tribunals?" Faith watched my reaction closely and I tried not to shudder. Nearly two months had passed since my tribunal had ended and I'd been cleared of all charges. Almost three years since the first tribunal when I'd also been cleared of all charges.

"That was a low blow," she said before I could answer. "Sorry."

"Why? You're right. The Councils, both Regional and Great, are responsible for enforcing our laws which sometimes means punishment instead of help."

"Well, the ones that are punished deserve it and it could be said the rest of us are helped by that, I suppose."

I shrugged. This wasn't getting us any closer to the real issue and we both knew it.

"So, I'm pregnant, right?" She wasn't asking a question, but I nodded and sipped my iced chai. My throat was dry and I wasn't sure I wanted to hear what was wrong with my birth pack. I had a suspicion I already knew and it was last goddamn thing I wanted to deal with. The conspiracy.

"I'm three months pregnant and I've been Alpha for seven months. Already the pack's talking about who should be the next Alpha pair like the minute I give birth, I'm out and they're in." Faith's chin jutted and her eyes sparked with indignation and something worse—humiliation.

"That would be weird. Alphas are usually Alpha for at least five years. More in small packs like Mayflower. If you're right, you'd have a year at best. Who's next in line?"

"That's just it. It's Rachel and Mark, or at least that's how the rumor goes. And they were Alphas before me and Scott." Faith sat straight in her chair and her voice vibrated with resentment.

"A second chance to have a baby? Rachel's got to be in her late thirties by now." I did the mental math and Faith bounced in her chair.

"That's just it, Stanzie, she has children. Twins. They're three. She'd be Alpha again for no reason except that she wouldn't be me."

"Alan..." I began. I referred to another young pack member and tried to calculate his age.

"He's twenty-one. He's not even bonded. Also, there's no one near his age to bond with in the pack, so when he finds a bond mate, he's going to leave and join her pack."

I blinked. "He's tenth generation. There's got to be some push back on that idea."

"No." Her hair fell in her eyes with the force of her headshake. "It's the other way around. He's being encouraged."

My mouth dropped open. This was definitely not standard operating procedure for Mayflower. It went against all tradition.

"That's why I wanted you. I need you to investigate this because you know Mayflower. You understand how freaky proud we are of our heritage, our status as the third-oldest pack in America. Alan is from one of the oldest families we have. Everyone should be falling over themselves to find him a bond mate who wants to join us."

I nodded because it was true.

"You know Paul renounced me, right?"

Faith waved that away with an irritated movement of her hand. The Mayflower pack ring, a band of twisted gold and silver, flashed from her finger. The story went that Paul Revere himself had designed the ring. That part of it I might believe. The part where Paul was a member of the pack was not quite as believable, but it was the sort of rumor people from Mayflower didn't discourage if it made the rounds at Regionals and Great Gatherings.

"Scott wonders if they don't like us because we're first generation and we have no history." Faith's shoulders slumped and a surge of anger pumped through my veins.

"New blood is vital for continuation. Otherwise you'd end up bonding with your cousin or uncle, for Christ's sake."

"All I ever heard growing up was that I wasn't true Mayflower. Not like you." Faith stole a look at me through her long lashes and I sat back in my chair, disturbed and astounded.

"You were the perfect child and I was the rebel. *Be more like Stanzie* was a constant refrain through my childhood. Until you shifted with that German boy in New Orleans." Faith's tone had started out aggrieved, but turned happy. "I was so proud of you for that, Stanzie. I never thought you had it in you. And then you gave the whole pack the finger and ran off with Grey Owens and joined Riverglow. God, I was jealous."

"I was always envious of the way Todd doted on you. Paul never did that with me," I confessed.

We exchanged rueful looks. The grass is always greener on the other side of the fence, for sure.

"When Alan was born, Todd wanted me to feel special." Faith's smile was affectionate and grateful as she thought of her father.

"Alan was Shane's son, not Todd's," I said.

"But Todd was still in Shane and Samantha's triad. Spare to the pair. He probably knew how it felt to be a little bit on the outside looking in. Although the three of them have been happy all these years, I wonder how different things would have been if my mother had lived."

Lily's face, the carbon copy of my mother's, flashed before my eyes. Unfortunately, in my mind her face was contorted with the agonized screams of labor gone wrong.

"I want you to come to Willoughby. Come see our pack. I'll say it's a family reunion. We ran into each other by accident in Boston and decided together you should visit. I've made you reservations at the Wishing Well Motel. You can check in anytime after three today."

Amy Lee Burgess

Motel? I wasn't welcome to stay with her and her bond mate? I guess it made sense since there was something wrong in the pack, but it still stung. Maybe she was mad I'd left Mayflower even though she said she was proud of me? Faith was the closest thing to family I had left. It was hard not to feel rejected.

Stanzie. Get a grip. You're an Advisor on a job. Act like one.

"Do you have a car?" Faith's loaded question broke into my self-pitying reverie.

I bit my lip. Technically, the answer was *yes*. The Prelude was parked in the tiny driveway on the side of the condo. The downstairs neighbors had no car so I got the space by default. Murphy had parked it there after we'd returned from Bethany's funeral. I hadn't been near it since.

"Yes, I have a car," I said.

Faith plucked a pad and pen from her purse and scribbled down a number. She ripped the page out of the notebook and slid it across the table toward me careful to avoid the wet spots of condensation from our drinks. "My cell number. Call me when you're settled. Bring your bond mate. I hear he's an Advisor too."

"He's in Dublin right now." My smile was evasive. Her eyes narrowed but she didn't say anything.

After a swig of water, she shouldered her purse and rose to her feet. The June sunlight illuminated her blond hair and turned it golden.

"Thank you, Stanzie. I feel better already."

I sucked down chai tea and watched her walk down Cambridge Street—a young woman in a short sun dress with blond hair and cheap Target sandals. Men drivers craned their necks to watch her go but she was oblivious. They were only Others, after all.

Chapter 7

"What a stupid, stupid thing to say, *yes I have car*!" I yelled two hours later. I'd managed to pack a suitcase full of clothes and an overnight case of just shoes, and I'd even been able to unlock the damn trunk and throw them both inside.

What I couldn't do was slide my ass behind the wheel. The front door was open and the smell of Murphy's cologne and the dregs of Dunkin Donuts coffee wafted out in a killer one-two punch to my gut. It wasn't bad enough I had to drive. I had to smell Murphy's goddamn cologne while I did it. I wasn't prepared for that too.

Fear. I fucking hated it. I tried to fight it but it just wouldn't stop. Relentless, without mercy, total annihilation.

I gave myself all the standard arguments—*You're an Advisor. It was three years ago. You've got to get a grip, you're not going to let this car win, are you, Stanzie?*

Nothing turned the switch in my head from *fuck no* to *let's go.*

Murphy's suit jacket was on the backseat where he'd casually discarded it after we'd walked back from the forest where we'd scattered Bethany's ashes. I'd folded it when we'd gotten in the car to drive home.

His empty coffee cup was in the cup holder between the bucket seats. His sunglasses tucked in the visor.

Tears blurred my eyes and I slammed the car door and ran back inside the condo. Halfway up the stairs I tripped and fell. I landed hard, my face two inches from the riser. Impact would have been a bitch. The warm trickle of blood down my leg let me know I hadn't escaped unscathed. My knee was shredded.

I sat up and clutched my bond pendant. Salty tears poured down my face and I sat there and bawled for a good five minutes, but they were not cathartic tears—they were the kind that scalded inside and out and made everything worse.

For the first time ever, the touch of my bond pendant did not comfort, but actively hurt me. As I had a hundred times before, I begged Murphy aloud although he couldn't hear. Just one more chance. I wouldn't be mean. I wouldn't be hurt because he wasn't there for the tribunal. I loved him, that was true, but he didn't love me and I had been unfair to hold him to expectations he could not fulfill. He'd done the best and only thing he knew how to do and I'd tried to accept it but had blown it.

Everything was my fault. I'd gotten angry and acted like a bitch. I'd hidden behind the trauma of Nate Carver instead of facing it with good grace. And as a result, I had nothing left.

I tried to remind myself that I did have a future. I was an Advisor and I would go on interesting cases that wouldn't always involve people I knew or places I'd been and I could be more of an observer than a participant. Someday.

I had the condo and all my shoes. I was young and not ugly. Maybe one day I might meet someone who did love me and wouldn't fucking die or leave me. One day.

With my eyes shut, tears hot on my cheeks, I forced myself to let go of the bond pendant and limped upstairs to wash the blood off my knee.

I brought a plastic bag back to the car with me and resolutely opened the door. My breath held, I reached in and picked up Murphy's coffee cup then Paddy's. I cleaned up the empty doughnut box and my own coffee cup. I stuffed Murphy's jacket and sunglasses beneath the driver's seat and threw the plastic bag in the trash can on the street.

My gladiator sandals slapped on the driveway as I approached the car, keys clutched tightly in my fist. If I didn't start to drive soon, I'd end up on the road after dark and I ardently wished to avoid that.

With fierce concentration I hammered all thoughts of Murphy, fear and the summer afternoon out of my head. There was only me and that damn car. And I would master it.

What's the worst that could happen, Constance? You could crash and die and what's the big deal now anyway? Who the fuck cares, right? You fucking baby.

Tears pricked my eyes again and I swiped at them viciously with the back of my arm. My arm came away streaked with black mascara and smears of eye shadow. Great. I probably looked like a fucking lunatic.

Get in the car, damn you!

I got in the car.

Ten minutes later I was still in the car, but that was all the progress I'd made. The door was still open, I breathed through my mouth to avoid as much of Murphy's ghost cologne as I could. The keys were still in my fist and not in the fucking ignition and it was now ten minutes after four in the goddamn afternoon and the sun set at eight. I had a two-plus hour drive that did not factor in traffic or my fucking fear and if I didn't get my ass in gear I would be on the road after dark.

Worse, I would be on the road at the precise moment between light and dark, when the shadows loomed low over the horizon and sifted through the tree tops. The moment when the front end of the Mustang had smashed into the guard rail and we'd begun the fatal plunge.

"*Liam Murphy, I fucking hate you!*" My throat nearly burst from the force of my scream and I felt an immediate rush of relief, resentment and regret. Why was it Murphy's fault I didn't have the guts to drive a damn car? He'd tried his damndest to get me to drive. He'd been endlessly patient with me and now he was gone and I had to suck it up.

Don't think about Murphy. I pounded my forehead on the steering for good measure to try to make the thought of him go away. *Do not think about anything but starting this fucking car and backing it out of the driveway.*

"Aw, man I would have to back up first after three years of not driving," I muttered and, before I could think about it, I stuck the key into the ignition. Score one for Stanzie.

Of course it took another five minutes of yelling at myself before I actually twisted the damn thing.

The engine roared to life. Damn it. I'd secretly hoped a month parked in the driveway would have killed the battery or something. I should have known Murphy's obsessive maintenance would have prevented any such mechanical travesty. The only reason there'd been empty cups and trash in the car was due to his mental perturbation. His normal routine was to clean the car out after he parked it—no matter what time it was.

Belatedly, I realized I did not have on my seatbelt and buckled it. After that I had what felt like a massive coronary but was really just a rampant panic attack. Grey and Elena had never worn their seatbelts. If they had, they'd most likely still be alive. I'd been the only one to survive, and I'd always worn my seatbelt.

The seat was too far back to allow easy access to the pedals, so I had to adjust it and then the mirrors. I chanced a look at the gas gauge then recalled Murphy had stopped to fill the tank just before we'd reached Boston. That had driven Paddy nearly crazy because it had been nearly one in the morning and he must have known we'd had a flight to catch the next afternoon. Or they'd had a flight. Not me.

I bit my lip, swore under my breath, pressed down on the brake and put the damn car in reverse.

"Oh my God. Oh shit, I hate this!"

I let up on the brake. The car moved backward one whole foot. I stomped on the brake so hard I nearly got whiplash. Sweat poured in rivulets down my face. The scent of my fear drowned any lingering whiff of Murphy's cologne. I couldn't even smell doughnuts anymore. Just me and my fear.

After I took a deep, cleansing breath then swore again, I gingerly took my foot off the brake. The car scooted back another few inches. A bit more. And more after that. Then, oh shit, the damn street. *Don't forget the damn street, Stanzie, and the other cars. That might help, oh, a little bit!*

Another stomp on the brakes. The next time, I looked for oncoming cars before I let off the brake.

I coasted into the middle of the street and panicked a little as I hastily shifted gears. Thank God the damn car was an automatic. Once in drive I had to actually put my foot on the gas. Make or break time.

With a small whimper, I pressed my toes down and the Prelude jerked forward. I straightened the wheel and pressed harder on the gas. It was as elementary and anticlimactic as that.

Navigation around the city proved easier than I suspected. Lights and traffic combined to make my progress slow. I maintained a murderously tight grip on the wheel and refused to contemplate the radio or a CD. I barely allowed myself to breathe so intent was I on the road.

Not until I had merged onto 495 did I dare relax my death grip on the wheel. No music yet, but I did switch lanes so I could pass a slow-moving truck.

It wasn't until I got off onto the smaller Route 2 I realized I was, no shit, driving. Me. Constance Newcastle, girl coward.

Of course I was petrified to stop, even though I really had to pee. I was afraid I would never be able to start the car again as if this was my only chance at driving. Maybe it was my only shot at getting unscathed from point A to point B without losing my nerve. Perhaps once I'd done that, I would be able to drive with impunity. Or least without so damn much sweat.

I blinked a drop of it out of my left eye and the road became less hazy. I chanced a look at the dashboard clock. Five twenty-seven. Nowhere near sunset and I was halfway there.

Boston was long gone and I was in the country. Farmhouses dotted the landscape. Red barns with rooster weather vanes. Stone fences and overgrown dandelions. Horses with switching tails in green fields.

My fingers cramped and I loosened my grip on the wheel even more. A slow sense of freedom sifted through my soul. I was really driving. I was doing this. Just me. No Murphy to cheer me on. No ghosts of Grey and Elena to point accusing fingers that dripped with blood. My heart skipped a beat now and again, and I would probably never stop sweating until the ignition was shut off, but I was driving. At the speed limit no less.

As I became more comfortable behind the wheel, my thoughts began to wander. When a black Mustang pulled around me and roared away at high speed, my mind stuttered and the black paint became gold and I swore I could see white-blond hair through the rear window and hear Elena's laugh just before it turned into a scream.

But it was fleeting. Three seconds, tops then it was gone, smoothed away, and I was distracted by a black-and-white cow who placidly chewed her cud, head hung over the top of a stone wall.

The contrails of a jet traced a white line in the blue sky, and I blinked more sweat from my eyes as a small spurt of happiness blossomed in my heart.

For the first time since the night Murphy and I had made love in the strange-angled room in Jossie's farmhouse in Vermont, I was happy. It wasn't anything sustained or huge, more like a brief pause between one breath and the next, but it was more than I'd felt for weeks. Better than the happiness itself, was the thin slice of hope that accompanied it. I was still in the tunnel, but there was light ahead. Maybe.

* * * *

The Wishing Well was the only motel in Willoughby. The town's population numbered under three hundred which made it one of the smallest in Massachusetts. Small enough that everyone knew everyone else except for the pack which, of course, kept to itself. Familiar faces at the local tavern but nodding acquaintance only.

When I'd been young here, we'd shopped two towns over in Wendell to avoid becoming known to the locals.

Still, when I drove into the small parking lot in front of the Wishing Well Motel, a strange sense of homecoming thrilled through me. Grey and I had spent nearly the entire summer before we'd bonded making love in room twelve. His room.

The night of my twentieth birthday, when I'd become officially adult by Pack standards, I'd come to room twelve just before midnight. When

Grey had opened the door, I'd smelled rose-scented candles. He'd lit twenty or thirty votives and spread them around the nightstands, dresser and desk. This had turned the small motel room into a sort of shrine or sanctuary that had been strangely beautiful. After cake and champagne, we'd fallen across the bed and torn each other's clothes off.

* * * *

"Stanzie." My name on Grey's lips is a prayer. I am on my back with my legs tight around his waist. He is inside me and I can feel the muscles strain along his arms and shoulders as he braces himself and looks down at my face. "Stanzie. Bond with me. Please?"

For a minute I am lost in lust, but his words penetrate me with almost the same physical thrust as his cock. I love this man. I love him so much.

"Grey, we're forever you and me," I tell him as I twine my fingers in his long dark hair. "Nothing will ever stop us, will it?"

"No," he promises before he finds my mouth with his. And for ten years to the day, nothing does.

* * * *

The woman behind the motel counter was thirty pounds overweight and in desperate need of a shampoo. Her greasy hair was drawn back into a slick pony tail. Potato chip crumbs dotted her lips and the jutting shelf of her ample bosom. She wore a blue sleeveless tank top and the flesh of her upper arms jiggled as she ran the key card to my room through the coding machine.

I held my breath and waited for her to tell me I had room twelve.

"Room seven," she said instead as she passed it to me.

"Is room twelve available?" I could not believe I had the guts to ask, but I did.

Irritation flashed across her doughy face. We locked eyes and she looked away first.

She ran the key card through the coding machine again.

"Room twelve." She handed it to me with a sarcastic flourish.

I froze, convinced I would not be able to reach out and accept it. What the hell had I been thinking?

But I somehow managed and, with the card clutched in my right hand, I went back to the Prelude and popped the trunk to retrieve my things.

Number twelve was the last room on the end by the vending machines and the ice maker. The belt of pine trees just beyond the room's side window had grown a few feet in the decade plus since I'd been here, but the two in the twelve on the door was still crooked. The lock was different. Thirteen years ago Grey had had a real key on a plastic tag instead of a key card.

When I opened the door, I smelled the pine scented cleaner. The same as thirteen years ago. The smell took me back instantly and I almost expected to find Grey sprawled across the bed, but it was empty. The bedspread was navy blue now. Thirteen years ago it had been a turquoise-and-coral floral pattern. A flat screen television on a black lacquer dresser replaced the boxy big TV in a built-in armoire. The mirror was different but still reflected the bed. Grey and I used to watch ourselves make love in the mirror. We'd left the nightstand lamp on so we could see.

The floor-length curtains across the windows were slate blue now. Thirteen years ago they'd been coral with turquoise circles. The desk and chair were the same and so were the cheap plywood nightstands. The lamp bases looked the same but the shades were different. Pearl gray instead of stark white.

The carpeting had been replaced but the wood panel walls had not. The bathroom was unchanged except for the light fixture. The shower still had a smoked glass sliding door instead of a curtain.

I sat on the edge of the bed and ran my fingers along the edge of the nightstand. Grey's fingers had touched the same grooves and indentations. He'd pressed the same button on the base of the lamp to turn it off and on.

He'd stood beneath the same shower head and rinsed off the sweat of our sated passion. Sometimes I'd showered with him—squealed when he'd pinned me against the cream colored tile with his soapy hands and kissed me beneath the warm spray until we were both dizzy.

I drew back the curtains and stared out at the pine trees. I half expected his arms to steal around my waist and draw me close but I felt nothing. Inside or out.

Twilight crept through the branches of the pines and slowly erased the light. I turned away and stumbled into the bathroom to take a hot shower. The water stung the shredded skin on my knee and the cheap motel soap slipped through my fingers and fell to the bottom of the tub. I turned my face up into the warm spray of the water and cried, my tears hotter than the water.

* * * *

Barefoot and wrapped in a towel, I padded out of the bathroom. I wound a second towel around my wet head turban style and rummaged in my purse for Faith's cellphone number.

Full dark was encroaching, but there was still a good half hour left of twilight. The pine trees outside the motel window were charcoal smudges against a dark blue-gray background.

Faith picked up on the third ring and I could hear voices and cutlery—she was at a restaurant.

"We're at the Stonewall Tavern. We usually meet on Fridays for dinner. Come join us," she invited. "We just got here. Tell me what you want and I'll order for you."

Grey and I had eaten many dinners at the Stonewall Tavern. Drunk our share of beer too. It was half a mile down the road from the Wishing Well, and most of the time we hadn't bothered to take his bike. We'd walked hand in hand along the side of the road in the moonlight. My heart had soared so high some nights, buoyed up by joy, my feet had barely seemed to skim the ground.

I told Faith to order me the fried clams and French fries and hurried into a halter dress with a bold brown-and-white batik design. I twisted my hair up and put on brown beaded dangle earrings. My fingers faltered as I tried to fasten my bond pendant on the heavy silver chain I used for evening wear. I went darker with the eye shadow than normal and ran a nude-colored lipgloss across my mouth before I grabbed my purse and stuffed my feet back into the gladiator sandals. A quick check of my watch let me know I had time to walk to the tavern if I busted ass, so I hurried out into the night.

Full dark descended a few steps out of the motel parking lot, but I had no trouble seeing my path. Heightened senses came in handy.

Walking alone was weird. Each time I saw my shadow, a dark shape against the road which glittered silver white with bits of embedded quartz, I jumped. Grey's absence was like a missing piece of the puzzle that was me. I didn't think of Elena or of Murphy, just Grey and the way things used to be before I left Mayflower.

But this wasn't a summer night thirteen years in the past, it was right now. Only when I looked at my shadow, I wasn't precisely sure who I was anymore.

The tavern's dirt parking lot was three quarters full when I dashed across the road and my sandals kicked up dust and small pebbles as I headed to the small deck off the front entrance.

The deck was large enough for three umbrella tables each with four chairs. Two of the three tables were occupied by a rowdy group of bikers in worn jeans and heavy metal concert t-shirts. Most of them had beards and sideburns of astonishing bushiness. Lots of silver chains pushed through belt loops and were secured to wallets tucked in back pockets. Scruffy boots discolored by the grime of motor oil and road dust were planted beneath the tables.

One of the men blew me a wolf whistle and when I ignored him, another one took up the call.

"What's the matter, darling, too good for us?" yelled a particularly hirsute gentleman in a Black Sabbath t-shirt with a leather jacket thrown across the back of his chair.

"You guys are way out of my league," I called back to their general amusement. A few of them lifted Budweiser bottles and drank to my health as I passed by. Nobody pinched my ass. A miracle. I should have worn my jeans. I was way overdressed. Things had changed a little in the past decade, apparently.

The restaurant was dark. Candles in glass jars flickered on the tables next to bud vases full of wild flowers. A massive oak bar ran the width of the room and a huge fieldstone fireplace sat cold and empty on the eastern wall.

Two tables were shoved together in front of the fireplace. Faith's blond hair gleamed in the candlelight. She and her bond mate, Scott, sat backs to the fireplace, with the younger generation of the pack ranged around them.

Those of my parents' age and above weren't there. I couldn't imagine Paul deigning to eat at an establishment that served bikers. A cold spurt of relief swept over me. I'd have to confront him eventually, but it wouldn't be tonight.

I'd grown up with six of the seven of the people gathered at the tables. The oldest, Tony, was fourteen years my senior but, of course, he could pass for anywhere from late twenties to mid thirties. He'd been Alpha when I'd left the pack, and he'd rescued my wolf the first night she'd shifted and had been scared of her own heartbeat. I'd crushed hard on Tony at one point in my life.

The youngest, Alan, was eleven years my junior. I knew it was him only because he looked so much like his father. The last time I'd seen him, he'd been nine or ten, a little brat of epic proportions. I'd been his primary babysitter and he'd driven me frigging crazy most of the time, but I had a soft spot for him anyway.

When he saw me, he leaped out of his chair and rushed me so he could envelop me in a huge bear hug.

"Stanzie Newcastle, my favorite sexy babysitter," he growled then hugged me again.

"Alan Perrault, if you don't cut the crap I'm going to kick your ass," I warned which only made him laugh.

"I couldn't believe my freaking ears when Faith told us you were here." He wrapped a strong arm around my shoulders and steered me to the table.

At ten, he'd been a skinny little kid with sly blue eyes who could run like hell when he was in trouble, and that had been nearly all the damn time. Now he was taller than me by at least five inches and, while still on the thin side, had muscles in all the right places. His innocent choirboy face had morphed into sensuality. He was a damn good-looking guy.

He nuzzled my ear with his nose. "Stanzie, don't trust anyone except for me and Faith, okay?"

I gave him a sharp look but didn't say anything. I found it extremely interesting that he hadn't included Scott, Faith's bond mate, in his short list of exemptions.

Pack structure centered on the Alpha breeding pair. Unless there were twins or triplets, generally the children in a pack were separated by five or more years. This made it a lonely time for only children.

My closet pack mates in age had been Mark Drake, who was five years older, and my cousin, Faith, who was five years younger.

Mark's cousin, Tony, the man who had been Alpha when I had left the pack, was bonded to Susan Driscoll, who at forty, was only eight years older than me but we had never had much use for each other. She'd been far closer in age to Rachel Costello, and they had been best friends forever.

Tonight they sat next to each other and I assumed things had not changed between them.

Proximity had led many pack children to bond with each other when they grew up. Mayflower was no exception. Mark, between me and Rachel in age, could have gone either way with us, but when he'd hit puberty I had definitely not been interested in boys. Rachel, five years older than Mark, had been a much more receptive target. Mark was more like a brother to me. Big and burly with dark brown hair and a moustache, he could have blended with the bikers outside in a heartbeat.

Rachel's hair was blue black and styled in short layers that framed her face becomingly. Not conventionally beautiful and far too strong-featured to be considered pretty, she stood six feet tall and was built like an Amazon. She and Mark were focused on fitness. They spent hours in their home gym and it showed.

Susan, by contrast, was small and plump with light-brown hair and a China doll lovely face. It was a mistake to be fooled by her demure exterior. She had a razor-sharp tongue that could cut anyone down to size in fifteen seconds or less. The only person in the whole world who could intimidate her was my father. My status as an Advisor and so-called member of Mac Tire would probably cut zero ice with her.

She gave me a frankly suspicious look as Alan and I approached the table. "It's crap that you're here to visit, Stanzie. You're wearing your Advisor cap, aren't you?"

Her bond mate, Tony, winced. Rachel grinned, clearly entertained, her dark eyes weren't hostile, they were curious.

"Could be," I said with my most enigmatic smile. Alan pulled out the chair beside him and I sat. Faith, seated almost directly across from me, sipped ice water and played with her appetizer of split pea soup. She avoided eye contact.

Susan's eyebrows elevated. "Since when did you get all dark and mysterious? Stanzie Newcastle, you've always worn your heart on your sleeve and blurt out everything you think the minute the thought hits your brain."

"I'm not twenty years old anymore." I unspooled my cutlery from my napkin and arranged it on the water-marked wooden table.

"Is it true your wolf tore out Nate Carver's throat?" Mark leaned forward, fascinated.

The table went dead silent. The only one who moved was me as I spread my napkin on my lap. My seat was close to an open window that overlooked a tobacco field in back of the tavern. The steady song of crickets was loud in my ears while the scent of growing tobacco and weeds stung my nose. I wished I had a drink.

"It was either that or be raped and tortured to death," I said. On my left, Alan shuddered. On my right, Tony's face hardened.

Mark sat on Tony's other side and he leaned around him so he could meet my gaze.

"I never liked that sorry sonofabitch in the first place," he said and raised his beer. "Good job, Stanzie."

The others raised their drinks in a strangely gleeful toast that made me uncomfortable.

It didn't seem right somehow to celebrate the fact that my wolf had broken Pack law and gotten away with it. Been commended for it.

"I have to live with Nate's blood on my soul for the rest of my life," I said.

"You're a hero." Was that mockery in Susan's voice or admiration? "Everyone says so."

I shook my head.

"I know. It seems a little weird that you, Stanzie, would grow up and become responsible instead of running away from your problems or ignoring them as usual, but maybe being an Advisor has been good for your character development," Susan mused. She contemplated the inside of her beer bottle before she swallowed the rest of the contents.

Okay. Mockery.

"Can we lay off her, Susan? Jesus." Faith's mouth tightened.

"You always worshipped the ground Stanzie walked on, but you were younger and didn't know any better. The rest of us weren't so blind, Faith." Susan patted Faith's hand and Faith jerked away from her. Before her ice water could tip over, Tony grabbed for it and managed to save it.

"I didn't ask Stanzie here so you could rip her to shreds."

"Why did you ask her here? Not that family reunion crap again, Faith. Please. She walked away almost fifteen years ago. We're not her family anymore."

"Paul renounced her as his daughter." Rachel's dark eyes turned judgmental as she looked at me.

"That's just so much melodramatic bullshit," argued Alan. A lock of wheat-colored hair fell into his blue eyes and he brushed it back with impatient fingers. "You can't renounce your own children, it's ridiculous."

"Stanzie walked away from Mayflower. She was fifteenth generation of the founding pack family. Paul waited twelve years to do it and it was only after Stanzie threw away her chance to come back after Grey and Elena died that pushed him to it." Rachel transferred her intense dark gaze to Alan. The breeze from the open window stirred the layers of her jet black hair.

My eyes bugged and I nearly expected to see them bounce on the table and roll into Rachel's sanctimonious lap.

"Come back to Mayflower?" I shook my head. "That was an option? Paul knew damn well I've been in Boston for nearly three years and not once did he deign to visit or even return my phone calls."

"You called?" Rachel was more surprised than she should have been since she knew Paul.

"Every month, regular as clockwork."

Rachel considered my answer. One thing about Rachel—she didn't rush into judgment. However, once her mind was made up, it was nearly impossible to get her to see the other side. Convincing a stone statue to dance would have been an easier task.

"He made it sound like he offered to take you back and you all but spit in his face. Wes still wanted to bond with you even after the way you treated him." She wasn't convinced I told the truth, but the slight doubt in her voice let me know there was still a chance she'd see my side and even believe it.

I couldn't repress a shudder of revulsion. Not Wes Hanover again. Rachel's sharp eyes missed nothing.

"Well, who else did you expect to bond with, Stanzie? Susan and Tony? You always had a thing for Tony, didn't you?"

A hot blush stole across my cheeks and I damned the fact I'd put up my hair and had nothing to hide behind.

"Well, you have to admit he's a hell of a lot closer to my age than Wes," I argued, although I probably should have kept my stupid mouth shut.

"A snowball has a better chance in hell than you do of bonding with us." Susan's mouth stretched into a sardonic grin, but her eyes sparked with jealousy. I'm sure if she'd known her jealousy had shown, she would have gouged out her eyes with her salad fork.

"I'll bond with you," Alan offered gallantly.

Susan snorted. "You're not old enough to bond with anyone. Why would Stanzie want a baby like you, Alan?"

Alan's blue eyes narrowed. "I've been old enough to bond for two years. Stanzie bonded with Grey at twenty. I'm twenty-one."

"Stanzie's almost thirty-three. Talk about an age difference."

"Wes Hanover is almost sixty-three. You should shut up about age difference, Susan." Alan gripped his beer bottle so tightly I feared for its continued existence.

"Bonding with someone because you have the hots for them is hardly a basis for sustainability, Alan." Susan's smile was condescending to the max. "At your age you think with your dick, not your brain. Just because Stanzie starred in your first wet dream when you were twelve doesn't mean you have to bond with her. She's here for a visit. You should sleep with her, get her out of your system."

"You're just jealous because you're nobody's wet dream material," Alan muttered and Susan threw her ice water at his face. Not only was he doused, but I was as well.

With a curse, Alan shoved back his chair and stalked to the back of the tavern to the rest rooms.

Ice water trickled down my cleavage. This was typical Susan behavior. I remembered it well. Dramatic bitch. I refused to give her the satisfaction of any sort of surprised reaction, but damn that water was cold.

"I have a bond mate. Can we stop this ridiculous discussion?" I asked. Tony handed me his napkin and I dabbed at my neck and chest. I wasn't precisely a liar. I did have a bond mate—at least for a couple more months.

"Where the hell is he?" Mark leaned around Tony again and I busied myself with the napkin to buy some time.

"He's in Dublin." The longer I stalled, the more curious they'd become. "My pack is Irish, remember?" Maybe they'd think Murphy was on pack business.

"What the hell possessed you to bond with someone Irish, for Christ's sake?" Mark's expression was baffled. "You're American."

"I met him at the Great Gathering in France. Not everyone at the Great Gathering is American, Mark."

"But Irish?" Mark shook his head.

"At least he speaks English," Tony remarked. Susan's eyes narrowed.

"Stanzie's always had a thing for foreigners. Remember that German boy?" Rachel said. "Paul nipped that in the bud, didn't he?"

Rudi's face flashed before my eyes. I remembered the feel of my hand on his taut stomach, the press of his mouth against mine. The way he'd said my name, as if I'd had the power to save him, just before he died.

"Whatever happened to him?" Mark asked and I stared at him in shock before I remembered Mayflower members never went to Great Gatherings anymore.

"He's dead," I said, and more deafening silence descended upon the table.

"We'd know all this if we went to Great Gatherings and Regionals." Faith pushed her cup of soup aside.

"We go to Regionals," Susan's smile was nasty. "At least you do, dear."

Resentment flared in Faith's brown eyes. "Three years ago. If I hadn't, I never would have met Scott." This was an old argument, I could tell by everyone's faces and body language.

Admiration warred with anger inside me. I was proud of Faith for defying the pack so she could attend a Regional, but angry that she'd had to do that. Everyone had a right to attend Regionals and Great Gatherings. The only thing that ought to hold someone back was whether they could afford it.

Faith and Scott had been Alphas for only a brief few months. Perhaps she was so stuck in the previous mindset of the pack she forgot she could now set policy. She didn't have to carry her resentment around like a smoldering torch any longer because she could do what she wanted and, even better, encourage the others to follow in her footsteps.

Just then the waitress appeared with a platter of food—including my fried clams and French fries. When she took drink refills I ordered a Stella Artois for me and another Bud for Alan.

"What's wrong with Budweiser?" Mark asked as he leaned around Tony again. I almost wished they would trade seats. Tony had barely looked in my direction the entire time I'd been there. That probably was so Susan wouldn't go off on him.

"Are you going to give me shit about the beer I drink?" I rolled my eyes and Mark grinned at me. I remembered how we'd always squabbled like brother and sister.

"If you drink that foreign shit, yeah."

"Oh, jeez, all right fine." I changed my order to a Sam Adams and Mark gave me the thumbs up.

Alan slunk back into his chair. His hair was damp from the ice water and his blue t-shirt had wet patches but his face was dry. He picked up his beer, discovered it was empty, and swore softly beneath his breath.

"I ordered you another one." I gave him a friendly nudge with my elbow but he didn't smile.

"If you're going to be pissy all night long, do the rest of us a favor and go home," suggested Susan as she dipped a chicken tender into a small bowl of honey barbecue sauce.

"Maybe I will." Alan shoved back his chair and stalked out of the tavern.

"I'm not paying his tab." Faith glared at Susan. "You do this almost every week, Susan, and I'm sick of paying for food he barely gets to touch before you drive him off."

"He's a big baby." Susan popped the dripping chicken tender into her Cupid's bow mouth and chewed with a blissful smile. "Samantha and Shane have spoiled him rotten. You and Todd haven't helped. He's twenty-one frigging years old and still hasn't initiated his wolf. I was bonded for a year at his age. If he can't make nice with the grown-ups, he should stay home and play WoW on his computer."

She gestured at me with another dripping chicken tender. "You're the one who gave him the idea he could pick and choose who initiates his wolf, Stanzie. He and Faith both looked up to you back in the day, but you never thought it was important to teach by example."

"Maybe I did," I retorted, stung. I dipped one of my fried clams into the paper container of tartar sauce on my plate and tried to enjoy it. "Not that I want to get into this discussion right now, but what the hell is wrong with wanting to choose your own partner for initiation?"

Tony pushed back his chair and mumbled something about the men's room before he beat a hasty retreat. It took every bit of self-control I had not to roll my eyes.

"You should be initiated by your pack, Stanzie." Rachel answered before Susan could finish her second chicken tender. "There's time enough to go out and choose partners for sex and fun or for bonding after you've been properly initiated. Look where rebellion got you."

A slow, simmering anger sifted through my blood. The first person who said anything derogatory about my wolf was going to get a beer bottle upside their head. "If I'd been allowed to have the partner of my choice, it would have been someone in the pack."

I stared hard at Susan. "My choice just wasn't the one everyone else wanted to make for me. If you'd let me do what I wanted, I wouldn't be getting this stupid lecture."

"It's not stupid," Rachel protested as she waved her fork in the air for emphasis. "Who knows you better than your pack mates?"

"I'm not arguing that point," I said with a sweet smile when I really wanted to snarl. I swirled another fried clam in the tartar sauce and wished like hell the waitress would hurry up with my goddamn beer. I was sure as hell going to claim Alan's too while I was at it.

"Because of you Faith snuck away to the Regional in New Hampshire and got initiated by Scott. Then she wanted to join his pack after they bonded. Luckily, he talked her out of that one. Can you imagine where she got an idea like that in her head?" Susan gave me a hard look. "She wouldn't let Wes initiate her. Wouldn't think of making a triad with Mark and Rachel. No, she had to go outside the pack for no reason."

I expected Scott to say something at this point but he just sat there and placidly ate his cheeseburger. He hadn't said a goddamn word all night. Not even hello.

When I reached across the table for the ketchup bottle, I took a better, longer look at him. Dark hair, silver gray eyes, razor stubble across his cheeks, dressed like a New England jock—Boston Bruins t-shirt, bond pendant tucked beneath the collar, baseball cap—another Boston team, the Red Sox, and while I couldn't see them I knew he'd have on a pair of well-worn baggy jeans and equally beat-up sneakers. He was heartbreakingly gorgeous and I don't know why that surprised me. Maybe because he made no effort to play it up.

He caught me scoping him out and gave me a frank appraisal in return. I'm not exactly ugly and I looked a lot like his bond mate, but not a flicker of appreciative lust flared in his eyes. He might have been looking at a not particularly interesting painting in an art gallery for all the interest he showed.

The waitress arrived with our beers and his face lit up. Beer he could appreciate—me, not so much. Tony was right behind the waitress and slid into his seat without a look toward me. He busied himself with his fried shrimp and kept his head down.

"Why is it so damn important to bond within the pack?" I asked. My voice was coated with an oil slick of bitterness which I'm sure they all heard. I hit the bottom of the ketchup bottle with the heel of my hand and used more force than strictly needed. Had to bleed off my aggression somehow.

"We are the oldest continuous pack in New England. Third-oldest in all of America. We have a heritage to preserve and protect." Rachel waved her fork again for emphasis, her dark eyes aglow with an almost religious fervor.

"Oh, God, not that old tired line." I snorted and someone kicked me hard in the shin. I pretended not to notice but it fucking hurt. I'd probably bruise.

"Bonding outside the pack brings in new blood. It doesn't dilute. If anything, it makes the pack stronger and gives it an opportunity for growth." I tucked my feet beneath my chair, out of reach.

"So speaks someone who couldn't wait to rush off to some no-name little pack in Connecticut. Someone with purer and older blood than any of us sitting here at this goddamn table." The blatant ire in Tony's voice surprised me, although I guess it shouldn't have.

"You had your chance," I said with soft malice and, when he shoved back his chair with explosive violence, I ducked because I expected a blow.

Instead he stalked for the door. He turned around halfway there and glared at Susan.

"You coming?" It sounded like an order she'd better not refuse.

"Nice, Stanzie. Some family reunion." Mark watched Susan gather her purse and walk after Tony who, once he saw her push back her chair, started for the door again. "You come in here and start shooting off your big mouth when you don't know a frigging thing about us anymore.

What gives you the right to judge us? Are you so goddamn successful and superior? Did your choice to leave lead you to some fairy tale happy ending?"

"You know it didn't," I snapped as the hot sting of tears burned my eyes.

Thank you, Mark, for pointing out just how shitty my life has ended up. Fuck you.

Mark got up and threw a wad of bills on the table. Rachel flung me a black look and got to her feet.

Scott drank his beer and watched them stomp out as a small grin curled the corners of his mouth.

Faith bit her lip and set down her forkful of broiled fish.

"Want me to go home now?" I took a gulp of my beer and contemplated my French fries. Was I or was I not hungry?

"Hell, no. You're picking up what's left of the tab. Cheapskate Tony and Susan didn't leave a dime and neither did Alan." Scott reached across the table and scooped up the money Mark had contemptuously thrown down.

"Seventeen bucks. Won't even cover their goddamn bar tab." He threw it back down with another grin.

"What is so funny?" Faith snapped at him. She pushed a lock of blond hair behind her ear and yanked on her silver hoop earring.

"You hate these Friday night dinners from hell. Why are you giving me shit about thinking it's funny your cousin got under their skin instead of them getting under yours for a change?"

"Can't make an omelet without breaking some eggs," I remarked and Scott guffawed into his beer.

"I don't like conflict," Faith muttered. She stabbed at her fish with her fork but didn't eat any.

"Babe, if you don't like conflict, you're in the wrong pack and the wrong place. Alphas don't get to cower in the corner at the first sign of tension. They get right up in the middle of it." Scott's eyes gleamed as if he relished the prospect of a good fight. He threw me a look. "They don't call in the goddamn cavalry before the first shot's been fired."

"Scott, we've been through all this. Stanzie's here and maybe she can help us. Why do you have to be like this?" Faith let her fork drop to her plate and pushed more hair behind her ears. Sweat beaded her forehead and I wondered if she felt sick.

Scott snorted. "Because we can handle this shit ourselves. You underestimate me, as usual. You always have. Thought I'd be an easy lay at the Regional, someone to initiate your wolf and get your ass out of Mayflower so you could join my pack. You saw how that went. So let's cut the crap. Your cousin is not going to waltz in here and magically solve all your goddamn problems. The biggest problem you have is you don't have the balls to be Alpha."

Tears glimmered in Faith's eyes then streaked down her cheeks. She swiped at them with the back of her hand. Scott gave her an impatient look devoid of sympathy. When he stared across the table at me, he shook his head.

"Yeah, I know. You think I'm an asshole. I read that loud and clear. What you don't understand is that I have to listen to this crap day in and day out. I don't even know why the fuck she agreed to be Alpha because she's hated every second of it."

"I wanted a baby. A baby." Her voice was vicious but clogged with tears.

"And you're going to have one."

"There is something wrong with this pack," Faith insisted in a low voice.

Scott's face hardened. "There's something wrong with your head. Jesus." He got up and drained the last of his beer before he walked for the door.

"I'm sorry." Faith groaned. More tears poured down her face. "I'll call you tomorrow morning. We...we can have breakfast."

She struggled with her purse and I held up a hand. "I've got the tab. Go on before he leaves you behind. I didn't bring my car, so I can't give you a ride home."

She looked like she wanted to argue, but in the end didn't.

As I waited for the bill, I drank Alan's beer. It tasted like shit.

* * * *

A man sat on the walkway outside room twelve, back braced against the door. He had a paper bag between his jeans-clad knees and swigged something from a bottle as I approached.

Alan.

"I followed your scent to the door." He kept his eyes downcast, as if he expected me to kick his ass, but I only slid the key card into the reader and unlocked the door.

He scrambled to his feet as I pushed it open and ducked into the room with me. Bottles jingled against each other when the paper bag shifted.

I flicked on the lights and threw my purse onto the desk before I drew the curtains against the darkness outside the window.

Behind me, Alan twisted the caps off two bottles of beer and handed one to me when I turned.

"Alan, you need to raise your sights a bit when it comes to beer," I said and took a swig of the Budweiser.

He reached into the bag again and pulled out a half-pint of Jack Daniels and handed it to me with a sheepish smile.

"Better." I put the beer on the desk and rummaged in my coin purse for change. When I had a handful, I took it and the ice bucket out to the vending machines.

Alan was sprawled across my bed when I returned with soda and ice. My beer was in his hand and his first two discards were in the trash.

I gave his bare feet a long look. "Make yourself at home why don't you?"

"Stanzie, can I ask you a huge, huge, mega favor? One that I can never repay but I'll always be grateful for?" A plaintive note made his voice crack and he cleared his throat.

I busied myself with the Jack Daniels. When I had a drink built, I leaned against the dresser and looked at him.

He probably had no idea in hell how damn hot he was. Wheat-colored hair, vivid blue eyes, flawless skin and tight muscles. He was even cuter than his father, in my opinion. Shane Perrault had made my girlish heart do somersaults when I'd hit puberty which had fucked with my head because I'd always looked to him as an uncle. The older men in Mayflower were all my uncles. Not by blood, but by pack proximity. All the older women were aunts.

"Can I?" He sat up straighter on the mattress and abandoned his depressed sprawl. I didn't like the look in his eyes, as if he expected to be slapped or belittled. I knew that look. I'd had that same one when I'd been around his age. Fucking Mayflower.

"Of course," I said, resolved to do whatever it was he wanted if it were within my power. And if it weren't, I'd do whatever I could to find someone who did have the power.

"Initiate my wolf? Please?" A slow stain of humiliation bloomed across his cheeks. It killed him to ask me. It pissed me off—not at him, but at the people who made him think asking someone for help to initiate his wolf would be such a horrible thing.

When I didn't say anything, he rushed back into speech. "I'm not hitting on you. God knows you're beautiful, but, really you're sympathetic. You know me but you're not patronizing and emasculating like Susan and Rachel. I can't ask Faith, she's like my sister, and I'd rather never shift in my life than be initiated by either of those two fucking witches. Please, Stanzie!"

I couldn't breathe.

"There's a Regional in August and I'm going, but I can't show up there and ask a stranger to initiate me. I'm almost twenty-two fucking years old. It's embarrassing, Stanzie. I'm not...shit. I'm not very confident. And I don't know anyone. In my whole life I've never met one person from the Pack outside of Mayflower except for Grey. Never been to a Regional or anything.

"Since I turned fifteen I've asked to go to one and everyone told me they had no idea when or where they took place. Bullshit, I know, but they didn't want me to go. Until now, suddenly, everyone's telling me I have to go to this one and find a bond mate. A fucking bond mate? I haven't ever even shifted yet! I have never even kissed a girl let alone had sex with one.

"I feel like such an asshole, Stanzie. And I can't talk to Faith about this because she already feels bad enough since she didn't take me to the one Regional she's ever been to. I'm so behind everyone else my age. It makes me feel like the world's biggest pussy because I'm scared. Faith had the balls to go alone to meet strangers and to find a bond mate, even if Scott is a douche bag. At least she didn't have to bond with Mark and Rachel like they were all planning."

When he said that, my heart gave a terrific stutter and a hot flame of fury ignited in my blood. Goddamned Mayflower.

"If I ask someone at the Regional and they turn me down, I don't know what the fuck I'll do." Alan slumped back against the headboard and covered his eyes with his arm so he wouldn't have to see my reaction.

I silently counted to ten to keep my temper in check and focused on Alan. Faith had gotten away from Mark and Rachel the same way I had gotten away from Wes Hanover—desperation and luck.

"It's an honor to be asked to initiate someone's wolf, Alan," I said gently. I had to put my drink down because my hand shook. "I think you'd find everyone sympathetic—in a good way—at the Regional."

"So it's no? You're going to say no, aren't you?" His mouth screwed up and for a moment I thought he would cry. What a shitty situation. This was so not fair.

I crossed to the bed and scooted onto the mattress so I sat close beside him and our shoulders brushed. He stiffened at first but soon leaned into me, although he didn't move his arm away from his eyes.

"You know about my wolf, right?" I chose my words with care because each one hurt more than the last. "You know she's not normal?"

He nodded. He didn't understand. He had no clue. How could he?

"If I were to shift with you, Alan, she wouldn't know how to help you. Initiation is when an experienced wolf guides an inexperienced one. My wolf can't guide anyone. She needs to be guided. She always has. It wouldn't be right for me to try to do this. Your wolf will be disoriented and scared, and my wolf won't be able to react the right way."

"She knew how to defend herself with Nate Carver." He said the name in a rush but I still winced and went cold.

"Oh, she thinks for herself. Of herself. Everyone else is someone to play with or someone to ignore. Look, Alan, if I could I would do this for you, I swear. But this is too important to fuck around with. Your wolf may need help and I can't rely on mine to give it. To even recognize your wolf needed it."

I swung my legs off the edge of the bed and buried my face in my hands. One more terrible reminder of the divide between my wolf and everyone else's. I'd never even contemplated what I'd do if someone asked me to initiate his wolf. It never crossed my mind it would be a possibility. How sheltered and willfully ignorant had I kept myself? Selfish. Alan needed me and I couldn't be there for him. That sucked so much I didn't even have words.

"I'm sorry." Alan touched my shoulder with a tentative hand and, when I didn't jerk away, he moved to sit beside me. He put his arm around me and I let my head drop to his shoulder.

"I'm the one who's sorry." I sighed.

"I'll suck it up and ask someone at the Regional." He forced himself to sound confident, but we both knew better. It made my heart hurt more than it already did. "I'm an asshole, Stanzie. I knew about your wolf being...different. But I never thought it would be an issue for initiation. That's my problem, you know? I never think. Everyone tells me that."

"Don't listen to them." I jumped to my feet and returned to the dresser for my drink. "How the hell would you know what to think about my wolf when they've kept you in the dark about what it means to be Pack? And then they dare to tell you that you don't think? Fuck them. Don't let them run you down, Alan. You used to be such a confident kid. Always laughing, always getting in trouble."

"Only so you'd chase me." He grinned, although futility lurked behind his blue eyes. "I used to love trying to outrun you. No one in the whole pack could catch me but you. You still faster than the wind, Stanzie?"

"Pretty much." I grinned back. We stared at each for a nostalgic moment.

"I really looked up to you, you know that?" Alan took a swig of his beer and moved back to his position against the headboard. His eyes darkened. "When you didn't come back from that Regional, I cried for three days. Remember how you took me out for ice cream just before the Regional and you told me you were leaving but I wasn't supposed to tell anybody?"

"I remember." I flashed back to a crisp autumn day in October. I'd taken Alan to the local ice cream shop in town where we could build our own sundaes and eat them on picnic tables by a stone wall. We had to be careful of the northern part of the wall near the oak trees because of the yellow jackets—they adored ice cream.

The trees had snapped with vibrant autumn colors and Alan and I had eaten sundaes in blue plastic bowls. He'd dripped his all over the picnic table—he'd been ten or eleven years old—and I'd been both apprehensive and completely entranced with the knowledge that I was about to bond with Grey. I hadn't known which pack we'd join. I'd only known I would leave Mayflower.

"I never told a soul," Alan whispered and the memory faded to be replaced with reality. The little boy who'd dripped ice cream all over had become a man.

I'd been younger than he was now when we'd eaten that ice cream.

"I knew you wouldn't," I said with a smile.

Chapter 8

A queasy headache thumped in the back of my head when I opened my eyes. My mouth tasted like the bottom of a stale bottle of whiskey and I grimaced.

Alan curled up against me on the other side of the bed, pressed close. His breath was warm against the back of my neck.

Careful not to disturb him, I staggered to the window. At some point during last night's booze fest I'd discarded my dress, but I still had on my bra and panties. I stood still for a moment, horrified, and tried to remember if I'd done anything sexually stupid.

My memory didn't supply me with any graphic details, but I sort of remembered the kissing. The idea that this gorgeous boy had gotten all the way to twenty-one without one kiss had outraged me. After several drinks I'd offered to teach him how to kiss so he wouldn't be entirely without weapons in his arsenal of seduction come the Regional.

It had taken multiple sessions with his enthusiastic participation to teach him the basics. From the feathery brush of lips to the playful nip, to full-on tongue wrestling. Oh God.

When I pushed the curtain aside, I recoiled with a curse. Fucking sun.

"You're killing me," moaned Alan from the bed. I turned around and saw he had a pillow over his head. A thrill of relief coursed through me when I realized he was still fully clothed.

Now it flooded back to me. After the tongue-wrestling kiss, I'd abruptly come to my drunken senses and retreated to the bathroom. When I'd returned, he'd been passed out on the bed. Then for some dumb reason I'd thrown off my dress and crawled under the covers. At one point during the night he'd burrowed under them as well, but he'd kept his pants on. Thank God for inexperience.

"The sun is harsh, huh?" I tugged the curtain back together.

"I mean you in those lace panties. I'm dying here," Alan complained. "So not fair. Maybe we could..."

"No," I yelped. I ran to the bathroom and locked the door between us.

Twenty minutes later, I emerged in a towel which was probably worse than the panties. Alan was asleep thankfully and I quickly threw on jeans, a lacy pink tank top, gray zippered hoodie and a pair of pink-and-white Nikes before I pulled my hair back in a ponytail. My stomach grumbled and, when I found my watch, I discovered it was nearly nine AM. Earlier than I'd thought it would be.

My phone chirped and it took me a moment to find it in my purse.

"Breakfast?" Faith sounded a lot more awake and a lot less hungover than me.

We agreed to meet at a Friendly's in Wendell, and I attempted to cover the hangover after effects with strategically applied make up while Alan showered.

Halfway to the Prelude I realized I would not be able to drive. Not with Alan riding shotgun. I was not ready for passengers yet. I tossed him the keys under the pretext he knew where the restaurant was better than I did.

"You lived here all your life until you bonded. Things haven't changed a goddamn bit." Alan's face was bitter as he snatched the keys out of the air.

"They did teach you to drive, didn't they?" I hesitated with the seatbelt half buckled.

He snorted. "Jesus, they kept me away from other people, Stanzie, but they did manage to teach me basic life skills."

"So if you knew how to drive and had a car, why didn't you just drive to some other pack at some point? Like to Riverglow?" I fastened my seat belt and tried to calm my erratic heart. Maybe I should have driven. No.

Alan adjusted the seat and mirrors before he started the car. My heartbeat calmed a bit. Checking the mirrors was a good, responsible thing. Let's hope he extended that to his actual driving.

"How the hell would I have found Riverglow? Connecticut's a small state, but I didn't even know where to start to find the pack." Alan glanced in the rearview mirror before he reversed the car neatly from the parking slot and zipped toward the road.

A little fast, okay, but I could handle it if he didn't pull into traffic and waited for the road to be absolutely clear before he... I squeezed my eyes shut until I realized there would be no impact. When I looked into the side mirror, the car behind us was a good four car lengths away, but I still would have waited for it to pass if I'd been the one behind the wheel.

"You okay?" Alan shot me a strange look.

"Can you not...can you keep your eyes on the road, Alan." My voice shook a little and I mentally cursed.

"I've been driving since I was sixteen." He gave me another look—this one offended.

"Yeah? So had I when I crashed the Mustang and killed Grey and Elena. That doesn't mean shit," I snapped and his eyes went wide with shock.

"Oh, damn it. I'm sorry." He fixed his gaze firmly ahead on the road and eased off the gas pedal. The Prelude's speed dropped to just under the speed limit. The car behind us crept up two car lengths.

"I'm a little weird about cars, Alan. Not your problem." I relaxed my death grip on the edge of the seat and forced my body to relax. My spine was uncooperative and stiff.

"Honestly, I'm a good driver. I've never even dented a fender," Alan said in a voice usually reserved for scared children.

Neither had I until the accident. But, for once, my thoughts didn't spill onto my tongue without a delay and I managed to stay silent.

The parking lot at Friendly's was nearly full and I held my breath until Alan had successfully nosed the Prelude into a spot between two huge SUVs. I barely had enough room to squeeze out the door.

Faith and Scott held down a booth in the back of the restaurant. She was dressed as casually as he was—jeans, t-shirt and sneakers. Her hair was pulled back into a ponytail and except for the color of our eyes and my slightly bigger nose, we might have been twins.

Scott's gaze missed nothing about Alan as we approached the booth. Neither did Faith's. They both registered he wore the same clothes from the night before and he needed to shave. Not necessarily indictments in and of themselves, but when paired with me, they screamed out that we'd spent the night together.

"Jesus Christ," said Scott as Alan slid into the booth bench opposite him. "Could it possibly be that the Virgin of Mayflower has had his cherry popped?"

"Shut the fuck up, Charest," Alan muttered as his face flushed dark red.

Faith darted a look at me.

"Come with me to the ladies' room." It was an order, not a request, and even though she had no real jurisdiction over me, I decided to be obliging.

After she ascertained we were alone in the bathroom, Faith whirled toward me.

"Tell me you didn't sleep with Alan. Tell me you didn't shift with him, Stanzie. You should have known better with the way your wolf is!"

It was my turn to flush. I saw my face in the mirror above the sink turn first red then stark, furious white.

Faith took a step backward. Her nostrils flared as she picked up the scent of my rage.

"You do not need to lecture me about my wolf. I am well aware of the fact I have no business initiating anybody. If you have that little trust in my judgment, maybe I'd better go back to Boston after breakfast." I reached out for the door handle and stiffened when Faith grabbed my elbow. She let go fast.

"Stanzie, I'm sorry. It's just I know how desperate he is and it's obvious he spent the night with you."

"We got drunk and passed out around midnight if you must know." I swung around again and she shrank away from my anger. "He's twenty-one years old and he's never even kissed a girl. What the hell is wrong with this pack? He has no clue where any other pack's territory is and he's never been out of Massachusetts and you people expect him to find a fucking bond mate and initiate his wolf at the Regional next month? How the hell is he supposed to pull that one off, Faith?"

"I did it!" she flared, mouth tight.

"Yeah, and look at you, stuck with that arrogant sonofabitch with the ball cap out there. Great job."

Tears glittered in her eyes and she blinked them back furiously, but still one escaped and tracked down her cheek. "You don't even know him. Scott's a great guy."

I heaved a sigh. "You sure? You let him walk all over you."

"I do not!" More tears escaped her brown eyes. "You have no clue, Stanzie, about Scott and me, so stop with the judgmental crap right now. You've been here for about five seconds. How the hell can you tell what the truth is yet?"

She had a point.

"I'll stop being judgmental about you and Scott if you stop leaping to conclusions about me and Alan," I offered and the ghost of a smile drifted across her mouth. I thought of Lauren again and my stomach clenched.

"So not even a little fooling around?" she asked. "He's twenty-one, cute as hell and he doesn't know it. Irresistible combo."

I snorted. "Let's just say that he can no longer claim he's never been kissed."

Faith chuckled and I rolled my eyes. "But that's it. That's all he can say. And I only did it because I felt sorry for the poor guy."

"*Mmm hmm.*" Faith peered at her reflection in the mirror and dashed the tears away with the back of her hand. "Tell that to your bond mate if you dare."

I don't know what I did, but Faith slowly straightened from the mirror and gave me a measuring look.

"Sorry," she murmured and I forced a smile.

"Not your problem," I assured her then cursed because I'd just acknowledged there was one.

Murphy's face flashed through my memory and I turned away so Faith wouldn't see the sudden tears in my eyes.

Get a grip, Stanzie. He's gone. It's over and you've got things to do here which don't include mindless bouts of self-pity.

Alan and Scott glowered at each other over mugs of coffee when Faith and I returned to the booth. Scott was more amused than pissed, which only served to infuriate Alan more. It would be a long breakfast.

"What's the plan for today?" I asked after the waitress filled my mug with steaming coffee and took my omelet order.

Faith examined her silverware to make sure it was clean before she stirred sugar into her tea. "Backyard barbecue at Tony and Susan's."

"I'm invited?" My smile was skeptical and Scott's mouth twitched.

Alan gave a theatrical groan and sank in his seat. "Shit. I forgot about the damn barbecue. Can I boycott?"

"If I have to go, you do." I nudged him with my elbow.

"Paul and Lauren are supposed to be there." Faith let that bombshell drop just as I took a sip of coffee. It went down the wrong way and I struggled not to gag and cough.

"Supposed to be means you don't think they'll show." My voice was weird and strained and I hoped they'd blame the coffee and not my nerves.

"They only found out last night you were in town," Faith said. "In view of what happened at your tribunal, I'm not sure what they'll do."

The word *tribunal* made my gut clench and I reminded myself it was over and done with.

"Will any of the elder generation show?" I tried to sound nonchalant as I realized it would bother me if everyone took Paul's side and ostracized me. But what else could I expect? Faith and Alan were probably my only allies in Mayflower. I reserved judgment on Scott. I hadn't figured him out yet although I thought he was a dick. The question was whether he was a smart one. Intelligence gleamed from his gray eyes but I wondered where his tired malevolence stemmed from. Was it Faith or was it Mayflower?

"It's the midsummer barbecue," Faith said then I remembered Mayflower's traditional kickoff to summer. Not only was this a barbecue, it was also a hunt.

Beside me, Alan played with his silverware. He kept his head down, but I could see the bright red blush as it slowly stole across his cheeks.

Scott looked between us both and grinned. "Found a partner to your liking at last, kid?"

Faith pursed her lips tightly.

Scott rolled his eyes. "What the hell'd I say now?"

"Look, I don't remember ever meeting you before, but you haven't got a Canadian accent so you're probably from one of the New England packs. Everyone in New England knows about my wolf, right? And if they don't, Mayflower pack members surely do." I met his gaze and decided I was through skulking around the issue of my wolf.

"So your wolf is a little on the wild side." Scott made no pretense he didn't have a clue. "This is a hunt. If your wolf goes wild, Faith and I will take care of both of you. This is a perfect opportunity for the kid so he doesn't go to the Regional next month a goddamn virgin."

"Stanzie doesn't want to shift." Alan said, but he kept his eyes down on his paper place mat.

"Wow," said Scott with a marveling, derisive grin. "You're so ashamed of your wolf you've got a twenty-year-old virgin defending you?"

"Scott," Faith murmured, her face tight. "Please don't."

"I keep telling you that you need balls to be Alpha, Faith. This is a golden opportunity. If Alan goes with her it solves everything. If he doesn't, every male in Mayflower is going to be sniffing around Stanzie's tail ready to seize the moment. She's our guest. She can't sit out with the grandmothers on the sidelines. If Alan doesn't partner with her, then as Alpha, I ought to. Is that what you want?" Scott leaned back against the booth and waited for her response.

Blood slammed to Faith's face and tears of rage and humiliation glittered in her eyes.

"Enough," I snapped. "I'm not going to shift with anyone. I'm just a guest and this is a Mayflower tradition."

"Oh, semantics. You were born here, Stanzie," Scott argued, but he was laughing at us all.

* * * *

Alan and I arrived at the barbecue a little after four that afternoon. The mouthwatering scent of grilling steak wafted over the redwood-stained privacy fence erected around the backyard of the tidy white Colonial Susan and Tony shared with Mark, Rachel and their combined children. The brick walkway to the front door was lined with beds of yellow and purple pansies, where bees hummed enthusiastically as they gathered pollen.

Alan led me to the gate rather than the front door and held it open so I could walk through first.

I'd changed into a bright blue-and-white tie dye long dress. The spaghetti straps and pattern made it cool and casual but dressy enough so my father, if he showed up, wouldn't get pissed. The women of Mayflower always wore dresses to barbecues and parties. It was like being in a scene from the goddamn *Stepford Wives*.

I paired the dress with white knotted thong sandals and silver hoops and bangle bracelets. My bond pendant made me feel like a fraud.

Alan had changed into a pair of tan Dockers and a black t-shirt. He'd shaved and looked impossibly young and irresistible.

The backyard was immaculately landscaped with colorful rock gardens and fountains interspersed between groomed hedges and pruned fruit trees.

The grill was set up on the bottom tier of the multi-level deck which blended into the sunken backyard seamlessly.

Tony, in crisp jeans and a white, short-sleeved button-down shirt protected by a bright red chef's apron, stood, spatula in hand, ready to flip the grilling steaks and burgers.

A wooden picnic table groaned under the weight of several baskets of chips, plates of pickles and olives, bowls of potato salad and baked beans. Two huge coolers packed with ice, beer, soda, water and wine coolers were propped by the deck stairs. Alan made a beeline for them.

The pack members already there drank water. It was obvious from the sexual current that snaked through the scent of grilling meat, there would be a hunt. They'd eat a plateful of food first, shift and hunt then come back ravenous for more.

Beyond the fence, the state forest beckoned.

I'd never participated in the midsummer's hunt when I'd belonged to Mayflower. In the end, I'd been the pack virgin just like Alan—only not really a virgin in the technical sense since I'd shifted with Rudi at the Great Gathering but refused to let Wes Hanover initiate my wolf afterward.

The last two midsummer barbecues I'd attended had been pure hell because they hadn't let me escape to Grandmother Elaine's house with the kids after we'd eaten. Instead, I'd had to watch the pack orgy before they shifted. I knew they'd wanted me to get caught in the sexual energy. The vibe had definitely affected me but Wes Hanover was the only male who would have responded to my sexual overtures, so I'd stayed firmly on the sidelines.

Alan stood by the coolers and gulped down a beer. My heart went out to him—I knew how he felt.

He held up a beer in a silent offer to get me one. I mouthed the words *wine cooler* and he obediently dug one up from the ice and brought it to me.

Everyone else drank water and, although I'd stood in the backyard for more than a full minute, no one had acknowledged me verbally, although everyone stared.

In addition to Tony at the grill, Susan sat at the picnic table with Rachel. Mark threw a toy football to a set of chubby toddlers—a boy and a girl—who I assumed were his twins, Ethan and Denise. Both had Rachel's blue black hair. They giggled together as they chased the football.

A pre-teen girl with a serious face and long brown hair was curled on a lounge chair with a paperback novel. She studied me over the top of the book and, when I smiled at her, she lowered the book and smiled back tentatively. When she did, I knew the smile and realized she must be Tony's daughter, Olivia. Susan had been pregnant when I'd left the pack.

On the way over Alan had told me about the children and their names.

Rachel's parents, Jennifer and Terry, sat in lawn chairs on the upper level of the deck along with Mark's parents, Dirk and Jill. Dirk's twin brother, Darren stood at the railing with a bottle of water in one hand, his dark eyes watchful.

His bond mate, Dorothy, chatted on her cellphone on the extreme end of the deck, her back to the rest of us. She was a real estate agent and loved her job so much she could never be far from her phone. The pack made most of its money from her small agency.

As a teen, I'd worked behind the reception desk and done filing. She'd paid me fifty dollars a week and my father had taken twenty of that and donated it to the pack fund. Since I was a teenager and not a contributing adult member of the pack, I technically did not owe the pack any money, but my father had wanted to instill a sense of responsibility in me. Most of what was left I'd spent on gas for my mother's car, since I used it to get back and forth from the agency, and on lunch at the local diner.

Lauren had packed me lunches at first, but Dorothy liked the diner and, when my father discovered she'd been paying for my lunch every day, he'd gone through the roof and demanded I pay my own way. Every Friday I'd paid for Dorothy's lunch too, at his insistence.

Dorothy had told me wild stories about her youth while we ate. Stuff she and Darren had gotten up to behind the rest of the pack's back. They were the resident rebels. They were also Tony's parents and sometimes she told me tales about Tony's childhood, which I loved because I had such a crush on him.

Today I smiled when I saw Dorothy's hair was an improbable shade of red no self-respecting stylist would have let escape the salon. The sale shelf at Walgreen's no doubt. Dorothy dyed her hair a different color whenever the mood struck her. I still remembered the Big Bird yellow spiked mullet she'd sported the summer I was five. I'd taken one look at her, along with her skin-tight spandex cat suit and thigh-high studded boots and screamed. It was one of her favorite memories. Or so she'd always told me.

Darren and Dorothy were in their late seventies, but Darren, at least, could pass for late forties, fifty tops. When Dorothy turned around, I saw that she'd pass for forty-five easily. When I was five she'd actually been around forty-five but could have passed for late twenties.

"Is someone going to help me with the goddamn cookies or do I have to do everything by myself?" The complaint came from an old woman—the only true elderly person left in Mayflower. My great-grandmother, Elaine.

"Elaine, I cannot do five things at the same time, can I?" Another woman, younger, but not young, answered her and my stomach clenched. My grandmother, Carolyn.

My bickering grandmothers were in the kitchen beyond the open sliding glass door off the deck.

"I can help," I offered, and raised my voice so they could hear me from the backyard.

Barbecue sauce sizzled on the grill as Tony deftly flipped one of the steaks.

"Stanzie?" Grandmother Elaine called. "If that's you, get your ass up here. Your grandmother is fucking everything up as usual."

"Mother!" cried Carolyn. She only called Grandmother Elaine *mother* when she was mortified or pissed off.

Alan sniggered into his beer and I took the stairs as quickly as I could.

Darren and his generation craned their necks to watch me as I rushed past.

The kitchen smelled like brown sugar and molasses. I trailed the scent to a huge crockpot of baked beans simmering on the counter.

Grandmother Elaine sat at the round kitchen table surrounded by jars of spices and a cookbook she'd made by hand, each recipe carefully copied in her neat handwriting. Recipes for food were in the front and recipes for medicines and other herbal concoctions were in the back.

Grandmother Elaine was nearly one hundred and forty years old, but she looked a spry seventy with curly gray hair and plump wrinkled cheeks. She'd looked the same all my life, but I'd seen pictures of her when she'd been younger and her hair had been blond and her face unlined.

The shocker was Carolyn. She'd crossed from middle to old age since the last time I'd seen her. Her once-blond hair was now gray and her beautiful face had sagged and wrinkled. She'd lost her goddess-like figure and was now on the scrawny side with stick legs and flabby arms.

The worst thing—she wore orthopedic old lady shoes in an ugly calf-brown color with tan laces.

She noticed my horrified expression and her welcoming smile turned into a grimace. "Gotten old, haven't I?" She sighed and I cursed myself.

"Your shoes are ugly as hell," said Grandmother Elaine. "That girl is more freaked out by your damn shoes than your wrinkles, Carolyn."

I couldn't help it—I burst into laughter. "She's right," I confirmed and a small smile tweaked the corner of Carolyn's mouth. Grandmother Carolyn. Once a Pack member passed into old age, they were always addressed as grandmother or grandfather by the younger generations.

"I've got bunions from years of high heels," Grandmother Carolyn confessed. "I figure I've earned the right to wear old lady shoes. You'll be the same way, Stanzie."

I shuddered. No fucking way. Not me.

"It's good to see you both," I said and sudden tears pricked my eyes. These women had helped bring me up. I'd learned everything I knew about herbs from Grandmother Elaine and everything I loved about shoes from Grandmother Carolyn. I hadn't spoken to either of them in more than ten years. When I'd left Mayflower, they'd shut me out. I'd always sent Christmas and birthday cards, but they'd never sent any in return.

Even after Grey and Elena died, I'd sent the cards. Sometimes I'd tucked photographs in too.

"I'm making my jam thumbprint cookies if someone can find a goddamn mixing bowl in this disorganized kitchen," Grandmother Elaine said. "I wanted to make the damn things at home where I know where everything is but Carolyn said it would be just as easy to make them here. That was a crock of shit. Susan hides things. Sticks them in the damndest places. You know where I finally found the fucking baking powder?"

"Elaine!" Grandmother Carolyn cast an agonized glance at the open sliding glass door. "Will you please stop swearing? You're worse than a teenage boy. You know how Paul feels about women cursing."

"Oh, for Christ's sake." Grandmother Elaine rolled her faded blue eyes. "Paul can go jump in a goddamn lake. I want to make cookies and I need a frigging mixing bowl!"

Carolyn winced and began to search through the cupboards. Grandmother Elaine was right. Susan was disorganized.

"Where's this new bond mate of yours?" Grandmother Elaine patted the chair next to hers and I sat. My fingers flew involuntarily to my bond pendant and when I didn't answer right away she snorted.

"Men are such sonsofbitches. I never was happier than when Jonas dropped dead of the red virus. Well, possibly I was happier when I realized I wasn't going to die of the fucking thing myself, but his death was a close second. Mean old bastard. You would have hated him if you could remember him. He held you once when you were a baby and you screamed like hell. Old buzzard couldn't get rid of you fast enough. Remember Jonas, Carolyn? What a bastard he was?"

"He was my father, Elaine." Grandmother Carolyn turned around from her so-far fruitless search.

"Big frigging deal. You were happy when Hank croaked of the virus, weren't you? Why begrudge your own mother the same thing?"

Grandmother Carolyn slammed a cupboard door shut and wrenched open the next one.

"I was devastated when Hank passed."

"Bullshit." Grandmother Elaine sniffed. "You were tickled pink. And happy to bond with Clarence when Grace died."

Grandmother Carolyn's cheeks flamed. "Elaine, you are being awful to me on purpose. Grace Keller was my best friend. I cried for weeks after she died. Clarence and I bonded because we were the only two left of our generation. It was either that or leave the pack."

"And you've been sad and suffering these thirty years and more with that man, I suppose." Grandmother Elaine winked at me. It was no secret Grandmother Carolyn was head over heels in love with Clarence Nott and had been even before her best friend Grace died.

The red virus was deadly to the Pack. The Others never caught it—it was species specific.

When my parents had been Alpha and I was eighteen months old, the red virus had swept through Mayflower and, by the time it was gone, more than half the pack was dead. Grandmother Elaine was the only one of her generation to be spared, just as Grandmother Carolyn and Grandfather Clarence were the only ones from theirs.

It had been a horrible test of Paul's leadership skills, but he'd brought the pack through the crisis and, to this day, people still deferred to and looked up to him.

I remembered nothing of being sick or of the twenty-five pack members who'd died. In the thirty years since the red virus had decimated Mayflower, the net gain of new members was a paltry six. Another reason why it was so weird that the pack encouraged Alan to bond outside of it.

"Why does everyone want Alan to leave Mayflower?" I asked.

Something slipped through Grandmother Carolyn's fingers and smashed to the ceramic tiled floor—a mixing bowl.

"Shit," she said then covered her mouth.

"Goddamned fool." Grandmother Elaine struggled out of her chair and knelt to pick up pieces.

I hurried to help her. Grandmother Carolyn found another mixing bowl and the broom, and Grandmother Elaine and I went back to the table so she could sweep up the smaller shards of glass.

"Tell me about your bond mate," Grandmother Elaine urged as we mixed the ingredients for her jam thumbprint cookies.

The broom stopped whisking across the floor for a moment but quickly resumed.

"It's complicated," I said. Grandmother Elaine snorted and reached out to pat my hand.

"Not like with Grey, hmm?"

"No," I said, blindsided by unexpected tears. My throat squeezed shut. The only thing complicated about Grey had been leaving Mayflower to bond with him. He had understood my dilemma, though and the complications had not been from him.

The pattern of our days together had been smooth and easy. Full of joy, both little and overwhelming. The difference between twenty and thirty. Between experiencing death and a second chance.

"Stop interrogating her." Grandmother Carolyn had stopped sweeping so she could listen. She was as interested in my story about Murphy as Grandmother Elaine but for some reason wanted me to believe otherwise.

I had no intention of sharing much with either of them. I wasn't a child any longer and they had been out of my circle too long. They no longer held much influence over me. They were not the all-powerful wise women of my youth. They were two old ladies tied to me by blood, but it could never be the same.

"You're unhappy." Grandmother Elaine patted my hand again. "Men are bastards, child. In a pack, you have sisters in all the women. There's where the real joy in life can be found."

"I need another wine cooler." I jumped to my feet before I lost my resolve and spilled my guts about Murphy and how much I loved and missed him.

The whisk of the broom began again as I darted out the door.

Late afternoon sunlight slanted across the manicured backyard and the gathered members of Mayflower.

More people had arrived since I'd gone into the kitchen. My parents, Paul and Lauren, were among them.

They held court at one of the circular bistro tables by the largest fountain. Lauren was breathtaking in a white cotton sundress with a sweetheart neckline trimmed with eyelet lace. Tan espadrille sandals turned her legs long and lean. Her golden blond hair spilled down to her shoulders in a loose wave that looked casual but had probably taken her an hour with a curling iron. The only jewelry she wore was her bond pendant and the Mayflower pack ring.

Next to her, I felt loud and overstated.

Wes Hanover and his bond mate, Maddie, sat with them, their posture submissive and eager. They all drank bottled water.

Susan brought them a basket of chips and a platter of olives and pickles. Maddie's plump fingers crept out for a fistful of chips which she crammed into her mouth. Her pudgy, sweet face lit up at the taste.

Maddie had always been on the *zaftig* side, but in the years since I'd left Mayflower she'd ballooned from pleasantly full-figured to obese. She wore a shapeless sack of a long dress in a hideous shade of coral that did nothing to flatter her form or coloring. Her hair was short and looked hacked by razors rather than scissors. Maybe she cut her own hair? It was hard to imagine a stylist had given her that look on purpose.

Wes was dwarfed beside her. He'd always been short, but now he was too thin. His elbows jutted, his kneecaps were bony knobs on his stick legs. He wore khaki shorts and a red polo shirt. His wispy fair hair floated on top of his skull and his watery blue eyes squinted against the slanting sun.

I shuddered. If my father had had his way, those two would be my bond mates right now.

Superficial. Shallow. Always reaching for the shiny things instead of the substantial. I heard my father's mocking voice in my head.

The ice was frigid against my skin as I dug in the cooler for another wine cooler. The second I had it open, someone reached his hand to snatch it from my grasp.

"You should be drinking water." Tony had abandoned the grill to abduct my wine cooler. His voice was soft and flirtatious as he inclined his body toward mine. He smelled of barbecue sauce and grilled meat which was not unappealing. His smile was the same as I remembered it back when it had produced butterflies in my stomach and a sensation of weightlessness.

I looked over his shoulder at Susan, who was headed in our direction, and braced myself for some sort of confrontation.

"Tony's right," she said as she drew close. She gave us both a friendly smile that put me on the instant defensive. "We're going to shift around sunset, Stanzie. No more alcohol, okay?" She winked and moved away.

I tried not to gape but Tony chuckled, so I knew my face gave something away. When he handed me a water bottle, his fingers brushed mine suggestively. He gave me another one of his heart-tugging grins, only my heart refused to respond and butterflies did not dance in my stomach. Somewhere in the past decade he'd lost his ability to reduce me to jelly.

I debated an attempt to retrieve my wine cooler but decided against it because he'd only think it was flirtation. Instead, I moved to the picnic table and grabbed a handful of chips.

What the hell was going on? Last night Tony and Susan had been hostile and cold, and today I was the object of their lustful desire? The hunt vibe was strong, but this was plain weird.

When I glanced over to the table where my parents held court, I saw Paul had disappeared and Lauren sat with Wes and Maddie. Sat was the operative word. No conversation. Maddie steadily demolished the bowl of chips while Wes watched Mark play with the twins. Lauren stared into middle space somewhere, her face blank, as if Paul's absence had rendered her inanimate and she would only spring to life when he was in her vicinity.

The sun was still bright, but low on the horizon as dusk approached. The temperature had dropped too and I wished I'd remembered to bring a sweater.

Drawn like a magnet, I approached the wrought iron table. Lauren gave a small start when she noticed me, but her face remained inert.

"Stanzie!" Wes Hanover jumped to his feet and nearly fell over his chair in his clumsy haste to intercept me. He grabbed my free hand with both of his and I restrained the urge to snatch it back. His palms were as clammy and sweaty as ever.

His lecherous gaze traveled up and down my body, a lascivious smile lit up his face. I gritted my teeth as he mentally undressed me the way he'd done since my sixteenth birthday. Maddie placidly continued to shove potato chips into her mouth. I knew Lauren would be no help, she never was. It was my own fault for walking into his physical sphere. He'd never approach me, that wasn't his way, but if I crossed the invisible line he considered within his space, he'd hound me and cling to me and undress me with his eyes until I felt coated with slime and dirty beneath the skin.

"How are you, Wes?" My voice was perfunctory but he danced around as if I'd evinced fascinated interest.

"I'm looking forward to the hunt tonight." His Adam's apple bobbed like a cork in his scrawny throat. I tried to extract my hand but his grip was too determined even though it was slippery. "I was thinking that maybe you and I could—"

"No." I shuddered with revulsion. "I'm not hunting tonight."

"Oh, but you are. Paul said." Wes blinked at me and scuttled closer like a roach. I took a step backward. The same old fucking dance.

"Paul doesn't speak for me."

"But he said you were." Wes let go with one hand so he could clamp his greasy fingers onto my bare shoulder. I flinched but he only tightened his grasp. Now he was a spider who weaved me into a slimy cocoon.

"I said no." I wrenched away from him and dropped my water bottle. Water gushed into the pristine green grass.

I threw an accusing look at Lauren, who sat still as a statue.

Wes made a grab for me as I escaped. A tumult of emotion washed over me. Humiliation, rage, futility. What the hell was I doing here? Why had I come? I touched my bond pendant and grief, sharp as a sword, pierced me. Why had Murphy left me? What was so wrong with me that he wouldn't even try to work it out?

Damn it, Stanzie, I cursed myself as I floundered toward the picnic table.

Scott and Faith were at the coolers. She had a bottle of water in her hand and he did too, although his gaze lingered longingly on the beer.

They both turned toward me, but Tony cut them off. He carried a platter of grilled steaks and burgers and herded me toward the large picnic table.

"You can sit next to me." He set the platter down and gave a shrill whistle, the signal that dinner was served. People began to drift from the deck. Paul emerged from the kitchen with Grandmother Carolyn on one arm, Grandmother Elaine on the other, and escorted them gallantly to the table on the deck. He told them to sit still and he'd fix them a plate.

"Lauren!" His gaze traveled across the lawn to Lauren. She came to herself with a start and leaped to her feet. She rushed to the table and began to fill two plates for the grandmothers.

"You can eat up there with them," Paul said to her as he approached the picnic table and sat next to Rachel. Susan passed him a heaping plate with the biggest, juiciest steak in the exact center.

Wes Hanover made a beeline for my side but was adroitly knocked aside by Dirk, who was elbowed away by Darren.

I reached out for a paper plate and Tony slapped my hand away with a flirtatious grin.

"Let me get your food." His voice was a low, sexy growl.

"I'll do it." Darren was quicker to the plates, his smile dark and seductive.

Shane Perrault, Alan's father, slipped onto the bench opposite me and gave me a lingering once-over, his sexual invitation clear.

The women sat on the other end of the table with Paul, not bothered at all by the way their bond mates were falling over themselves to seduce me.

"Alan, go eat with the grandmothers," Paul suggested when Alan tried to sit at the picnic table.

"Oh, for Christ's sake," muttered Scott from behind me. "Do you want Faith and me to go sit with the grandmothers too, Paul?"

Paul surveyed the jam-packed picnic table and didn't say a word.

Scott snorted and put a hand on my shoulder. The men around me stiffened, their eyes turned hostile.

"You have Faith," Darren's tone was a challenge and the whole table went silent. I braced myself. If Darren pressed it, there'd be a fight. Over me. And I'd be expected to go with the winner. But in a situation like this, challenging the Alpha was wrong. What the fuck was this?

"She's pregnant, remember? She wasn't planning to shift tonight. I'm a free agent." Scott's smile was easy, but his fingers pressed into my shoulder painfully.

I could stop the fight by accepting his overture or Darren's and everyone knew it. I ought to accept Scott's, since he was Alpha. Scott knew damn well I didn't want to shift, why was he doing this? I could have played the men off each other without it coming to violence and, in the end chosen none of them. Now I was trapped.

Paul lifted his plate as he got to his feet.

"Constance, shall we eat at a bistro table?" He gestured toward a secluded one in front of a burbling box-shaped fountain. He walked away from the picnic table secure in the belief I'd follow.

If I didn't, I'd have to deal with the testosterone-fueled egos of all the men. Was Paul actually helping me?

He'd devastated me when he'd renounced me in front of the tribunal. I should ignore him—after all, I didn't exist to him anymore, did I? But he'd talked to me and acknowledged me. I was here to investigate weird shit happening in this pack and Paul talking to me after he'd renounced me fit right into that category. Of course, I was rationalizing. I would have followed Paul regardless of the Council's investigation. Eager as ever for crumbs of attention off his table. The more things change, the more they stay the same—wasn't that the saying?

I took my plate from Darren's hand and followed Paul to the bistro table. Scott's gaze burned into my back the entire length of the yard and I smelled his frustration. I also felt Faith's gaze and smelled the sharp scent of betrayal, as if I'd deliberately set out to seduce her bond mate.

The role of Advisor sucked sometimes.

After I took the chair opposite Paul, he sliced into his meat with a sharp steak knife while I busied myself with a mouthful of baked beans. After we'd both chewed and swallowed he said, "Constance, in view of the circumstances, I'm lifting my renouncement."

I considered his words for perhaps three seconds. How big of him.

"Because the tribunal didn't put me to death you mean?" I curled my lip in derision but he pretended not to notice and sliced himself another bit of steak. "I'm a hero, Paul. So now I'm good enough to be former Mayflower and your acknowledged daughter?"

Paul chose to ignore that and said, "From what your grandmothers tell me, there's an issue with your new bond mate. I wondered that myself when he wasn't there at the tribunal. At first I thought that rude man with the mop on his head was your bond mate but I was mistaken."

"That was my Alpha." I nearly choked on the word. Liar. Paddy O'Reilly. "And I didn't tell the grandmothers a damn thing."

He winced at the word *damn*. He despised it when women swore. He didn't much care for it when men did either.

"You didn't have to." He chewed his steak and swallowed. I looked at his cold, handsome face and tried not to think of him as my father but it was impossible. I was here on Mayflower territory and he had the same haircut for Christ's sake that he'd had nearly thirteen years ago when I'd left with Grey. Nothing had changed. Tony and Mark had done more landscaping of the yard, but this fountain was not new. I remembered sitting on the edge of it and watching the Mayflower wolves stream out the back gate into the forest on a midsummer's eve much like this one.

I felt trapped between time and didn't know if Grey would be waiting at the motel room for me tonight or Murphy would suddenly walk through the back gate.

Loneliness swamped me. I was so tired of being alone and, even among my former pack and my blood relations, I didn't feel like I belonged. Yet everything was strangely familiar and I struggled against the notion that I had to please the man sitting across from me. Please him or defy him. Why was there no middle ground? Why couldn't he just sit there and have a rational conversation with me where I didn't become defensive?

"I'd like you to know there's a place here in Mayflower for you if you want to come back." Paul calmly continued to eat his steak while my entire body tingled first with icy cold shock waves followed by roaring hot ones.

Next he would tell me how much Wes Hanover still wanted to bond with me and I would scream. I could feel it building up in my throat in a choking wedge of panic.

"Susan and Tony would welcome you into a triad. So would Mark and Rachel, if you'd prefer, although I know you and Mark have always been more like brother and sister. You could have your choice, Constance. Your birthday is in two months and everything could be arranged so there'd be a seamless transition if you severed the bond with this absent Irish man. What do you think?" Paul reached out for his water bottle and his Adam's apple bobbed as he swallowed.

My food congealed on my plate. I couldn't eat. My stomach was a hard, tiny ball in the pit of my gut. How long had he planned this? A week? A year? This morning? Since he found out I was here? Or was this spur of the moment? Only Paul was never hasty. He always considered all the angles before he came to a conclusion. How much did he really know about Murphy and me? Who the fuck would have told him? He was guessing. He had to be guessing.

"Last night Susan told me hell would freeze over before I ever bonded with her and Tony." Somehow my voice was normal. Paul smiled genially.

"Oh, Susan always protests a bit at first but I think if you spoke to her today you'd discover she was fine with the idea."

Great. I was playing right into his hands. Instead of a forthright refusal, it now seemed as if I'd actually entertained the idea. Stupid. Well, not go all the way then?

"What if I preferred Alan?"

The genial smile faltered. "He's very young. You need someone with experience. Or do you prefer to babysit your bond mate? That's your relationship dynamic, after all, and he's still following you around like a puppy, isn't he?"

Paul had no doubt heard about how Alan had spent the night in my motel room. Fucking pack grapevine. Insidious.

"But what if I wanted?" I pressed.

"I'd rather not, but it might be possible." His words were clipped. I'd pissed him off. Surprise, surprise.

"Well, the thing is, Paul, I've got a bond mate."

"Your birthday can take care of that." His smile was smooth and bland. He cut another bite of steak. "Think about it. That's all I ask. Just as I ask you to listen to Faith with a grain of salt. Her hormones are making her unpredictably emotional. She's had difficulties coming to terms with being Alpha. I know she invited you here to confirm her paranoia but as you can plainly see, there's nothing wrong with Mayflower." Paul took a forkful of baked beans and smiled at me, one adult to another. Not our usual exchange.

Was he scared of something? Or was I the paranoid one?

* * * *

A hand came down on my shoulder as I tossed my half full plate into the trash can by the gate. Flies buzzed over the plastic rim enthusiastically.

"Really, I can fix it so you shift with Alan tonight, Stanzie." Scott's voice was low. His mouth nearly brushed my ear as if he whispered something seductive. "I'll watch over your wolf and Faith will watch over his. Just say the word. Say *something* because if you don't there's going to be a fight."

He was right. The men of Mayflower prowled around each other with clenched fists and hostile stares. They enjoyed it, though. This was the most exciting midsummer's hunt for years. They hoped for a chance to fight. It was like a choreographed dance, only I wouldn't play my part.

"I don't want to hunt," I snarled and his fingers tightened on my bare shoulder. I winced but he didn't let up the pressure.

"For someone who had the guts and audacity to rip out a guy's throat, you're a real coward. What the fuck is your problem? You want to shift with me then? Leave Alan out of it? That's a stupid waste of resources, don't you think?"

"What? You aren't panting for the opportunity to fuck me like the rest of the pack, Scott?" I shifted my shoulders to dislodge his hand, but failed.

"Come on, be serious." Scott's laughter should have been insulting but it wasn't. "You're hung up on your bond mate, I get that, but he's not here and you are, and there's going to be a situation if you don't stop acting like an idiot. I thought you were an Advisor. Aren't they supposed to be smart?"

"No. Allerton picked me for my stunning looks and tractable personality," I said and he laughed again, this time definitely in admiration.

"If I tell you you're hot, will you shift with Alan?" He nudged the side of my face with his nose and I twisted away. This time he let me go.

"What the fuck do you care about Alan anyway? "

The amused admiration died out of his face and he took an exasperated breath. "I'm on your side, Stanzie, believe it or not."

"Not," I decided and he shrugged.

"Fine. You're on your own." He walked away.

The second he left my side it was open season for the other men to approach me. I cursed my stupidity as I searched the backyard for a neutral zone.

Alan and Faith stood on the lower level of the deck together, so close their shoulders brushed, while Rachel and Susan hovered near. I watched Rachel reach out to comb her fingers through Alan's blond hair and grin at the shudder her touch produced. He edged closer to Faith and stuck to her like a burr. She and his mother were the only safe havens for him, and his mother, Samantha, was as far from him as the yard allowed.

Alan endured his own mating dance just as I did. Maybe Scott had a point. Then I thought of my broken wolf surrounded by the Mayflower pack and not understanding who they were. I pictured her frantic search for Murphy's wolf and the realization that he'd betrayed her just the same as every other creature she'd ever known. No way. Fuck that. I'd hurt her enough. I wouldn't do this to her too.

While I stood there and tangled thoughts of my wolf clogged my brain, Darren Drake took the opportunity to box me into the fence.

Darren was just over six feet tall and lean, with dark good looks that he played up with black jeans and a tight black t-shirt that revealed a tattoo of a stylized carrack—a four-masted sailing ship—on his left biceps. The Mayflower, of course.

The pack had its ring, but over the past twenty years or so it had become a rite of passage for the men to tattoo the Mayflower somewhere on their bodies when they came of age. I imagined the women did it now too, although I hadn't seen one on Faith's arms or legs.

Darren's tattoo was bigger than most and darker somehow. To fit his edgy image.

Darren was Tony's father. Tony had inherited his father's smile, but otherwise resembled his mother, Dorothy.

Tony was conservative and reserved where his father was liberal and outspoken. Darren took what he wanted with a grin and tonight he wanted me.

"Scott struck out. Too bad." Darren's right hand rested palm flat on the privacy fence above my shoulder. His left hand played with a stray strand of my hair that had escaped the clip.

He was close to eighty yet he looked like a man in his forties—a fit and sexy forties.

My body, alert to the pheromones that danced in the air and coated the backyard like invisible paint, gave a responsive leap. My brain shrieked in outrage. Sometimes it was pure hell to be Pack when my body craved one thing and my brain demanded another.

Darren smelled my reluctant arousal and a gorgeous grin lit his dark face. He leaned closer so his dark hair brushed my forehead and I could smell his breath. Minty. He'd popped a handful of breath mints after he'd eaten. Considerate. Yet, the smell of meat was just as heady to someone Pack. Maybe more. However, we lived in twenty-first century America and were not immune to the commercials that told us to mask our natural body odors.

Grandmother Elaine's generation barely tolerated the notion of deodorant and despised manufactured perfume. Once in a great while, she would dab some rose oil behind her ears, but it was rose oil she'd made from roses she'd cultivated in her own backyard."Hunt with me." It was a demand, not a plea or an invitation. Darren was always so cocky and damn sure of himself. Arrogant sonofabitch.

"Excuse me." I tried to duck under his arm and irritation flashed over his face as he realized I was not playing hard to get and he'd overestimated his appeal.

"Wait," he said and, for a moment I thought he would physically restrain me. My blood iced over in a moment of blind panic, but he allowed me to get free and watched me flounder toward the picnic table.

My panic melted. *Nate Carver is dead*, I told myself as I headed for the wine coolers.

"Stanzie!" Wes Hanover waylaid me halfway to my goal and I gritted my teeth. He blocked my path with his scrawny body and his gaze crawled all over me. I resisted the urge to cross my arms over my chest and instead stared him down.

"Can I please get by, Wes?"

He cleared his throat nervously and his spidery, clammy fingers brushed my bare arm. "Mosquito." It was a blatant lie but I let it pass, determined to break his fucking arm if he touched me again.

Violence. The flip side of the sex coin. The backyard was poised to become both an orgy and a sparring ring.

The sun had stained the sky purple and red a few moments ago, but now it was pearl gray. Dusk was fast deepening into night.

A chaise lounge scraped against the cement patio and I glanced sideways to see Todd Marshall, Faith's father, and his bond mate, Samantha, Alan's mother. She was beneath him on the chaise lounge, her skirt hiked up to her waist as his fingers probed beneath her yellow silk panties.

It was beginning. The midsummer's hunt was not far off.

A few feet away Scott watched them. He drank bottled water as his gaze switched between the passionate couple on the chaise and me and Wes.

Solar lights planted at even intervals around the yard glowed to life and with my enhanced Pack sight they made everything as clear as if the sun still shone.

The children were gone and I didn't hear or see the grandmothers either. No doubt they'd taken the kids to Grandmother Elaine's house. Everyone called it Grandmother Elaine's house even though Grandmother Carolyn and Grandfather Clarence had lived there with her for more than thirty years. When Mark, Faith, Alan and I had been growing up, we'd always had fun sleep overs at Grandmother Elaine's on hunt nights. We'd help her bake cookies and watch movies and play board games together. Pack didn't hide sex from children, but neither were they blatant about it.

I saw Lauren's face in an upstairs window then my father's before he drew her away. Bedroom. Paul had never liked sex in the grass or on a chair or chaise lounge. Too undignified.

Susan's mother and father, Karen and Ralph, kissed on the deck. Both her hands were clamped tight on his ass as he ground against her. As I watched, they began to shed their clothes and back toward one of the chaise lounges near the sliding glass doors to the kitchen.

The other men of the pack, Shane, Dirk, Tony, Mark, Darren, Terry and Wes stood in a loose group by the picnic table and stared at me.

The women, Susan, Rachel, Dorothy, Jennifer and Maddie waited beyond them. Their eyes, like the men's, glittered with lust. Maddie had a bowl of strawberry shortcake and moaned slightly as she nibbled from her spoon. It was clear she found the food much more erotic than the men. I could hardly blame her with Wes for a bond mate.

On the chaise lounge, Samantha cried out as Todd thrust into her, eyes shut tight with ecstasy.

"Take your pick, Advisor." Shane's blue eyes danced as he looked me up and down and liked very much what he saw. The way he said *Advisor* sent a reluctant shiver down my spine as if the word caressed me. "Tell us what you want and we'll do it. Anything you like."

A soft breeze fluttered across my body and I realized I was hot with instinctual desire. My nipples were hard and I was afraid to look down at my chest for fear it was apparent.

"I don't want to hunt," I said and was answered with disbelieving, seductive smiles.

Scott rolled his eyes and continued to watch. I wondered what he'd do if I went to him. He'd said I was on my own, but would he turn me away and refuse to help? But then, I didn't know what I wanted him to do. Escort me to my car or throw me across one of the chaise lounges and fuck my brains out?

I ground that thought into dust. Lust could not be allowed to cloud my judgment. My wolf was not ready for this pack, even if she agreed to come out. I wasn't going to do this to her. I owed her more. Just because I hadn't gotten laid in two months didn't mean I had to give in. Besides I didn't want sex. I wanted to make love. With Murphy.

Which was never going to happen again. Was I supposed to remain celibate forever while Murphy found some other bond mate and went on with his life? Why shouldn't I indulge in some carnal pleasure? What else did I have? A fucking condo? I couldn't even be an Advisor very much longer. Once I didn't have a bond mate I had three months to find a new one or I forfeited everything the Pack offered. It was our law. Maybe I should take Paul up on his offer. Maybe I should bond with Tony and Susan. Then I could still be an Advisor and I could be with my mother and my cousin and have a family again. Maybe someday I could even have a baby of my own, someone who would always be tied to me by blood, no matter whether she stayed in my pack.

Baby? I could not fucking believe myself. I could not have a baby. I could not risk that. No one else should have to suffer a wolf like mine— broken, defective, half of what she could be.

I squeezed my hands into fists, my nails dug into the soft flesh of my palms. I *wasn't* ashamed of my wolf. No. Not *ashamed*. Just not ready to inflict another like her onto someone else. But if that wasn't shame, what was it?

The pain in my clenched fists punched through my swirl of self-pity.

Get a grip, Stanzie.

Faith and Alan looked down on us from the middle level of the deck. She was apprehensive while he was both excited and despondent because he knew he would sit this hunt out as he'd sat out last year's. He probably wanted to retreat inside, but he wouldn't do that until I chose a partner. There was a slim chance it might be him after all.

Dorothy approached Darren from behind and wrapped her arms around his waist. She whispered something into his ear. He struggled to keep his attention on me, but she continued to whisper and when her hand crept to his crotch, he gave in. With a snarl, he turned on her and gave her a brutal, punishing kiss which she returned with equal fervor.

A moment later they were on the grass, oblivious of everyone else but each other.

The scent of their passion was thick in the air and I steeled myself against it. The others drank it in and allowed it to inflame them so their eyes burned with it.

If I didn't choose soon, they'd all, men and women, converge on me. It wouldn't be rape, but it would turn into a brawl or an orgy. Maybe both. Part of me wanted that.

The forest beyond the fence beckoned. The scent of pine and earth filled my senses and added a layer of complexity to the smell of sex and pheromones. The charcoal briquettes had been allowed to go out, but they still gave off their unique scent, as well as that of marinated steak and burgers.

I contemplated the men in front of me. Say I would choose one of them—which one? Wes Hanover I dismissed without hesitation. Mark went next. He was like an older brother. Shane, Dirk and Terry were more like uncles, much as they wanted me to forget that. I suppose if I'd stayed with Mayflower I might have been able to do that after I'd been accepted into the pack as a contributing adult versus a nurtured child, but I hadn't stayed with the pack.

That left Scott, Tony and Alan.

Alan was so cute, but he needed a teacher and a guide, no matter what Scott and Faith promised they'd do. They shouldn't have to. If I shifted with somebody, that was the wolf I wanted with me and that wouldn't be fair to Alan's.

Scott was technically hotter than Tony and my girlish crush on Tony had faded. Plus Tony had been a prick the night before. But then Scott had too and attraction for me was not just how cute a guy was. I actually did value substance over shiny no matter what Paul said.

Still, I took a step toward Scott because my pulse raced and the sounds that escaped Dorothy and Darren made me wish I hadn't been so hasty to turn Darren down.

Scott and I locked gazes and a small, satisfied smile curled the corners of his mouth.

Before I got more than three steps, Tony moved forward to block my path.

"Stanzie." His voice was husky with desire. "I want to talk to you."

"Oh, yeah?" I drawled and someone sniggered in the background. Talk was the last thing on his mind from the way the front of his jeans tented. My tone was sardonic and just the slightest bit flirtatious.

Tony wrapped his arm around my shoulders and guided me away from the rest of the men. The back of my neck tingled as their hungry gazes followed us.

He sat me down on a chaise lounge and rocked back on his heels as he assumed a semi-kneeling position so our heads were level. He handed me a bottle of water and his eyes dared me to drink it.

If I did, I was his. Simple.

I took it, but didn't drink. Frustration flared in his dark brown eyes but he smiled and braced himself with a hand on the arm of the chaise lounge.

"It's been a long time coming between us. You know that. You had to feel how much I wanted you ten years ago. I still do. Now we can finally find out what we're like together. Pretty hot, I'd guess." His eyes caressed my body with a slow, seductive deliberation.

He smiled and my stomach did flutter. A little. I pictured his mouth on mine, his hands all over me, and a slow flush heated my body. His smile became wickedly sexy and he leaned in to kiss me, but I turned my head so his lips brushed my cheek.

He chuckled, not the least put out, especially when he saw me raise the water bottle to my lips.

Fuck Murphy. Fuck everything. My participation in the midsummer's hunt did not mean I needed to decide my entire goddamn future in one stroke too. I could just have sex, shift, hunt with my former pack and fuck everything and everybody else. Including my own fear of what my wolf would do.

Three things struck me in the few seconds before the bottle touched my lips.

The bottle, while cold, was dry, not covered in an icy slick of water.

Tony's expression of triumph was due to more than just the fact I would hunt with him.

There was no cap.

I remembered the first bottle of water he'd given me. It hadn't been wet or capped either.

The inevitable conclusion? Neither of them had come from the coolers. Tony had given me bottles of water from a different supply.

Cold panic doused the fire of passion in my head and my body. He'd put something in the water. Damn him, he'd done something to the water.

Rudi's contorted dead face swam before my eyes. The bottled water with the blue label he'd drunk from at the Paris Gathering had been laced with poison.

Was Tony trying to kill me?

I dropped the bottle and as Tony's gaze automatically tracked its downward trajectory, I went backward over the chaise lounge and scrambled awkwardly to my feet.

He called out my name urgently, as I bolted for the gate. He chased after me, but Scott moved in a blur of speed and held him back. As I fumbled with the gate latch, Tony snarled and swung at him and they went down in a tangle of fists and curses.

My purse was on the front seat and, after I leaped behind the wheel and power locked the doors, I scrabbled in it for my keys. They were there thankfully, and not in Alan's pocket, and twenty seconds later I zoomed in reverse for the road, as I barely avoided sideswiping a late-model Malibu.

Tires squealing, I raced the car down the street and skidded around the corner. My heart thumped so hard in my chest I thought I might puke and, when I caught sight of myself in the rearview mirror, I barely recognized my own face—pale, stained with sweat and tears. I swiped an arm across my burning eyes and refocused on the road, desperate to escape.

Chapter 9

The double locks on my motel door did nothing to ratchet down my terror. Neither did the security bolt. I looked at the windows suspiciously and pictured Tony crashing through them and shuddered. I wrenched the curtains across the dark expanse of glass and hugged myself but found no comfort.

I needed something. Someone. I don't remember how my phone ended up in my shaking hands, nor do I remember scrolling through the contacts to Murphy's number. But I do remember hitting talk and the interminable span of seconds between that and the sound of ringing. If I could just hear his voice, just for a moment. He'd talk me down. He'd tell me my fears were unjustified and, if they weren't, he'd be there for me. I knew he'd get on a plane and come get me and when he got here, he'd kick the ever-loving shit out of Tony and make me feel safe again.

"Hello?" The man on the other end of the phone did not sound remotely like Murphy and I froze until he irritably repeated himself.

"Is...can I speak with Liam Murphy?" I wanted to hang up, but somehow didn't.

"Who?" The man's irritation doubled. "Look, lady, you've got the wrong number."

"Wait!" I shouted before he could hang up. I recited the phone number and asked him if that was right.

"That's my number, but there's no Lee Murphy here. Just got this number a couple weeks ago, sounds like it might have been that guy's before it was mine. Sorry, lady." He hung up.

The phone dropped unheeded onto the bed I'd once shared with Grey and I stood there for a long moment. It was a struggle to pull air into my lungs because I felt as if I'd been sucker punched.

The last vestiges of hope that someday Murphy would come back melted away. This was not a dream. This was not a test and, no matter how much I wanted or wished for it, Liam Murphy would never walk through my door again with a smile just for me. He was not my bond mate.

With a grief-stricken wail, I yanked the silver chain around my neck until the clasp snapped. I threw it and my bond pendant on the floor and ran to the bathroom to lock myself in. A part of me knew I was being irrational, but a bigger part wanted to keep my head down and hide so no one would find me.

I was alone.

A noise outside in the parking lot sent a bolt of panic through my body. I remembered Tony and the suspicious water bottles. As I huddled in the bottom of the tub with the shower curtain pulled, my knees drawn up to chest, I shivered and waited for my doom.

Time crawled past. My phone rang several times but I made no move to answer it. I was marginally safe behind the locked bathroom door and my phone was all the way out on the bed. No way was I going to retrieve it.

More time inched by. My legs cramped but I wouldn't straighten them. My head ached but I wouldn't shut my eyes. I just wanted it to be dawn and then I would go home. Escape. Leave. Run away.

At first whoever knocked at my door was patient, but gradually he or she became demanding, until the knocking was more like pounding.

"Stanzie, I know you're in there. I can see the light under the door and your car is parked two spaces away. Open the goddamn door."

I turned my face toward the sound of his voice. What the hell was Scott doing here?

"Stanzie, I will break down this fucking door if you don't open it." He sounded like he meant it and, after a pause, he pounded again. I scrambled out of the tub and nearly fell down. My legs were all pins and needles. I lurched to the door, braced myself against it for a moment until I had more feeling in my feet and went into the bedroom.

When I peered through the security peephole in the door, I confirmed it was Scott and he was alone.

"Jesus," he said when I opened the door. "Are you all right?" He pushed his way into the room and made me sit in on the edge of the bed. I panicked a little as the word *rape* flashed across my mind, but he moved away and dragged the desk chair closer to the bed before he sat.

"What the hell happened back there? You ran like your ass was on fire." He had a bruise high on his left cheek and the knuckles of his right hand were bloody and red with abrasions.

"Poison," I choked out. "In the water."

He stared at me, his gray eyes wide with shock.

"You smelled it?" His brow furrowed in confusion. Anger gave his skin a faint reddish glow.

I shook my head.

"Then how do you know? You didn't drink it."

"The bottles weren't wet with melted ice. No caps. He gave me bottles with something in them. Twice. Two times he tried to get me to drink poison. I dropped the first bottle by accident and he tried again with the second."

Scott scrubbed at his face and when he looked at me again, he shook his head. "Shit. What makes you think poison? Roofies are more likely, don't you think?"

I puzzled over the word for a moment until it clicked. The date rape drug.

"They didn't want me or Alan to touch you but they didn't care which of the rest of them did. And they definitely wanted you to hunt tonight."

"How could I hunt if I was paralyzed with date rape drugs?" I protested and his brow furrowed again.

"Good goddamn point." He stared at me for a moment. "Why poison then? You couldn't hunt if you were poisoned."

The conspiracy. The words tingled at the tip of my tongue, but somehow I was smart enough not to say them. Maybe I was too tired to think straight and, for once, I didn't just blurt out my thoughts.

"Maybe we're both way off base here," he suggested, but I could tell he didn't believe it. "Damn it. Something weird was going on tonight."

"Is it over? The hunt," I prompted when Scott only stared.

"How the hell should I know? After you wouldn't answer your goddamn phone I was out of there. Last I saw, everyone had paired up and was going at it. I guess the damn hunt's still on." He checked his watch. "Is that important?"

I didn't know.

"Did you win the fight?"

A smile curled the corners of his mouth. "Damn right I did. Tony knows dick about throwing decent punches."

"So what's that?" I reached out to touch the bruise on his cheek and he laughed.

"Lucky shot. I was distracted by the sound of your tires squealing and was waiting to hear the fucking crash."

I shuddered and a flash of irritation passed across his face. With himself, I decided when his expression softened into concern as he looked at me.

"At the risk of sending you screaming into the night, do you want a drink? I've got a six-pack in the trunk. Warm as shit but it might do you some good."

While he retrieved the six pack, I took the ice bucket to the vending machines and filled it.

"Gross," he said five minutes later as he contemplated the ice cubes floating in his beer filled plastic motel glass.

I gulped down my glass in two swallows and refilled it.

"Labatt's," I said.

"Better than frigging Bud, which is all the assholes in this pack drink." Scott refilled his glass too and gulped it down.

"Why?" I asked after I finished my second beer and was well into the third.

Scott cocked an eyebrow at me.

"Are you here? Why are you here?" I clarified.

"Your stunning good looks and tractable nature?" He tried and a small giggle escaped me. I thought I might be a little drunk. Two nights in a row. Mayflower drove me to drink. I stifled another giggle and tried to look serious but suspected I failed.

"I'm walking a fine line here, Stanzie." Scott poured the rest of my beer into my glass and watched me drink it. I waited for him to go on. "You told me I didn't look familiar but my accent wasn't Canadian so you figured I was from a New England pack; right?"

I nodded.

"Guess which one?"

"Honestly, I have no idea." At first I was exasperated and impatient, but he'd posed a challenge and I always rose to challenges. "Not Wolfsong. You don't have a Maine accent but all the other New England accents sort of blend together so I don't have a frigging clue, Scott. Not Maplefair."

"Oh fucking please." Scott rolled his eyes so far back in his head I thought he might hurt himself.

"I said not. And not Nightclaw. Your clothes aren't good enough."

He burst into laughter. "Fuck you."

"It's true." I calculated for a moment then ventured, "Snowmoon?" He knew enough about Nate Carver to be disparaging and he seemed disdainful of the whole pack. Even though they both were from Vermont, Snowmoon and Maplefair were rivals more than allies.

"Not even close," he snorted.

"No clue." I gave up and looked around for more beer. One bottle remained of the six pack and I reached for it.

"That one's mine," Scott pointed out.

"You're driving," I responded and he rolled his eyes at me again.

"What? You aren't inviting me to stay the night?"

It was my turn to roll my eyes and he grinned again. He was a prick, but he was sort of rubbing off on me.

Scott made a sound like a buzzer and said, "Time's up. You fail, loser. I'm from Darkhunt thank you very much. Greatest pack in New England."

"It's shocking that you, as Alpha of Mayflower, would say Darkhunt is the greatest," I said. But I smiled. I certainly couldn't take offense at the slight to Mayflower since I'd run away from it as soon as I'd been old enough.

"Mayflower sucks," he declared.

"Then what are you doing here? And if you tell me it's because you are madly, passionately in love with my cousin, I'm going to call bullshit."

His grin edged toward enigmatic. "You don't think I love Faith?"

"I didn't say that. I said madly, passionately. As in 'I'll follow you to this suck-ass pack, baby.'"

He nodded slowly. "Would you believe I did it because someone asked me to? Faith was all for joining Darkhunt, and that's what I actually wanted, but as you can plainly see I'm here."

"This is not another round of Guess the Right Answer or You're a Big Fat Loser is it?" I groaned. "Because, once again, I have no clue."

"You sure?" Scott's eyes gleamed with amusement.

"Shit." I gulped my beer which tasted disgusting because it was warm as melted butter. "Someone asked you to join Mayflower. You mean Paul? Why the hell would you listen to him?"

"I wouldn't. You are approaching this from the wrong side," he hinted and I contemplated that for a moment as I took a fistful of ice from the bucket on the nightstand and transferred it to my plastic motel glass.

"Someone from Darkhunt asked you to join Mayflower? What? They want to get rid of you, you jerk?" I gave his shoulder a push with the flat of my palm and he snorted.

I remembered how Alan had warned me to trust no one in the pack but him and Faith. He'd left out Scott for a reason and here I was drunk and sloppy, and about to fall for his brash charm.

As usual, I spoke without thinking. "Alan doesn't trust you. Why should I?"

"Alan doesn't trust anybody."

"He trusts Faith."

"Okay, anybody but Faith. The guy's a little fucked up, Stanzie. Concentrate on the question I asked you or I'm drinking that beer."

"Go to hell." I snatched the bottle before he could and set it out of his reach. "Someone from Darkhunt wanted you to join Mayflower but not because you're a frigging jerk. That's a tough one. Can I ask for a hint?"

"No. You don't need one. You're drunk and not thinking straight, loser. You do not get help because you're a light-weight."

I thought about Darkhunt. It was the Rhode Island pack. They lived in and around Providence. For some reason I started to crave butterscotch squares.

"No." I gaped at him. "Not her. Not Kathy Manning. No freaking way."

"She initiated my wolf," Scott confessed with a secret smile that made me wonder if he might have a little bit of a thing for her. The thought boggled my fucking mind. Scott and Kathy Manning. Two steamrollers on a head on collision course. Or maybe two rams butting horns. Only that wouldn't work. Kathy was female. Two jousters on horseback with lances? The thought of Kathy in chain mail brought another giggle to my lips.

"She was grooming me to become her next Advisor."

My giggle became incredulous laughter and Scott sat there and endured it.

"You done?" He took my glass and drained it before I could protest. "Then came the Regional in New Hampshire and I met Faith. I went to Kathy before I went to my Alphas to see what she thought of Faith joining Darkhunt. That's when she suggested it be the other way around."

"God, so she'd have a spy in the pack," I guessed with such rancor that Scott grinned. "It galls her that Mayflower's so insular and private, doesn't it? She can't get her greedy Counselor fingers in any of Mayflower's pies."

"Until three years ago," Scott shrugged with blatant false modesty.

"You know she's looking for a new Advisor. Her old one just became Alpha of Darkhunt and stepped down."

"I know," he said. "Although as of last week she's no longer looking. She found her new Advisor." He waited for my reaction.

I let myself fall back onto the back with a groan.

"She's evil. That woman is pure evil. And you're her wicked minion, Scott."

"That's one way to look at it, I guess. So, Stanzie, we're two Advisors and we ought to stick together, don't you think?"

"I'm an Advisor to the Great Council. I outrank you."

"Fine. You are the lead on this one. I bow to your vastly superior experience."

"She's going to make you dance. You'll be her puppet." The thought of Scott suspended from wires while far above him Kathy pulled the strings was deliciously funny.

"Laugh it up. Maybe you'll laugh yourself sober." Scott wasn't offended, he was amused.

"You let her initiate your wolf? For real?" I sat up, fascinated.

"Let her? I practically begged," Scott confided. I could not picture him begging, but then again, we were talking about Kathy Manning. "She was a great teacher, Stanzie. You're making a face at me, but it's true. You just don't know her."

"Ha. That's a good one. You obviously don't talk much if you think I don't know her."

"She likes you. A lot. I can't see why myself, but I'm just the wicked minion, maybe it's beyond my puny powers of perception." Scott ducked when I hauled off to hit him. "Seriously. She likes you. She trusts you. If she's okay with you, I am too.

"At first I didn't think it was a hot idea to bring you here because I've been working on what's wrong with this pack for three years now and to tell you the truth, Stanzie, I was pissed as hell at the thought of some Advisor from the Great Pack swooping in here and fucking everything up. But Kathy says you have this knack not for fucking things up, but blowing them up. And then all the little missing pieces of the puzzle come raining down and fit together and the mystery's solved." Scott sat back in his chair and his expression grew thoughtful.

"Damned if she doesn't have a point. You're here less than forty-eight hours and you've got all the men at each other's throats for the chance to screw you. Not that you aren't beautiful, but there's way more behind it than your face and body, don't you think?"

"Femme fatale I am not," I agreed, somewhat ruefully.

"We gonna pool our knowledge or are you going to hold out on me?" Scott's tone was easy, but there was an underlying edge to it as if he suspected I wouldn't tell him everything. I cursed in my head but maintained my smile.

"You first."

"Yeah, right." He snorted then rubbed his hands through his dark hair and messed it up. He didn't seem to give a shit. "Look, I know you're an Advisor to the Great Council and I'm just one to the New England

Regional, but I'm Alpha of this pack. If there's something I should know, you'd tell me, right? Fuck the rules?"

"What rules?" I asked. "Did you get a handbook or something? Because I sure as hell didn't."

"Come on. The Great Council knows shit they wouldn't share with a Regional. The New England Regional doesn't even represent a big population. So you have to know some secrets, right?"

"And what if I do?" The beer sloshed uneasily in my stomach. I should have eaten more at the barbeque, but I'd only managed a few bites thanks to Paul's weird machinations. "You expect me to tell you everything because you're Alpha? Of what? Mayflower? Twenty people? Please."

"Not everything, just things that pertain to me and my pack. Things that might sneak up and bite me in the ass, Stanzie. I hate that." Scott was persuasive but I steeled myself against him. If he didn't already know about the conspiracy I sure as hell was not going to enlighten him. And, stupid me, what if he were a part of it and I played right into his hands?

Advisor or not. Alpha or not. That meant shit.

"You first." I found my purse and rummaged for change and dollar bills for the vending machine. Scott watched me for a moment, sighed, and took out his cellphone so he could order a pizza for delivery. I guess my gurgling stomach gave me away.

I went to the vending machine anyway for sodas and chips. Scott followed me, as if he thought I might try to escape.

Once back in the room, I kicked off my espadrilles and unscrewed the cap to my soda.

"Still waiting." I crawled onto the bed and crossed my legs Indian style. Scott tried for a half-hearted peek up my skirt, but I pulled it down over my knees and tucked it under my legs primly.

He bent down and fished something off the floor. My bond pendant.

"Clasp's broken. You could get it fixed. Nice chain." He tossed it in my direction and I caught it automatically, but flung it away as soon it hit my palm.

He picked it up again, only this time put it on the dresser, where it was out of my reach and I couldn't throw it anywhere.

"You've been here almost three years, you must have some theories," I prompted. The soda was cold and it tickled my throat and tongue.

"No one makes a move without checking it with Paul Benedict." Scott's expression was flat and sour, and building resentment seethed beneath the surface of his eyes. A resentment I knew all too well, since I'd felt the same way since I'd turned seventeen. But Scott was at least ten years older than that and Alpha. The fact his pack turned to Paul rather than him must be galling.

"Well, you make yourself such a disagreeable prick it's no wonder," I commented and took another swig of soda.

"Believe me I've tried other approaches and they all lead to the same destination. Paul." The brooding anger was for him, not me, but I still treaded lightly.

"It's always been that way." I frowned. "At least as long as I can remember. He's either been Alpha or Alpha Emeritus since the day I was born."

"There's no such thing as Alpha Emeritus," Scott pointed out. "Sure, you can go to past Alphas for inspiration and advice, but I should be the one going to him. The rest of the pack should come to me and Faith."

"When you joined Mayflower, Mark and Rachel were Alpha, right?" I watched him stare at the framed drawing of the state forest hung above the bed. "Did everyone go to them?"

"Sometimes." Scott shrugged, but the truth simmered beneath his flushed skin.

"Because while everyone eventually did it Paul's way when I was growing up, it was pretty subtle. The Alphas went to him, not the rest of the pack usually. Paul would state his opinion on something and, within a few weeks, it spread so it was everyone's opinion. Like he never said the pack couldn't go to Regionals or Great Gatherings, but he didn't like them. It was a huge deal when we went to the New Orleans Great Gathering and I gave him all the ammunition he needed to persuade the pack that Gatherings were a waste of time and a potential pitfall for the younger members."

"Except for Faith sneaking off to the Regional three years ago, Mayflower hasn't shown up at a Regional or a Great Gathering since New Orleans," Scott said. "Faith and I told everyone we're going to the Rhode Island Regional next month and you know what? Nobody else is going. They all have things to do. Except for Alan. They want him to go. They want him out of the pack. Which is bullshit. He's a good kid and I think he'd make a decent Alpha in a few years. He's staying right here."

Determination made his eyes glitter. He rubbed his fingers across his cheek and they made a rasping sound against his beard stubble.

"I went to one Regional after New Orleans as a member of Mayflower," I whispered. Vermont in the autumn nearly thirteen years in the past.

"Only so you could bond and get the hell out of Mayflower. And if you tell me you left for any other reason than to spite Paul Benedict, I'll call you a goddamn liar to your face." Scott's gaze jerked away from the improbably pastel colored forest print and focused on me.

"You know my story." My voice trembled slightly and I worked hard to steady it. I'd be bawling in a minute if I weren't careful.

"That was my first Regional. The one in Vermont." Scott's eyes crinkled when he grinned as he obviously replayed some good memories. "I had the wildest crush on Deanna Martin, you know her? From Snowmoon? She was nineteen and hated the idea she couldn't join the adults, so she bossed all us kids around like she was a grandmother or something. One really, really hot grandmother. I made a pass at her and she smacked me in the mouth. Made me bleed. And gave me a hard on."

I snorted.

"I remember you and Grey," he went on. My heart gave an uncomfortable lurch and it was suddenly hard to swallow the soda in my mouth. "You two were way into each other, huh?"

I nodded and my own memories of that Regional woke and began to play for me.

* * * *

"This is the best day of my life, Stanzie." Grey looks at me and I can see the adoration in his eyes and feel it when he touches my cheek. We stand together in the largest room at the Autumn Leaf Inn, owned by the Vermont pack, Snowmoon, where all Regionals in Vermont are held. He is wearing a dark blue suit with a red-and-blue tie I'd picked out at the mall in Stowe on our way to the Regional from Willoughby. The only person I'd said goodbye to was Alan. His little face had crumpled when I'd told him I wasn't coming back. He hadn't even been able to finish his banana split and he loved them. He usually ate half of mine too. He hadn't cried because he was ten years old and wanted me to think he was a big boy, but he had been close.

I am going to miss him. And my cousin, Faith. I'd tried to find her to say goodbye but at fifteen she is moody and unpredictable and incredibly sulky. She knows there is a Regional and it would have been her first opportunity to attend a Gathering, but naturally no one from Mayflower is going. Thanks to me and my wolf at the Great Gathering in New Orleans.

Heat blooms in my cheeks. Tonight Grey and I will make love. Not for the first time or even the hundredth—we've spent the entire summer in bed together. But I've only shown him my wolf three times. All since September. It is October now. Tonight there will be a hunt and I'll participate in it for the first time since I've begun to shift. I am scared but I know I will have Grey with me and that makes all the difference.

The tag on my dress says the color is sea foam. A sort of strange, gorgeous blend of pale blue and green. It shimmers. It is not an autumn color. I found it on the summer clearance rack at the mall for nineteen dollars marked down from forty-nine. I have exactly fifty-seven dollars left to my name after buying the dress, the tie, the small black wooden box, tiny peridot gemstone and the double setting for my new bond pendant. My stash of babysitting money. Technically I shouldn't be paid for watching Alan, but Todd always slips me a few bucks behind everyone's backs. He knows how notoriously short Paul keeps my leash.

All summer long Grey has paid for nearly everything—all the burgers and fries at the Stonewall Tavern, the beer, the gas for his motorcycle. I've chipped in when I could, but it hasn't been much.

And now I am down to fifty-seven dollars and twenty-two cents.

But I am bonded to the best man in the whole world and it is forever. My life as an adult, as someone separate from Paul Benedict's daughter, can finally start. Here. Tonight.

* * * *

"It's not like that with your new guy, is it?" Scott interrupted my stroll down Memory Lane and jolted me back to the present. He glanced back at the broken chain and my bond pendant on the dresser.

I wished I had Grey's little black wooden box. He'd kept his spare chain in it, and his bond pendant when he took it off, which wasn't often. But of course the box had been smashed to splinters during Vaughn's rampage through my house after Grey and Elena died in the car crash. I remembered finding it squashed flat on the bedroom floor. One violent stomp with heavy boots had destroyed it.

Then I thought of the seashell box I'd given Murphy six months ago in Paris. It hadn't been among the things he'd left behind, so he'd taken it with him. Force of habit, probably. No doubt he'd smashed his too. With a stomp of his Timberland boots, the ones I'd bought him once upon a time. Had there even been enough anger in him to smash his box? Or had he just stuck it in a drawer somewhere to come across years from now and have to pause to think before he even remembered what it was and where he'd gotten it? That thought hurt twice as much.

Scott watched me, his expression open and sympathetic, and all at once I wished there was one person in the world I could tell about what it was like between Murphy and me. I couldn't talk to Vaughn or Jason Allerton. I felt so alone, especially since I was in Willoughby and it had once been my home. Scott's was the only new face in the pack, the only one who didn't know shit about me or about Murphy, except what other people had told him.

I tried to keep silent, but the story poured out of me and he listened without saying a word. Halfway through, the pizza arrived and he went to the door to pay for it. He set it down on the desk but made no move to eat because I wasn't done.

When I was, I took a deep breath and held it a moment before I released it. He still made no move toward the pizza even though it smelled fucking delicious and I could barely resist the urge to stuff the whole thing in my mouth at once.

"What do you think?" I asked as I walked to the desk and opened the pizza box. The pieces were square, not triangular. That meant it was from Gus's Pizza, my favorite pizza in the entire world. I hadn't tasted it in over a decade, but the first bite brought me back to my childhood. Tears burned my eyes that weren't entirely due to Murphy and my story. "Do you think I have a chance to get him back or did I blow it?"

He winced, and I knew the answer before he opened his mouth.

"He changed his phone number. He's made no effort to contact you in almost six weeks, and you let him walk out, Stanzie."

"I...*let* him?" For a moment I forgot the pizza in my hand and stared, uncomprehending, at Scott.

He nodded. "You didn't even try to get him to stay. That told him all he needed to know. A man doesn't walk out like that unless he's ninety percent convinced it's the right way to go. You pushed it to one hundred when you just sat there and didn't protest. Sorry, babe, but, yeah, I think you blew it."

"He took his bond pendant box. He took all the things I gave him." The pizza tasted like ashes and I set my half-eaten piece aside.

"He's not a fucking bastard," Scott said. "He wasn't going out of his way to be vindictive when he left. Which, again, sounds more like a man who's made up his mind instead of one who wants convincing he's doing the wrong thing."

"Maybe it's a good thing you never said you loved him. You still have your pride." Scott finally approached the pizza and took a slice. As I watched him eat it, I thought about how he would go home to Faith and she would have a companion and a lover to spend her life with. I would have three quarters of a pizza and whatever I could find to watch on TV.

When I started to cry, Scott swore softly and put down his pizza. He wrapped his arms around me and I went willingly because he was somebody to hold onto even if he was a stranger.

116

Amy Lee Burgess

"We need to figure out what's going on in this pack, Scott," I said after a while. I tried to pull away but he wouldn't let go until he gave me a hard squeeze.

"No, I need to go home and you need to get some sleep. We can talk more tomorrow, right?" His smile tugged on my heart and I was pretty sure I'd revised my opinion of him.

"I think maybe you aren't such a prick as I first thought," I said and he laughed as he ruffled my hair.

"Oh, hell yeah, I am. After what you just shared with me, you're going to hate my guts twice as much in the morning. If you were a guy you could punch me in the mouth and things would be cool, but you'll settle for being cold and distant like you wished I were dead."

"No, I won't," I argued. "I'm not such a bitch."

"Okay." I had a feeling he humored me, but let it go. He kissed my cheek and walked for the door. "You're sure you're okay?" He hesitated at the door and for a moment, I wondered what would happen between us if I said no. Sex outside bonds was not a big thing in Pack culture, but it would be a betrayal just the same. Sleeping together was probably a sure route to cold and distant too. I had begun to believe I wanted Scott's friendship, not a quick, empty lay that would feel good at first but rapidly sour.

"I'm okay," I said and, with a last glance, he was gone. I ate two slices of pizza, washed them down with soda and stripped to my underwear.

Murphy's Faneuil Hall t-shirt was packed in my suitcase and I held it in both hands for a moment before I slipped it on. Scott hadn't told me anything I hadn't already known.

After I crawled beneath the covers and turned off the lights, I pretended Murphy was there. I turned on my side so he could put his arm over my waist and move up against my back, but of course he wasn't really there at all.

Chapter 10

I dreamed I was in danger. Amorphous, unsubstantiated and invisible, but danger all the same. I was not alone.

With a gasp, I thrashed awake and scrambled up in my bed just as something moved in the corner of my eye. I whipped my head around and made out the shadowy figure of man who lurked just inside the door near the bathroom. The room was illuminated by thin rays of morning sunshine which penetrated through the cracks in the draperies, but I couldn't make out the intruder's face. He stayed just far enough in the shadows to make his features indeterminate.

"Get the fuck out of here!" I screamed and launched myself for my phone, which was on the desk next to the stale pizza box.

The shadowy figure moved faster, intercepted me and we went down in a tangle of sheets onto the bed.

When I tried to scream, he clamped a rough hand over my mouth and I drew in a deep breath. His scent went down my throat and filtered into my nasal cavities and I knew who it was a split-second before he spoke to me.

"Stanzie, don't scream, it's me." He cautiously lifted his hand away.

I snarled, "What the fuck are you doing in my room, Darren? How did you get in here?"

He chuckled and made no move to let me up. His body pinned mine to the mattress and he was heavy. I couldn't move and panic began flashing bright pinpricks of light behind my eyes.

"Have you forgotten how I contribute my share to the pack funds?"

The panic made it hard to think, but a few seconds later the answer filtered into my brain.

Darren was a master at breaking and entering. He'd always fancied himself a modern-day lupine Robin Hood who stole from the rich to give to the pack. I suppose getting into my motel room had been child's play to him.

When I'd worked for the real estate agency, he'd frequently stopped by to "borrow" keys to certain properties. He'd never actually steal from them while they were under contract, but he'd always told me I'd be surprised at the number of new home owners who didn't bother to change the locks after they'd bought a house. And guess who had copies of the keys?

Anger began to burn through the panic.

"I thought Paul had talked you out of your life of crime," I spat and he chuckled again.

"Paul has decided that what he doesn't specifically know can't specifically bother him. So the topic never comes up between us, Stanzie."

"Well, I don't appreciate this. Let me up."

He shifted his body so I was even more trapped. One of his knees nudged between my thighs and I froze. His face lowered until it was three inches from mine, and he could stare into my eyes.

"What's the rush?" He brushed hair from my cheek and let his fingers linger on my skin.

I gulped back a scream and tried to think because it was hard to believe this was happening. I had to still be dreaming. Wasn't I?

"I used to fantasize about you, you know that? I wanted to be the one to initiate your wolf. We all did. You had to be aware of that." His voice was a smooth caress and I fought against puking.

"I thought of most of you as my uncles," I said. "And I do not remember anyone but Wes drooling over me, so no, I was not aware of it. I think it's disgusting."

"I don't drool." He laughed. "Unlike Wes, I can keep my lustful thoughts to myself. But I still had them. I'm having them now." He lowered his mouth to mine and kissed me. I went wild beneath him, tried to buck him off me, but that only seemed to inflame him.

"Oh, Stanzie, this is going to be so good. You'll see. Stop fighting it, you know you want it." He found the hem of my t-shirt and swarmed his hand beneath it to tug on my panties.

"No!" I screamed as I twisted and tried to escape. He had me at a wrong angle and was so much stronger than me. "Darren, stop. No!" I managed to get one arm free and used it for leverage to push away from him. He wrapped his fingers around my panties, so when I moved, they slid down to my thighs.

He let me get halfway off the bed before he dragged me back up and flipped me onto my stomach. He used his weight to pin my legs which prevented me from kicking.

The sound of his zipper and the rattle of his belt buckle as he hastily thrust off his pants sent icy waves of dread through my blood.

"No!" I screamed. "No!"

I got free again and managed to flip myself off the bed, but my fucking panties were tangled around my knees, so I couldn't get to my feet before he was there. His pants were gone and his erection was huge. The pungent scent of his excitement mixed with the acrid tang of my fear. I knew his character and I'm sure he understood he was wrong, but that only made him want to do it more. He'd always lived on the edge, always walked on the wild side, and rape would probably be just one more notch on his belt of forbidden acts.

He hauled me to my feet and I hit him in the face. He backhanded me across the mouth and the hot gush of blood when my lip split tasted metallic.

"I'm going to do this, so stop fighting!" He snarled at me and shook me until I was dizzy then threw me across the bed. I couldn't focus enough to move and screamed when he climbed on top of me.

"Stanzie!" Scott shouted. Scott? Where had he come from? He was on the wrong side of the door and pounded frantically. "Open the door! Are you all right?"

"*Scott!*" I shrieked and Darren backhanded me again.

"Shut up!" His lips curled back from his teeth and his eyes were black and pitiless, on fire with lust. He thrust my legs apart with brutal force.

"*No!*" I howled and Scott threw himself against the door.

"If someone doesn't open this door right the fuck *now*, I am getting the manager and calling the cops. I mean it. I'm calling the cops. I'm dialing right this fucking second!" Scott kicked the door.

"Fuck." Darren got swiftly to his feet and didn't bother with his pants. He stalked to the door and unlocked it.

Scott burst through, his eyes wild, phone in hand. He took in the scene and his face darkened until I thought he'd burst all the capillaries under the skin.

"You bastard," he said and took a roundhouse swing at Darren.

Darren danced out of the way, but had nowhere to go when Scott threw his second punch. It took him under the chin and turned him halfway around. Scott dropped his phone and grabbed Darren's arm so he could wrench it behind his back. Darren sucked in a scream and the air in his lungs escaped with a tortured hiss.

"You're overreacting." He gasped, and Scott gave his arm another wrench. This time Darren did scream.

"Let me explain," he begged and Scott threw him into the wall where he sagged and slid down to the floor.

"Get your fucking pants on." Scott hurled them at Darren's head and Darren made a half-hearted attempt to shield his face. "When they're on, you and I are going outside for a little conversation. So fucking move your sorry ass."

Scott spared me one glance. "Did he hurt you, Stanzie?" He meant, had he raped me? Scott could see for himself my lip was split. Blood still gushed freely and I used the edge of the sheet to wipe some of it away. Murphy's Faneuil Hall t-shirt was stained with gore and that, almost more than anything, pissed me off.

"Just a split lip," I said and Scott's fists clenched. Darren had his pants half on, but he fell back down when Scott kicked him viciously in the shin.

"If you want me to get dressed, you'll need to let me keep on my feet, Scott." Darren rubbed his shin and glared. When Scott held his ground, Darren stood and pulled up his pants.

"Out," Scott pointed at the door. "Go to the side of the building and get ready to have the shit kicked out of you, you sonofabitch."

"Don't you even want to hear—" Darren began.

"After. If you have any teeth left," Scott interrupted. He pointed again at the door and, with a sigh, Darren limped outside into the bright morning sunlight.

By the time I put on my jeans and grabbed the key card, the fight had started.

Darren fought well, but Scott was younger, fitter and angrier. Darren tried to use Scott's anger against him, but Scott plowed through his defenses.

I stood far enough back so I didn't get in the way, but close enough so I saw and heard every punch.

They didn't talk, they just fought. Blood spattered and there was the occasional groan, but it was a viciously silent battle.

Ten minutes after they began, Darren was on the ground, bleeding and beaten.

Scott's nose bled, but it wasn't broken. Besides being winded, he was in pretty good condition.

He stood back from Darren's body and looked at me. "Stanzie? You want a piece of him?"

I wasn't going to kick a man who was down but then Darren choked out, "Oh, what's she going to do? Shift and tear my throat out?"

I lost it. My bare foot connected squarely with Darren's gut and he spluttered out a weak curse. I kicked him again and then again. He tried to crawl away, but I followed him. I kicked him in the ass, in the thigh and would have kicked him in the head except he covered it with his arms, the fucking coward.

"You fucking piece of shit, Darren, you really said that to me? You motherfucker. You goddamn, cock-sucking prick!" With every curse, I kicked him. My foot ached like a bitch but I was beyond that. I existed in a veil of red hot fury and it didn't go away, it only got hotter.

Scott stood back, arms crossed over his chest, and a savage grin threatened to split his face.

"Stop," begged Darren when I kicked him in the side so hard I swore I heard something crack. His ribs, my toes, I had no idea and I didn't give a flying fuck either.

"Oh, yeah? Like you stopped when I begged you?" I didn't recognize my voice so coated with ferocious glee. It was if I were outside myself and I didn't really know who I was anymore. This was a side of me I'd never seen except once before in Grandmother Emma's root cellar, and that had been my wolf, not me. Hadn't it? "You like this, cocksucker? This feel good the way you said you'd make me feel good?" I kicked him again in the ribs and he tried to shriek but had no breath to do it.

"You done?" Scott didn't rush me, he was just checking.

I considered. The red veil still wound tightly around me, but I could push it aside if I wanted.

I gave Darren one last kick in the ribs and his body gave a miserable leap. When he rolled over and let his arms fall away, tears leaked out of the corners of his eyes. I grinned spitefully.

"Can you get up?" Scott asked him and Darren cursed at him breathlessly. Scott snorted laughter and moved to drag him to his feet. He draped one of Darren's arms over his shoulders and grabbed him around the waist so he could drag him back into my motel room.

I led the way. It was hard not to limp. My foot was already bruising and I was pretty sure my pinky toe was broken but it was all good. In fact, it was fantastic.

* * * *

Darren's face looked like shit. Even after we'd given him a wet towel and ice, he still looked like a refugee from a boxing ring.

I wouldn't let him near my bed, so he sat on the desk chair and steadily cursed as he cleaned the blood off himself.

Scott sat on the edge of the bed with a washcloth full of ice pressed to his nose. I'd insisted. My pinky toe sang a painful song but I ignored it and kept most of my weight off that foot. I would not sit, not with Darren in my room. I had another wet wash cloth pressed to my mouth. The bleeding had stopped, but my lip had started to swell. Not to mention throb.

"So this explanation you wanted to give me? I'm listening." Scott tossed the wash cloth full of ice onto the bed and gave Darren his full attention.

"I'm past the point of cooperating," said Darren. He shifted uncomfortably on the chair and it was clear his side hurt. I couldn't see the bruises, but I knew damn well they were there.

"Huh," Scott scoffed. "Funny. Oh, well, guess I'll have to kill you now."

Darren threw him a startled look before he decided Scott was kidding.

"You think?" Scott elevated his eyebrows and a very dangerous smile quirked the corners of his mouth.

"You wouldn't dare. How would you explain my death to the Councils?" Darren's bruised face turned sullen, but he was scared too.

"I'd think of something," said Scott with an evil grin.

"Go to hell." Darren tried to stand, and his face drained of color until I thought he might pass out. The idea was not unattractive.

"That's original." Scott snorted. He got to his feet and Darren cringed then flushed. "Tell me what the fuck possessed you to try to rape Stanzie? I'm not screwing around, Darren, I want a good answer."

Darren pressed his lips together and turned his face away.

"She grew up in this pack, you bastard. She's family," Scott shouted.

"She's not!" Darren yelled and grimaced. "She's a traitorous bitch. She turned her back on us."

"And so you decide to rape her in retaliation? Thirteen years later? Try the fuck again." Scott's voice was perilously dark.

"I don't have anything else to say. Either kill me or help me out to my car, Scott." Darren's eyes blazed as he tried again to stand up.

"I'm your Alpha, you sonofabitch," Scott reminded him.

"Not for much longer, hopefully." Darren sneered and Scott almost punched him, but pulled it at the last second.

"I want you out of this pack," he said and Darren's eyes became huge. "You can't do that!"

"I can't?" Scott's smile was merciless. "The fuck I can't. I'm Alpha. You either tell me why the hell you did what you did or you get in your frigging car and you drive it the hell out of my territory."

"I can't." Darren's voice was a small, choked wheeze.

"What?" Scott tilted his head as if he hadn't heard right.

"I said I can't tell you," Darren repeated.

"Can't? Or won't?"

"Can't," Darren whispered. He wasn't lying. I smelled the truth oozing from his pores and the despair at the idea of losing his pack. "Mayflower's my home, Scott. My family's been here for generations. My son. My granddaughter."

"I don't give a shit," Scott snapped. But he was shaken because he could smell Darren told the truth too. "I want the goddamn reason you did this, Darren."

Darren bowed his head and fought tears.

"What did Tony put in the water he gave Stanzie last night?"

Darren's face creased in confusion. He clearly had no idea. "He put something in her water?"

"Oh, balls." Scott whirled and kicked the wall. "Get out of here, Drake. Stay the fuck away from me and especially from Stanzie. If I see your fucking face, I'm going start thinking about kicking your ass out for good. You understand?"

Darren nodded and dragged himself to his feet. With a lurch, he moved for the door and clutched his stomach as if afraid his intestines might fall onto the floor if he didn't hold them in.

Scott made no move to help him. Darren fell outside the door and cursed, but after a moment we heard him drag himself up then, a moment after that, the start of an engine.

"That bastard. I hope he kills himself on the way home," Scott spat and I forced visions of the Mustang flipping over and over out of my head.

"Get your things, you're checking out." Scott swung back to me after he was sure Darren's car was out of the parking lot. "You're coming to stay with me and Faith."

"But Faith wanted me to stay here." My protest was automatic. If I were welcome at their house, she'd never have reserved me this room.

"That was because of me," Scott explained. "I didn't want her calling you in, remember? But now I am pissed as hell, and you and I are going to figure this shit out if it kills us. Right?"

I wondered if it just might. My experience as an Advisor had nearly been the death of me on more than one occasion.

"I need to call Jason," I told him as I grabbed my stuff and shoved it haphazardly into my suitcase.

Scott swore and scrubbed at his face. "Can you hold off on that? If he's as protective as I think he is, he'll haul your ass out of here. Or is that what you want?" He didn't sound angry, but I looked at him suspiciously.

"No, I'm not pissed," he said. "If you want out, Stanzie, you go. I don't want to be a fucking ogre or anything. I can handle this on my own."

"Do you think they can overthrow you as Alpha?" I asked and his face tightened.

"Faith is pregnant. They can hate my ass all they like and want us booted out of the Alpha position, but they won't do it until after she has the baby. Otherwise, they'd be forcing her to have an abortion. That's not right, Stanzie. As fucked up as everything is, I don't think they'd do that."

It rarely happened, but Alphas could be forced out if the entire pack voted against them. It had to be unanimous, and it couldn't be done without the Regional Council's involvement. That, more than Faith's pregnancy, made me think they wouldn't play that card just yet.

"Can we at least call Kathy?" I limped into the bathroom for my toiletries.

He swore again. "Yeah. When we get home we'll call her. We probably should, I guess, only I have nothing to tell her except negatives. I have no frigging clue what's going on. Do you?"

"No. Except that all the men in this pack seem hell bent on fucking me. And it doesn't seem to matter what I want." I swept my cosmetics into my makeup bag and zipped it shut before I retrieved my shampoo and conditioner. I looked up at the shower head and thought once again of Grey—his body wet and slick, his mouth hot and demanding as his hands roamed over my soapy body. I let the memory play out then put it out of my head.

* * * *

Faith was in the front garden when Scott and I parked our cars in the driveway of the house I'd grown up in. The small Cape Cod brought back so many memories I could only stare through the windshield at first. It looked exactly the same as I remembered it, down to the gray shingles and black shutters. The front yard was dominated by a birch tree that towered at least twenty feet high. Flower beds full of bright purple pansies, orange and white zinnias, and pink impatiens were meticulously maintained. Faith, in shorts and a white t-shirt, knelt by a bed of zinnias, a trowel in her gloved hand as she eradicated stubborn weeds.

Scott and I had stopped at the local drugstore for some medical tape for my toe and cotton balls to keep my toes from rubbing together and chafing.

Faith heard the car doors slam and straightened up, her hands going to her back.

"Hey, babe." Scott crossed the flagstone path that led from the driveway to the front steps and bent to brush his lips over the top of her blond head.

She saw me and her brown eyes narrowed in confusion and then dawning horror. I was acutely aware of the blood all over my shirt and my split lip. At the drug store I'd waited in the car so Scott could go in and buy the stuff for me.

"Stanzie, are you all right?" She looked between me and Scott. His nose had stopped bleeding and the abrasions on his knuckles could have come from last night's scuffle with Tony, but I could tell by the flare of her nostrils she'd picked up Darren's scent and the last traces of Scott's fury.

"Thanks to Scott," I said and went to the trunk to get my luggage.

He explained while I pretended I had more suitcases than just the two and, when I slammed the trunk back down, he had both hands on her shoulders as she listened to him, her face pulled tight with shock.

"You can't kick Darren out. If you do, everyone will vote us out as Alphas. I'm pregnant," she wailed and he bent his head closer to hers so he could whisper something in her ear. Whatever it was pulled her up short and her face flooded with shame.

"Stanzie, I don't mean to make light of what happened to you. I think it's awful. I can't even believe he'd do something like that."

"You know him. Likes to experience the forbidden. Walk on the wild side." I slung the strap of my overnight bag over my shoulder and Scott sprang forward to take my suitcase.

"Rape?" Faith shook her head, eyes dark with doubt. "That's a little much even for him, don't you think?"

"Faith, if Scott hadn't pounded on the door at the exact moment he did, Darren would have raped me. No, I don't think it's a little much even for him. He's very capable of it."

She blanched.

"Faith's the reason I was there. I was at the store picking up the Sunday paper when she called and suggested I bring you over for brunch. I was in the neighborhood so I stopped by instead of calling." Scott started up the flagstone path.

Once inside the front door, he continued on up the stairs to the second story while Faith turned right to cut through the dining room and into the kitchen where I smelled seafood. I followed Scott up the stairs and into the room to the left of the staircase. It was an obvious guest room now, although when I'd lived here, it had been mine. A bright aqua comforter detailed with subtle branches and leaves in silver thread covered the brass bed. Sheer aqua curtains fluttered at the window to left of the bed and the one in the recessed eave in front of it.

Beneath the eave was a built-in window seat covered in silver fabric and silver-and-aqua striped throw pillows. A small walnut bureau stood to the right of the eave and built-in drawers were to the left. A bright white aluminum cover concealed the radiator beneath the other window. A bowl of potpourri in a clear bowl with the faintest tint of aqua rested in the center.

A white-and-aqua floral rug covered most of the hardwood floor and a bookcase stained in the same walnut as the bureau sat just to the side of the door. I saw mostly murder mysteries on the shelf although there was a smattering of urban fantasy that featured werewolves and vampires.

Across the narrow hall was the nursery. Save for Winnie the Pooh curtains and bright yellow walls, the room was bare.

"You own this place?" I asked as Scott set my suitcase on the bed.

He smiled. "Nah. Paul does. We rent it from him."

Faith had painted over my purple walls with an eggshell white, but the radiator cover was still the same and my full-length mirror was still nailed to the closet door. I wondered if another reason Faith had booked me into the motel had been because she wasn't sure how I'd react to her living in my old house.

Scott had no idea, but when I went to the radiator and drew my finger along the top of it, his eyes narrowed.

"You lived here," he realized. "Duh."

"Yeah," I agreed.

"Is it a lot different?" He sounded genuinely curious. I shrugged.

"This room is."

"Yours?" he guessed and I nodded. This trip was slamming me headfirst into my past whether I liked it or not.

"You look like shit," he said and laughed when I grimaced. "You know where the bathroom is. Take a shower, get into some clean clothes. Throw that shirt away, it's ruined."

My hand crept up to the neck of the shirt and sudden tears burned my eyes.

"Ah, fuck, it was his shirt, wasn't it?" Scott swore. "Look, don't toss it. We can wash it. What's a few blood stains, right?"

"You said yourself he was gone for good," I whispered and he winced.

"Since when am I such an expert on relationships? I've had exactly two in my life."

"Tell me one of them was not Kathy Manning."

Scott snickered, genuinely amused. "Dude, she was my mentor. My initiator. She was not my girlfriend. Shit."

"Well, Jesus Christ, how am I supposed to know?" I curled my lip at him and he continued to laugh. For a moment I thought he might even fall on the floor, the dramatic bastard.

"Kathy Manning," he choked and went off into a fresh gale of laughter. I winged one of my sandals at him and he dodged it. There were actual tears in his eyes.

"Shut up," I took aim with my remaining sandal. "Goddamnit, Scott, you're going to hurt yourself if you don't stop. It is not that funny."

"Bullshit." He wheezed and wiped the tears from his eyes. I threw the sandal at him and this one hit him in the ass. He was such an idiot.

* * * *

It was a good thing I came out of the bathroom dressed and not in a towel. The only bathroom in the house was inconveniently located between the master bedroom and the kitchen, so I'd prudently brought in a pair of fresh jeans and a long-sleeved t-shirt.

I'd taped my pinkie toe to the one next to it and cushioned the space between them with a cotton ball. The only shoes I had that I thought would be halfway comfortable were my pink-and-white Nikes so I put them on over a pair of white socks. My toe hurt like hell but I ignored it.

I'd managed to put on some makeup but my hair was wet because I'd forgotten my hair dryer in Boston, and didn't know where Faith kept hers. I French braided it wet and secured it with a fabric band I found on the shelf above the toilet. I was pretty sure Faith wouldn't mind.

I couldn't wear lipstick with a fat lip so I felt acutely ugly when I walked out of the bathroom, my dirty clothes balled up under one arm.

I had to pass through the living room to get to the stairs and my room, and was confronted by Tony, Susan, Rachel and Mark. Faith sat with the women on the black-and-white plaid sofa while the men were spread around the room—Scott in the recliner by the window, Tony in a kitchen chair and Mark on one of the sofa arms by Rachel. They'd left the rocker by the stairs for me.

"Jesus H. Christ." Mark got to his feet when he saw my lip and his dark eyes got even darker. "What the hell, Stanz?"

"I'll be right back," I said and escaped to my room to dump my dirty clothes. I'd had no idea brunch meant them too and a rush of humiliated anger scorched through me. I didn't want everyone seeing my lip nor did I want them all to know what had happened. So much for keeping it under wraps.

Before I'd finished stuffing the clothes into the closet, Faith, Rachel and Susan were behind me.

Susan reached out to touch my lip and I fought hard against the urge to push her onto her ass. Instead I allowed it. Her fingers were cool and gentle and there was real anger in her eyes.

"He went too far," she said. So much for keeping what Darren had done under wraps. I gave Faith a "what the hell" look and she winced.

"Are you sure you didn't lead him on, Stanzie?" Rachel asked and Faith squeezed her eyes shut in horror.

"Oh, fuck you, Rachel," I snarled and Rachel took a step back.

"I'm only saying that because Darren likes it rough. Doesn't he, girls?" She looked at Faith and Susan.

Faith sighed and Susan nodded, but anger still danced in her eyes.

"Of course, Faith only knows that by watching, but Susan and I, we know firsthand," Rachel continued. She ignored my spiraling anger and Faith's obvious discomfort. "Faith won't sleep with anyone but Scott. Cute, but kinda weird."

"By rough do you mean when the woman is screaming no and actively trying to escape?" I asked bitterly.

"No, I meant the fat lip," Rachel said. "Sometimes he gets carried away. But he always stops when you say no. Doesn't he, Susan?"

"I've never said no," Susan mused. "He's never given me a split lip, though."

"Me either," Rachel said. "But he's been rough. I've bruised and once he did slap me. But I had it coming." She grinned reminiscently and I slammed the closet door shut so hard they all grimaced.

"I don't want to talk about this," I said. "Can we change the subject? Also, I can't breathe. Can you give me some space please?"

They backed away and I felt a little less crowded.

"Why'd you run out on the hunt last night?" Rachel asked. I went to the window seat and sat so I could look out into the branches of the birch tree. It had grown a few feet in the past decade. I could no longer clearly see the small pond across the street.

"Honestly, I'm not going to be mad if you sleep with Tony," Susan said in a placating voice. My fingers tightened around the throw pillow I'd clutched protectively to my stomach. "Honey, I know about things between you and the Irish guy and, really, I didn't mean what I said at dinner Friday night. If you want to bond with us, that's okay."

"Or with me and Mark," Rachel added.

"Bonding with Mark would be like bonding with my older brother," I snapped.

"Okay, so bond with Tony and Susan."

"We have plenty of room at our house. Mark, Rachel and the twins can move out and you can have their rooms all to yourself. After Faith's baby is born we can even be Alphas and you can have a baby. Wouldn't you like a baby, Stanzie?" Susan wheedled.

"A baby?" I choked. My fingers mashed the pillow. "You've got to be shitting me. I can't have a baby with a wolf like mine. You think I'm going to risk my child having to put up with the crap I've had to take?"

"Stanzie, it will all work out. Believe me," Susan said with a Stepford wife smile that made my blood run cold.

"What is going on here? Stanzie's not going to bond with you and Tony, Susan. She has a bond mate," Faith protested. Her fingers worried the pleats in the lavender skirt she'd put on while I was in the shower.

Susan and Rachel gave her pitying looks.

"The grandmothers both told us that Stanzie and her bond mate are on the outs. Her birthday is in August, Faith, wouldn't it be wonderful if she came back to Mayflower?" Susan patted Faith on the shoulder and her expression turned both sly and fake compassionate. "Or are you worried about Scott? He does have a thing for her, doesn't he?"

"Shut your mouth," I snapped before Faith could say anything. "I'm not bonding with you and Tony, Susan. I'm not bonding with anybody in Mayflower."

"I'm sorry to hear that," Susan said and she looked like she wanted to cross the room to pat my shoulder but the snarl on my face kept her at bay. "What can we do to change your mind?"

"I've got to check the casserole," said Faith and darted from the room.

I escaped after her before the two harpies from hell could converge on me.

The living room was deserted. Scott had taken the men to the cellar where he had a wet bar. From the sounds of it, he also had a television. The Red Sox versus the Brewers. An excited yell went up from the men, and so I assumed the Red Sox had done something right.

Amy Lee Burgess

Rachel and Susan were hot on my heels, so I dodged into the kitchen to ask if I could give Faith a hand.

* * * *

Brunch was a difficult meal. My split lip made eating a chore, not a pleasure, so after a few bites of Faith's delicious seafood casserole I mostly moved food around my plate rather than eat it. The lobster bisque had gone down much easier, so I didn't starve, it was just hard to watch everyone enjoy their meal with such gusto while mine was more of an ordeal.

The white wine was chilled and delicious, and I made sure to watch everyone around the table take a sip of theirs before I drank any of mine. The bottle was on the table and I kept an eye on it. A full glass of water had been poured and on the table before I took my chair, so I avoided it on general principle.

Halfway through the meal, Scott's cellphone buzzed and he excused himself to answer it in the kitchen.

No one made any pretense they weren't straining to listen to at least his end of the conversation.

"Did he tell you *why* I kicked the crap out of him?" Scott snarled once he could get a word in edgewise. Whoever was on the other end of the phone made sure to keep the conversation nearly one-sided.

"Dorothy," said Susan, eyebrows elevated as she helped herself to a second serving of the casserole.

"Mad as hell about Darren. He must be in bad shape," Rachel remarked as she buttered a crescent roll.

Tony ran a finger along the line of his jaw and I wondered if it still ached from the fight he'd had with Scott the night before. Mark grinned and gave me a wink from across the table.

"What?" He feigned complete innocence when Faith sighed.

"It's not funny, Mark. What happened is very serious."

"Serious enough for Scott to get it into his head to kick Darren out of Mayflower?" Susan launched the offensive around a mouthful of food.

"Maybe," said Faith with a grim glint in her eye. Susan knew just how to rile a person up. She'd done it to us when we were kids and she was a teenager, and she did it now that we were all adults.

"Well, maybe he doesn't want to stay Alpha then." Rachel reached for her glass of wine. "Instead of supporting this ridiculous notion, you ought to be using all your influence to calm him down, Faith. Unless you don't want the baby."

"Shut. Up." Faith spat the words through her clenched teeth and the whole room vibrated with her fury. Rachel grinned, unperturbed, and drank her wine.

"Nobody's said anything about kicking anybody out." A worried frown pulled the corners of Tony's mouth down.

"You are not going to threaten me." Faith pushed back her chair so hard it slammed into the wall behind her.

Everyone's attention instantly focused on her.

"Darren Drake almost raped her. Stanzie is not only a former member of this pack, but an Advisor to the Great Council. Do you not comprehend that she could start a tribunal against him right now if she wanted to? Who's to say she won't? And you're going to sit there and threaten me and my baby? You go fuck yourselves, all of you. Get out of my house. Scott and I are Alphas of this pack. You four had your shot at it and, when you were in my position, I supported you with everything I had and I expect the same back from you in return. I don't expect to be stabbed in the back every single time I turn around. This shit is over. "

"Faith, sweetie," began Susan in her most placating voice.

"Get out!" Faith shouted and pointed toward the front door.

Susan gave her a pained smile and threw her cloth napkin on her plate.

"We support you," Mark said, but his eyes were downcast. "We want to support you, Faith."

"Then do it," Faith yelled. Her brown eyes blazed with rage.

When Rachel, who sat next to me at the table, got out of her chair, she gave my shoulder a gentle squeeze before she moved behind me to get to the archway that led to the front foyer and the door. I tried not to flinch, but it was hard.

Faith stalked to the dining room window to make sure they got into their cars and left.

"Jesus H. Christ, that was hot," said Scott from the kitchen archway. "I knew you had it in you to be Alpha, babe. That's what I'm talking about." He approached her from behind and wrapped his arms around her waist so he could nuzzle behind her ear. His hands spread protectively over her still-flat belly.

"I am so mad I think I might fly apart," Faith said in a shaky, thin voice. "Those assholes. They're all I have. All I've ever had and this is what I get?"

"Not true," said Scott. "You've got me. And I've got your back, babe. Always will, okay?"

From the choked sound of her breathing, I knew she'd started to cry.

With my wine glass, I retreated out the back door onto the flagstone patio to give them some space. And maybe so I could cry too.

* * * *

An hour or so later, the screen door creaked open and Scott bounded down the back steps, the bottle of white wine in one hand and his cellphone in the other.

His smile was self-satisfied and I could see a touch of his wolf's eyes reflected in his—a silvery white glow that made his eyes unearthly. If I hadn't already known he'd taken Faith to bed, his eyes clinched it.

The silver glow would gradually fade in a couple of hours, but he would be able to shift for up to forty-eight.

I sat beneath the shade of a green umbrella at a small white wrought-iron patio table.

Scott tipped the wine bottle over the rim of my empty glass and filled it to the brim before he settled in the lawn chair next to mine and took a swig from what was left in the bottle.

"Faith okay?" I asked and his mouth quirked.

"She's taking a nap," he said and laughed.

I rolled my eyes and took a sip of wine. It wasn't quite as chilled anymore, but it was still damn good. "You shouldn't drink that." I gestured at the wine bottle and he winked before he guzzled more. "You'll pay for it after you shift."

"I'll risk it," he decided. He pushed his cellphone into the center of the table. "You want to call Kathy now? Wasn't that the plan, partner?"

Kathy answered on the second ring and Scott put her on speaker. Gulls screamed raucously in the background.

"Where are you? On the beach?" I asked after Scott told her I was with him.

"It's an absolutely glorious day and I live in Providence, Rhode Island. Of course I'm on the beach," Kathy retorted. I pictured her in a sexy full-piece bathing suit—some jewel tone like emerald or ruby—with a floppy straw hat and a romance she'd read beneath the rims of her Dolce and Gabbana outsized sunglasses. Chaise lounge, coconut-scented sunscreen and definitely something sweet and homemade to nibble on. Chocolate-covered strawberries?

"Are you eating chocolate-covered strawberries?" I couldn't resist.

There was a moment of silence. "White chocolate-drizzled raspberries steeped in Grand Marnier actually. Why? Are you hungry?"

"Figures you wouldn't do ordinary chocolate-covered strawberries," I muttered and she chuckled.

"Did you call to discuss food, Stanzie?"

"No, I called to bring you up to speed on what the hell is going on in this pack. Your planted spy wanted to go through you before I went to Jason and, for some reason, I agreed. Wasn't that nice of me?"

"Incredibly." She sounded like she spoke through gritted teeth.

"You fighting with Jason?" I asked sweetly. Okay, I experienced a secret, savage glee when I asked this because it seemed as if I'd waited a lifetime to be able to put her on the spot, while every time she turned around she managed to gut me.

"I'd have to be speaking to him in order to be fighting with him, don't you think?" Her teeth were definitely clenched and I grinned.

"What did he do? Something heinous like ask you to bond with him?" I wondered.

"What on earth does this have to do with what's going on in Mayflower?"

"Not much, but inquiring minds want to know."

"Nice try. Let's move on, shall we? Scott, Stanzie is an incurable romantic at heart. Don't let her vicious exterior fool you. Incurable romantics have an uncanny knack for trying to fix other people's love lives while completely screwing up their own. How's Liam, dear? I don't hear his snide laughter on the other end, so I presume he's not there, is he?"

It was my turn to grit my teeth.

"Oh, go to hell. You know damn well where he is."

"I do?" Kathy feigned ignorance and failed pitifully. "Oh, well, I had heard this little rumor that he's in Dublin and you're pining alone in Boston, but I thought to myself, no, that couldn't be true. Surely Stanzie wouldn't let a man she absolutely adores get away from her because of a silly argument. But I was wrong, I take it?"

"Where the hell do you hear this shit? You're like a fucking spider sitting in the middle of a web with sticky-ass strands connected to every goddamn pack and person in the world. It's disgusting and unhealthy, you know that? Obsessive."

"Informative," she corrected. "And not every pack and person, just the ones I care about. Really, Stanzie, if I were you, I'd get my butt on the next plane for Dublin and tell that idiot he's being, well, an idiot. He might listen to you. He never listens to anybody else, but he sometimes does listen to you, although I don't know why."

"Not anymore," I snapped. "And you might have been nicer to Jason. You know damn well you love him."

"Which is precisely the reason I couldn't bond with him. It was an absurd idea, Stanzie. Imagine me the bond mate of a Councilor with nothing to do but paint my nails and make him dinner while he gets to do all the important work in this Pack. No thank you. My one shot at the Great Council blown because of his old-fashioned sentiment. It's appalling."

"What do you mean your one shot?"

"How many Great Councilors do you suppose there are at any one time from New England? Why do you think Rosemary Young is sitting on the Great Council now instead of me?" Kathy must be pissed off to discuss this with me. Or she really did think of me as a daughter. And Scott must be important too. He listened with growing incredulity to our conversation, the bottle of wine forgotten.

"Because you were Jason Allerton's mistress?" I guessed.

"Bingo. I knew the appointment was coming, but I had no idea it was so close. And he never said a word. Instead, I have to find out when Rosemary comes rushing up to me, glowing, to tell me that she has been selected. Not me. I was flabbergasted. Completely crushed. And then what does Jason do? The minute his bond mate dies, he's proposing that we bond together. Us! He knew damn well I wanted that slot on the Council. If he'd truly cared about me, he would have broken things off between us in time for me to have a shot. Sick bond mate or not, he knew damned well when the Council began considering candidates. I'll never forgive him for that."

"But you love each other," I objected.

"Stanzie, once I was on the Council, we could have picked up where we supposedly left off, but no, he had to get greedy and want me for his bond mate. I already have a bond mate. It's insulting."

"I'd rather be with someone I loved than serve on the Great Council," I said and she snorted.

"If you wanted to be with someone you loved, you'd be in Dublin. Instead you're in Massachusetts investigating your birth pack."

"You make it sound like all I have to do is get on a fucking plane and he'd be there at the airport with flowers and we'd live happily ever after. Get real, Kathy. You had a great thing with Jason and you threw it away for nothing because if you're right, you'll never get on the Great Council now and so what do you have?"

Scott slowly pushed his chair back in preparation for escape. I glowered at him and he froze.

"I have my position on the Regional Council and a devious Advisor placed in the most secretive and isolated pack in New England. I have Jason Allerton's Advisor as a close, personal confidante. I have my beautiful son who is going to Yale in the fall. In four years, he'll come back to Darkhunt with a degree and the means to obtain a lucrative and powerful business position. This will enable our pack to one day own our own corporation which I intend to govern behind the scenes. The Great Council can go screw itself, I'll have it all anyway."

I listened to Kathy's plans and knew without a shadow of a doubt she'd achieve them. She scared the hell out of me on so many levels I couldn't even count them all.

"I'd have both of Jason Allerton's Advisors in my pocket if you'd stop being a ninny and get on a plane," she added and I gave the phone the finger. Scott turned his laughter into a strangled cough but Kathy wasn't fooled.

"She just made an obscene gesture at the phone, didn't she?" she guessed irately.

"Well, it wasn't actually at the phone," I said and this time Scott couldn't disguise his laugh.

Kathy waited for him to finish while the gulls continued to shriek in the background. If I listened hard enough I could hear the waves crashing to shore. The weather was still too cold for swimming, but I'm sure there were sunbathers on the beach—none as chic and composed as Kathy Manning, however.

"Tell me what's going on," Kathy demanded and Scott sobered enough to tell her. When he got to the part where Darren nearly raped me, she actually swore. Kathy Manning never swore.

"That sonofabitch," were her exact words. "Stanzie, are you all right?" The concern in her voice wasn't feigned and unexpected tears burned my eyes. I blinked them away, aware of Scott in the chair beside me with his gaze fixed on the phone in an attempt to give me some privacy.

I reached out to touch his shoulder in gratitude, and the smile he flashed me was at once so beautiful, friendly and compassionate it took my breath away.

Scott Charest was the most gorgeous man I'd ever seen. Murphy was handsome, but Scott was breathtaking, especially when he smiled.

"If you tell Jason this, he'll have you out of there so fast your head will spin," predicted Kathy and I knew she was right. A part of me wanted nothing more than to get the hell out. Scott put his hand over mine on the table and gave it a gentle squeeze as if to say he was fine with that decision.

But he needed all the help he could get because something sinister was wrong with the pack. What I didn't know was whether the strangeness festering within Mayflower had anything to do with the conspiracy. I also didn't know if Scott was aware of the conspiracy.

"Kathy, something is going on here. Not sure what it is. Scott wants to pool knowledge with me. You know, my vast experience as an Advisor to the Great Council?" I injected a little sarcasm into my tone but really, what I asked was whether it was safe to tell him everything.

"If I were you, I'd listen to what Scott has to say about this specific pack rather than conjecture with things you've run across in other packs right now. Concentrate on where you are instead of where you've been. What do you think?" Kathy didn't want me to talk about the conspiracy. Scott didn't know.

He listened to us and frowned. He wasn't sure, but suspected we kept things from him.

"Fine. And I'll hold off telling Jason since you know what's happening, and you're a Councilor." I decided. "I'm staying."

"You make sure Scott sticks with you. I don't want you alone and vulnerable," Kathy lectured.

"She's not going anywhere without me." Scott's uncanny gray eyes darkened to glacier blue.

When we finished the conversation, Scott disconnected and played with his phone for a moment, his face grim.

"Are you two doing some sort of end run around me?" He looked up and his eyes sparked with frustration. "I can't work in the dark."

"You've been working in the dark for three years," I pointed out. "And I'd tell you anything you needed to know, Scott."

"When I need it, but not right now I guess." He spun the phone around on the table and took a deep, unhappy breath.

The abrasions on his knuckles had turned an ugly red.

"Did you clean those out with peroxide?" I took his hand with both of mine so I could look more closely at his wounds. Twin bruises on his face had turned a livid, brutal blue. I had purple bruises in the shape of Darren's fingers on both my shoulders, a nasty one on my right inner thigh from his knee and my lip throbbed like a bitch. We both looked like refugees from a war zone.

"No, Mom. I'll get to it." He ruffled my hair with his free hand and, when I stuck out my tongue, he grabbed me into a friendly headlock. "Ha. You're trapped, loser. What are you gonna do now? Cry?"

"Kick you in the balls as soon as I stand up," I promised, but I laughed and so did he.

We tussled together in our chairs as I tried to free myself and he held me prisoner.

When my wine glass went over the side of the table and smashed into bits on the flagstones, we both burst into guilty laughter and he released me.

As we gathered the broken shards, I fought against sudden tears.

"Did I hurt you?" Scott, of course, saw my struggle and got upset.

"No." I shook my head. "It's just...it's been so long since I've been in a pack and goofed around like that. It's been years since I've done it. I miss being in a pack, Scott."

Vaughn and I, of course, had touched and been close while he'd lived in Boston with us, but I had been there for him and had not derived the uncomplicated pleasure from the contact that I had with three minutes of horseplay with Scott. And, Murphy, of course, didn't like to be touched first. We'd never scuffled around for fun, except in bed or in wolf form. We'd never even held hands when we walked down the street together.

Scott gave me a sympathetic smile. "You'll find a new pack, Stanzie, you'll see. Fuck that Irish guy. He didn't know what he had and it's his loss, not yours, okay?"

I thought of Paddy sitting on the grass in Gina and Ron's backyard after Bethany's funeral. The casual way he'd leaned against my legs and the way I'd played with his dark curls. Touch. Pack to pack.

Little tastes just made me want huge gulps, and the reality was a condo in Boston that reeked of fresh paint and lost hope.

Chapter 11

Someone's shrill scream yanked me out of my nightmare. Drenched with sweat, yet shivering with chills, I scrambled upright and threw panicky looks around the four corners of my dark room in search of intruders.

The scream, of course, had been mine.

I half screamed again when my bedroom door burst open, but it was only Faith in a short ivory nightgown. Her bare legs flashed white in the near dark as she rushed to my side.

"Are you all right?" The erratic thump of her heart all but deafened me.

"Fucking nightmare." I was mortified. My hair stuck to the sweat on my face and my split lip ached like hell.

"Scoot over," Faith ordered and before I could object, she was under the covers with me. "You're not alone, Stanzie, okay?"

I burst into ugly tears. Yes, I was.

"If you don't stop crying, I'm going to start. I hate it when people cry." Faith's voice wobbled and I tried hard to stop my tears but they continued to pour down my face. They tasted of salty despair.

"It's always the same thing. Nate's lying there in a pool of blood and I can taste him in my mouth, only I'm not my wolf, I'm me. And then Murphy comes down the ladder and he sees Nate and tells me I'm bad and that he hates me and he asks how many more people am I going to kill? Grey wasn't enough. Elena wasn't. All the blood, it's filling up the room and sloshing around and it's over the tops of my feet and to my ankles and then it's to my waist and Murphy's on the ladder, yelling he's not going to die too, but he's swept off the ladder in a tide of blood and I see his hand, fist clenching, and then he's gone and I'm choking, I'm drowning and the blood isn't cold like water, it's warm and thick and tastes like iron and I don't want to die. I don't want to die alone, Faith."

"You know it's just a dream, Stanz." Faith reached for my hand under the covers.

"Some damn Advisor I am. I can't do anything but frigging cry," I sobbed.

We both stiffened when we heard rapid footsteps on the staircase then Scott rushed into the bedroom.

"Jesus Christ, what the hell is going on?" he demanded in a hoarse whisper. His chest heaved and his hands were balled into fists. He looked wildly around the room as if he expected to see an army of assassins but there was nothing but shadows.

"Stanzie had a nightmare," Faith explained.

"Oh." Scott blinked at us in the faint moonlight then stalked to the bed. "Move." He crawled over me so he could be in the middle and gathered me and Faith close so our heads rested on his shoulders. "Now shut up and go to sleep. I'm frigging tired, you guys."

Faith obediently closed her eyes but I stared into the darkness, body stiff and alert.

Scott's fingers squeezed my arm.

"Don't get any ideas. I'm too tired to fuck," he warned me and I snorted.

"You wish, Charest," I moved closer so my body fit tight against his and put my palm flat on his chest so I could feel his heartbeat. Faith's breath was feather light on the back of my hand.

"Tomorrow morning I should be up for anything though." He chuckled and I kicked him in the shin with my good foot. If I dreamed again that night, I didn't remember.

* * * *

I woke first the next morning. Scott and Faith were dead to the world. None of us had shifted positions during the night so I carefully slid from beneath Scott's arm and out of the bed.

I shuffled down the stairs in my gray sweats and white *J'aime Paris* t-shirt I'd bought from a street vendor on the Champs Elysees and inspected the refrigerator and cupboards for breakfast ideas.

I'd just poured a quarter teaspoon of vanilla extract into a bowl of eggs and milk in preparation for French toast when someone knocked on the bottom half of the screen door. I'd opened the back door to let the fresh breeze into the kitchen and now I regretted it.

I whirled around, teaspoon clattering to the floor, to see Dorothy and Darren on the back steps.

Dorothy wore a bright green short-sleeved blouse over a pair of light brown linen trousers. Chunky gold earrings dangled from her ears.

Darren was in pair of gray Dockers and a crisp black button-down shirt with the sleeves neatly rolled. An expensive TAG Heuer watch gleamed from his right wrist. Stolen no doubt. No way he could have afforded it on his own. He stood tall and erect, his dark eyes watchful.

"May we come in?" Dorothy essayed a nervous smile. Her lips were coral red and almost but not quite clashed with her hair.

Darren's dark gaze pleaded eloquently with me. I bent to retrieve the teaspoon and carried it to the sink. It rattled against the stainless steel when I threw it in. I moved back to the counter so I could see them through the screen again. I said nothing, just stared at them.

"Stanzie, we want to apologize," Dorothy begged. A large taupe hobo bag was slung across one shoulder and she played with the zipper.

The bruises on Darren's face were greenish yellow and I had to strain to see the faint abrasions on his knuckles through the screen. I'd thought Scott and I had kicked the shit out of him, but he looked in better shape than both of us. My broken toe throbbed and my split lip felt huge and swollen, although it probably wasn't half as big as it felt.

Scott pounded down the stairs and barreled into the kitchen in just his sweat pants, chest bare. Livid purple bruises traveled from his chest down to his flat stomach. The bruises on his cheek were still dark blue.

"What the hell are you doing here?" he snarled as he stepped between me and the screen door.

"Please let us in," Dorothy pleaded. "Scott, we're sorry."

"*We're* sorry?" he repeated. "What the hell did *you* do?"

Dorothy bit her lip. "If you kick him out, you kick me out too."

"Did I say I was going to kick him out?" Scott raked a hand through his dark hair. "I haven't made up my mind yet. Showing up at my door and harassing Stanzie isn't helping your case, by the way."

"We're not harassing her."

"You sure look like a couple of fucking stalkers to me. Lurking out the back door like that."

"She won't let us in."

"Good for her. I'd kick her ass if she did. Dorothy, your bond mate tried to rape her yesterday morning."

"I know. And we came to apologize."

Scott sneered at them. "That fixes everything, doesn't it? You came to apologize. Jesus H. Christ."

"It looks like Stanzie's making breakfast. Can we join you? We could eat out here on the patio. We brought the coffee. French vanilla, Stanzie, for you. We remembered." Darren held a cardboard carry case from Dunkin' Donuts. Five large coffees rested within. He held it up and I got a better look at the light abrasions across his knuckles and felt like an idiot for thinking I'd actually hurt him. No, my puny strength had obviously done very little.

He screamed, Stanzie, a little voice inside reminded me, but I shook it away. My memory had to be faulty.

When I'd worked behind the reception desk at Dorothy's real estate agency, Darren would stop every morning with Dunkin' Donuts coffee for us all. Ten AM on the button. Plain black for him, extra sugar, extra cream for Dorothy and a French vanilla flavored for me.

The three of us had gathered around my desk and joked and laughed as we consumed the coffee. Dorothy was usually in a rush to show a house, but Darren was never in a hurry. I'd told him all about my favorite music, the books I read, my harp practice, problems with Paul. My revulsion for Wes Hanover and his creepy, sweaty hands.

He'd listened sympathetically. He was the rebel of the pack. I'd expected him to encourage my own teenage rebellion, but he'd generally counseled I should listen to my father.

"I wish I'd listened to mine when I had him here," he'd declared more than once, his eyes dark with old grief. His parents, Trevor and Stella, had died in the red virus epidemic that had swept through Mayflower when I was a baby.

More than once I'd gone home halfway resolved to do things Paul's way, only to get there and discover Lauren sobbing in a corner because she'd packed the wrong sandwich in Paul's lunch bag or forgotten to buy something at the store that he expected to be served at dinner that night.

I'd tell her I'd make his lunch the next morning or I'd run out to the grocery store for the last-minute item and, by the time I had her calmed down, my teenage rebellion had bloomed hot and dark again. A never-ending loop that had played out time and again the last few years I'd been a member of Mayflower.

"Are you on a construction job this week, Scott?" Dorothy strove for a normal tone but failed miserably.

"It's none of your business, Dorothy," Scott growled. He glared at Darren. "And take your coffee and shove it."

"Please. You don't know how hard it was to come here." Darren's face twisted.

"Are you going to give me one good reason why you did what you did?" Scott demanded as Faith appeared in the hall archway by the cellar door, one hand to her throat. She'd thrown on a pretty floral robe that skimmed just above her knees. Her blond hair was tousled and her eyes still a shade sleepy.

"I...can't." The words seemed to drag out of Darren's mouth. Shame made his cheeks burn and emphasized the yellowish green bruises on his face.

"What the fuck is this *can't* shit?" Scott exploded. "I'm so fucking pissed off, Darren. I don't want to hear *can't* from you!"

"That's all I can say."

"Then why the fuck are you here?" Scott took a threatening step toward the screen door. Dorothy backed away, but Darren held his ground.

"I'm doing what I can do. It may seem inadequate, but I am trying, Scott." He switched his gaze to my face. "I'm sorry, Stanzie. I can't always control the things I do."

"Darren." Dorothy put a trembling hand on his arm. "Let's go. We're making things worse, I think."

Darren locked gazes with me once more then abruptly turned away. He put the coffees on the patio table and left without a backward look.

"What the fuck was that?" Scott paced around the kitchen like a caged wolf. His fingers scraped across the dark sprinkling of course beard hair along his jaw and winced when he encountered a sore spot from Darren's fist.

"Why can't he control the things he does? That makes no sense and it's insulting." Faith moved into the room and knelt to the cupboard beneath the stove to retrieve a frying pan. "He's an adult, for God's sake. He knows right from wrong."

"Unless he's trying to confess he's a sociopath losing his grasp on reality," I mused. But that was ridiculous. Nate Carver had been an aberration. Darren was no serial rapist. The idea was absurd.

* * * *

Access to Wendell State Forest was across the road and fifty yards to the east of Faith and Scott's house. The narrow dirt trail led to a small metal entrance gate meant to bar vehicles, not pedestrians. This way into the woods was rarely used and then generally only by the houses on Scott and Faith's street. Most people entered the state park in Wendell. Willoughby was strictly for locals or cars passing through on their way somewhere else.

I managed to limp as far as the first set of ancient picnic tables and rusted grills before my broken toe screamed no more and refused to cooperate any further.

Faith and Scott set me up near the picnic table I'd used for countless tea parties when I was a little girl and Paul and Lauren had brought me to the woods for picnics. Today, we'd packed in a camp chair, a cooler full of soda, water, beer and sandwiches. I'd brought one of the urban fantasies from the bookcase in my room and a small pocket knife. Scott had slipped me the latter while Faith made sandwiches.

They were going to shift and I was going to read and pig out on ham-and-cheese sandwiches. Possibly peanut butter and jelly too.

Before they melted away into the woods to shift, they perched on the picnic table bench and drank bottles of cold water. Faith was excited and her energy fairly crackled around her head. Her eyes glowed more amber with every sip of water as she unconsciously called up her wolf.

Scott sat close beside her on the bench so their thighs touched and once when Faith impulsively kissed the side of his face, he turned to intercept her mouth with his and the kiss turned nearly pornographic. His hands found the bottom of her t-shirt and roamed beneath then upward while her fingers found the crotch of his jeans.

I took a sip of beer and focused my attention on a pair of squirrels frolicking in the branches of a pine tree across the clearing. Great. Everyone had a partner.

We'd spread a blanket on the grass and pine needles by the picnic table and when Scott and Faith sprawled across it and her t-shirt ended up in my lap, I decided, toe or not, I might want to take a little walk.

"You can join us, you know." Faith's smile was beautiful and so was her lacy pink bra. I never seemed to get underwear anyplace other than Target, although I'd been tempted in Paris but repelled by the prices. Faith's bra definitely didn't come from Target even if her clothes and shoes did. Weird what women indulged themselves with sometimes. "It'll be fun, Stanzie."

"No shit," I muttered as Scott grinned at me and his uncanny gray eyes issued a definite challenge. He didn't think I would but he clearly was open to the idea.

"We can all three shift," Faith continued and that poured a whole lot of cold water on any idea I'd entertained about sex with Scott. "We'll watch over you. We promise."

"I'm technically not supposed to let you out of my sight, remember what Kathy said." Scott gave my shin a playful nudge and curled his fingers around my ankle. His touch was electric hot and I gulped. Damn. Damn, damn, damn.

"You're not scared cause of Darren, are you?" Faith's brown eyes became troubled and she sat up. Her jeans were unbuttoned and I glimpsed a silky pair of matching pink panties. Definitely not from Target.

I hadn't been up until she mentioned it, but it was only a brief blip of uneasiness and soon gone. Scott was not Darren and anything I did with him, I would do willingly. Very willingly.

"I can work around that fat lip of yours," said Scott as his gaze traveled up and down my body. My pulse gave a leap and my blood began to hum. This was not good. All it would take would be a gentle tug on my ankle and I'd be down on the blanket with them and that would be it.

I opened my mouth to say yes and Murphy's face flashed before my eyes.

"No," I said instead. "I don't want to shift."

They didn't argue. Faith stood up and shucked off her jeans and underwear and walked for the cover of the trees to shift. Scott watched her ass for a moment before he rose to his feet.

"Dare you to watch me strip," he teased.

"I'm not so weak that the sight of your naked body is going to change my mind, Charest," I said, but I wasn't so sure. Especially since he was aroused and, when he stood up, he was placed at a very strategic angle for my line of sight. He did a little striptease dance for me as he shimmied out of his jeans and grinned at me. I grinned back and resisted the urge to touch him.

The bruises on his body made me wince but he didn't seem to feel them.

"You're an idiot, Constance Newcastle," he told me before he sprinted after Faith. The sight of his bare ass made me agree with his assessment, but at least I had beer.

* * * *

I heard the person on the path before I smelled him. My book dropped to the ground as I scrambled for the jack knife tucked into the pocket of my gray hoodie. A frantic glance into the trees where Faith and Scott had disappeared more than two hours ago revealed nothing. They were not conveniently back. I was alone.

The scent of familiar cologne underscored with a whiff of the wearer's personal odor drifted over. I relaxed my grip on the jack knife.

"Alan, what are you doing here? It's two o'clock on a Monday afternoon. Shouldn't you be working?"

Alan stepped off the path and made his way across the dirt and grass to my picnic table. His expression was both worried and furious.

"You think I'm going to show up at the agency for work after what Darren did to you? Fuck that. Fuck him and fuck Dorothy too." He flung himself down on the blanket so he could stare moodily up at the blue sky.

"Jesus, news travels fast," I muttered. I reached into the cooler by my chair and dredged up a beer. Alan took it, but didn't sit up or look away from the sky.

My job behind the reception desk at Dorothy's real estate agency had passed to Faith and, after her, to Alan. Someday it would go to Olivia, Tony and Susan's daughter. Before I'd worked there, Mark had. The job belonged to the youngest members of the pack who inherited the position when they turned sixteen.

"I don't understand dick in this pack anymore," Alan complained. As I watched his face, a tear trickled out of the corner of his eye. I thought of the French vanilla coffee Darren had left on the patio table and how I'd poured it down the kitchen sink.

I remembered, Stanzie, Darren had said.

Children were cherished in a pack. Nurtured by everyone. And when they grew up and became adults in the pack, they had bonds with everyone. Deep ones.

When I'd left Mayflower to be with Grey and escape my father, a part of me had always understood why no one had ever responded to my cards and letters. Why no one had called me. I had broken the bonds. It wasn't a crime to leave the birth pack, but there were ways to do it so people didn't get hurt. Ways I hadn't taken.

Alan had grown up in this pack and been loved and indulged by everyone—including Dorothy and Darren. That Darren could do something so awful to a former pack member was almost impossible for him to believe and devastating to contemplate.

"That bastard's like a father to me," Alan whispered. He put one arm over his eyes so I couldn't see him cry.

I crawled across the blanket next to him. When I reached out for him, he rolled into my arms and we held each other.

"You disappeared. You fucking left and never looked back. And now you show up and everyone starts acting like goddamn aliens. They've been acting weird ever since I turned twenty, but this is worse than ever. They want me gone too. I grew up here. This is my pack and they want me gone. The same people who two years ago loved me. I don't understand."

"I sent you birthday cards every year. Christmas presents too." I stroked his blond hair. He buried his face in my neck and burrowed against me for comfort.

"I got shit from you," he said sullenly. "Shane got me my own post office box when I turned sixteen. Made a big production out of it. All I ever get is junk mail. I suppose he did that so he wouldn't have to give me a key to his and Sam's box, huh?"

"I think so," I agreed. It didn't surprise me his parents had kept my cards and presents from him. If he'd known, he would have responded. "I always put my address on the envelopes and hoped someday when you learned to drive you'd show up on my doorstep. I did look back, Alan. I never forgot you or Faith or anybody here."

"And you come back and this is what you freaking get." Alan pushed away from me so he could sit up and gulp his beer. He appeared so adorable and young I could finally see the ten-year-old-boy I'd left behind. He looked at me over the top of the beer bottle. "Why, Stanzie? Why would he do that? Why were they all so weird at the hunt Saturday night? I've seen people pair up outside their bonds before, but never have almost all the guys gone after just one of the women. It was like they were stalking you. Jesus. And the worst part was..."

"You wanted to join in," I finished for him. He nodded, guilt flushed his cheeks red.

"Pheromones," I told him. "And the hunt itself. You're old enough to feel it now, Alan. Something happens during group hunts. Lust, desire, pure and plain sex. It's passed from one to the next like..."

"A virus?" It was his turn to finish my sentence. I tried not to laugh but it was impossible.

"A virus you want to catch," I said when I caught my breath. "I was into it, Alan."

"No, you weren't." He threw his beer bottle at a rusted trash bin and made it just over the rim. "You bolted like a terrified rabbit. Scott and Tony got into a fight when Tony tried to go after you."

"That wasn't because I was scared of the sexual current," I told him, but he didn't believe me.

"They were stalking you. And you got the hell out of there like any sane woman would have. And everything I thought I knew about the people in this pack is wrong and I don't have a fucking clue. Is there more beer?" He made a desperate lunge for the cooler and scrabbled inside until he found one.

I wished I could explain the conspiracy and my paranoia over poisoned water bottles but I couldn't. It was hell being an Advisor sometimes.

"Isn't there anybody in this pack besides Susan or Rachel that could initiate you?" I leaned over him to get a beer and Alan rested his head against my shoulder as I reached. In times of stress especially, Pack craved touch.

I took a swig of beer as Alan settled on the blanket and positioned himself so his head was in my lap. Idly, I smoothed back his hair with my fingers and wondered what he saw besides the blue sky when he gazed upward.

"Like who?" Alan was inclined to be sulky but my touch calmed him.

"Dorothy? Karen? Maddie? Jennifer?" I named all the women in his mother's generation, except for my own mother, Lauren. She never slept with anyone but Paul. Ever. Plus, the idea of her initiating anyone's wolf was ludicrous. I tried to imagine her in the role and failed. Unless Paul was there too so she could look to him for cues.

"They say I have to choose between Susan and Rachel," Alan answered.

"Who are *they*?" I had my very deep suspicion. "Not your Alphas, I bet."

"No, Faith and Scott tell me it could be anybody," Alan allowed. "But nobody listens to them, Stanzie, you know that."

"Which is bullshit. You ought to. Show everyone by your example how a pack is supposed to function." This was hypocritical advice since I had never been one to listen to my own Alphas. I could see Paddy's eyes roll even as I spoke and gritted my teeth. Paddy O'Reilly. He didn't deserve my respect, the lying sonofabitch.

Alan snorted. "Like anyone is going to look up to me. Stanzie, you're being ridiculous. I know you've been gone from this pack for over a decade, but you remember how it works here. Paul has an opinion and pretty soon it's everyone's opinion. And Paul's opinion is that I ought to choose between Susan or Rachel. So when I asked Dorothy to initiate my wolf she turned me down. Nicely, of course, but she said no. And she was my one shot. She and Darren are the rebels of the pack. If Dorothy said no, can you imagine what Jennifer would say? Or Karen? At least Dorothy didn't tell anyone I'd asked her. Any of the other women would have run straight to Paul."

"Paul Benedict should not get to decide who initiates everyone's wolves." I almost threw my full bottle of beer at the trash can just to hear it smash. Anger boiled through my blood.

"Ouch, you're pulling my hair," Alan yelped and I realized I had a fistful of it.

I hastily let go and smoothed my hand across his forehead in apology. He settled back into my lap, but remained tense for a moment, as if he expected me to attack.

"Where are Faith and Scott? Shifted?" Alan answered his own question so I took another sip of cold beer and contemplated the tallest pine tree beyond the picnic area. Majestic and old, it towered a good ten feet above the other pines, and the top limbs shivered in the summer breeze. I wondered how many times I'd stared at this exact same tree during the years I'd spent in Mayflower.

When I'd been a child, I'd named the tree Sir Piney and I smiled to remember it now.

Movement just behind the tree caught my eye and I held my breath when I saw a large silver wolf emerge, closely followed by a smaller wolf. Her fur was also silver but tipped with black. As I watched, I saw her lower her front legs so her butt stuck up in the air. She pounced on the unsuspecting larger wolf. Only he was not quite as unsuspecting as he pretended to be and whirled when she was in mid leap and knocked her to the forest floor with playful ease. They scuffled in the pine needles, mock growling, first one then the other on top.

Alan sat up so he could see them and his whole being radiated such intense longing my heart clutched.

"I want to meet my wolf so bad." The words came out in a bitter whisper, faint, accusatory and hopeless.

The wolves were a silver blur as they tumbled together. The female broke away and ran. The male gave chase and flew past her. He changed course so he headed straight at me and Alan. I braced myself for the collision, but at the last second he gave a powerful leap and cleared my head by a three-inch span.

Alan whipped his head around so hard I heard his neck crack then the male wolf landed on him and drove him down to the blanket, tail wagging furiously.

Alan's arms came up to the wolf's ruff and laughed helplessly as the wolf slobbered his wet tongue across Alan's face.

"You bastard, get off," he wheezed, but the wolf continued to lick his face.

The female wolf approached me at a much more sedate pace and sat so she leaned against me. I draped a companionable arm over her back and she rested her muzzle on my shoulder.

She had lovely orange-amber eyes and I wondered what color my own wolf's eyes were. I'd never seen them in color. I'd only seen her reflection in puddles and brooks. I knew her fur was very light with dark tips, but I didn't know what color her eyes were.

She saw in black and white, gradations of gray, but her focus was sharp and clear, and her sense of smell made up for the lack of color depth.

Of course since I hadn't had sex in months my wolf was nowhere near the surface. Dormant beneath the skin, she waited for release. Or perhaps she was oblivious of everything and was aware only when sex and opportunity woke her.

The spark that was human dimmed to a glowing ember when she was in control. With Murphy's help, the small ember of me burned hotter and I remembered more of what happened when my wolf was free as it happened instead of in fragmented pieces that came to me after she was gone and I was back.

She resented that, disliked me looking over her lupine shoulder because I forced her to do things she didn't want to do. I'd started her down the path of acquiring words for everything and she'd taken it over with a vengeance, but she never would have cared about what things were named if I hadn't called it forth within her.

Faith and Scott's wolves were at peace and full of joy. Faith's wolf watched Scott's wolf wrestle with Alan and I didn't know how much of Faith saw the play versus her wolf. a combination to be sure, but the ratio was much closer to fifty-fifty than it was for me.

Scott's wolf finally let Alan up and bounded a few feet away. He curled up on his side and seemed to blink in and out of focus. Fur receded and skin emerged. Fingers replaced paws. Back legs became longer. His tail disappeared.

He gave a final shudder and was human again. Also, buck naked.

Faith moved away from me and underwent the same metamorphosis then climbed to her feet. Dirt smudged her left cheek and her brown eyes glowed.

Her belly was still perfectly flat but there was something about her naked body that made her pregnancy more apparent than when she wore clothes.

"Hand me my shirt will you, Alan?" She reached out her hand and Alan handed back her t-shirt.

Scott rose to his feet, totally unselfconscious, and approached the cooler for a bottle of water. He used most of it to wash his hands and face and gave the rest of the bottle to Faith who did the same thing.

Alan had enjoyed playing with Scott's wolf, but now his mouth was sulky again and he abruptly lunged to his feet and stalked away, hands stuffed into his pockets, head down.

We watched him go until he disappeared around the turn in the path. Scott found his jeans and pulled them on.

There was something so self-satisfied in the slant of Scott's smile, I grew suspicious. The more I thought about it, the more it became clear what he'd meant to do with his wolf and Alan.

"You did that on purpose," I accused and he paused as he donned his t-shirt to give me an unconvincing confused look. "You could have shifted back in the woods, but no, you had to stay in wolf form to show him what he's missing. You fucking prick."

Faith's mouth dropped open but she didn't say anything. Scott shrugged and continued to dress. I walked away.

* * * *

"Why is Faith working? She's pregnant." I gripped the railing halfway down the cellar stairs and waited for Scott, who had the ball game on, to mute the volume.

The cellar was finished with glossy pine paneling and pale brown carpeting. Scott had furnished it with a battered leather sofa that had seen much better days, as well as a brown recliner. He lounged in the recliner, the foot rest up, bottle of water on the end table next to him.

A full wet bar with a mirrored back and brown leather bar stools completed the room's decor. Well, there was also the flat-screen TV mounted to the wall beneath the stairs and some framed sports posters— all New England teams.

Scott's sanctuary obviously. He'd descended into it after he'd returned from the forest and taken a shower.

Faith and I had spent the remainder of the afternoon in the garden before she'd showered and put on a pair of black pants and white blouse with a name tag. Sensible black flats, hair put up in a messy bun, minimal makeup, no jewelry except for her bond pendant tucked beneath the blouse.

Her work clothes for a restaurant in Wendell.

Each adult member of a pack contributed part of their wages to a pack fund administered by the Alphas. Some of it went back out to the pack to help subsidize their rents or property taxes, some of it was invested, but most of it went into reserve to maintain the Alphas. Once the female Alpha was pregnant and after she gave birth, she was not expected to work a paying job until she gave up Alpha status.

"She's only two months along." Scott's voice was neutral but I thought he might be pissed at me. Good.

I didn't answer, I just stared until he sighed and kicked the foot rest down so he could put his feet on the carpet.

"If you tell me you give most of the pack money to Paul I'm probably going to throw myself down these fucking stairs in protest."

"No." Scott shook his head. He was silent, but I could see by his expression and the impatient way he drummed his fingers against the arm of the recliner that he waged an internal debate with himself. There was something he didn't want to tell me, but in the end he gave in and said, "Todd's been gambling again."

"Oh, goddamn it," I said. "I thought he'd given up the casinos."

His chin jutted angrily. "It's the only way he knows how to make money, Stanzie."

Exasperation made my voice sharp. "Not the casinos. You can't beat the casinos. Everyone has told him that. Friendly card games, sure, but not the casinos."

"Last year he made thirty nine thousand dollars at the casinos," Scott said.

That stopped me for about ten seconds.

"Which the state taxed half away, right?"

Scott blew out his breath. "Listen, when you're Alpha of your pack, you do it your way. Todd is Faith's father and sometimes he has a bad streak and we let it slide. He never developed any sort of skill so what else is he supposed to do?"

"Work his ass off at a fucking restaurant as a waiter, maybe?"

"He's tried that. Gets fired within a couple weeks. He's not cut out for that kind of job, Stanzie. He's a gambler, okay? It's in his blood. And most of the time he's a damn good one."

"Which is why his pregnant daughter is hauling heavy trays of food around and walking her ass off between tables tonight?"

"Construction's slow thanks to this fucking economy." Scott raked a hand through his hair and glared at me. "You think I like sending my pregnant bond mate out to work at some crappy restaurant surrounded by selfish Others who stiff her on tips and send half their dinners back just so they can watch her ass as she walks away? I'm doing the best I can. Jesus. Since when were you able to afford nice clothes and expensive cars? It's because of your bond mate and his pack, isn't it? You better scale down your lifestyle, babe, because it's about to come to a screeching halt and you won't even have a pack to help you with the mortgage on that fancy condo of yours."

"I own that fucking condo outright. I paid for it in cash," I snarled. "And everything I wear I bought with my own money that I earned as an Advisor."

"You get paid for that?" Scott stared at me, incredulous.

"Don't you?"

He grimaced. "Sure. Not enough to buy a loaded Prelude or designer shoes."

I looked down at my Juicy Couture wedges. "How the hell do you know these are designer shoes?"

"Faith," he said. "She's managed to mention your shoes and your clothes, oh, about a hundred times in the past forty-eight hours. She drove past your condo too. Your jewelry is real gold and silver, real diamonds, real everything. Mayflower is not hurting for money, but we're not in your league. And I resent you storming down here to fling in my face that you think I'm not providing for my bond mate or my pack. Who the hell are you? You can't even hold onto your bond mate. You can't even stick to a pack without being thrown out on your ass, so don't you even start the bullshit lectures with me. Got it?"

Scott was so mad his face was white. Shame darkened his eyes, both for what he'd said to me, and because a part of him believed I had a point and that he wasn't a good Alpha.

Good going, Stanzie. It's always nice to criticize the Alpha. I let go of the railing and retreated up the stairs and out the back door.

Dusk choked the sky with gray. Crickets chirred at the fence line and I pulled out one of the chairs at the patio table and sat. Someone had lowered the umbrella for the night and I played with a bit of the fringed edge as I thought about what we'd said to each other. He was right. I couldn't hold onto my bond mate and I had a terrible track record with being a pack member. Who the hell was I to tell him anything about the way he ran Mayflower? I was an Advisor. I was supposed to be here to help, wasn't I?

Ten minutes later Scott came outside. Without a word, he took the chair next to mine.

"I'm not doing shit to help you," I said. "I'm making things worse."

"No, you're not." He stretched his legs out beneath the table so one of his bare feet rested against my ankle.

We sat in silence together for a long time. The dark had brought cooler temperatures and I was glad for my gray hoodie. I thought of Scott's bare feet and wondered if he was cold. My mind conjured up a vision of Faith as she bussed tables and counted her damn tips. Alan too, trapped between childhood and adulthood while he waited with quiet desperation for a chance at initiation.

I saw my grandmothers in the house they shared as they baked cookies and argued in their steady, good-natured way. There was no pleasing Grandmother Elaine yet Grandmother Carolyn never stopped trying.

Lauren barricaded behind the doors and windows of Paul's house condemned to live half a life if that. Did she love him or had she convinced herself that she did, afraid to press too hard, delve too deeply because there was no escape no matter what she felt for him?

In the Mayflower pack, no one ever quite made it to where they wanted to go. Some of them didn't even have a plan and drifted along, but even they must sometimes look up at the night sky and wish for just a little bit more.

I was the just the same. If I wanted to be a good Advisor I had to put my personal issues aside. Hell, if I wanted to be a decent person I needed to work through my own bullshit instead of hanging onto it and torturing myself with my own failures and insecurities. What could I do to move forward instead of stagnating in my own self-pity and doubt?

"You and Faith." I forced myself to go on even though I wanted to run, not talk. "You'd stay with us if I helped Alan shift? My wolf won't be any help at all."

"I already told you Faith would take care of Alan and I'd stay with you," he reminded me. If he was surprised at my words, he didn't let it show. He closed his eyes for a moment then opened them. "And you're right. I did act out that scene this afternoon on purpose. I wanted him to see our wolves. You too. I wanted to guilt you into doing this for him. It was a bullshit move, Stanzie."

"No," I said. "It was something an Alpha would do. You're looking after your pack, Scott."

He pressed his bare foot into my ankle, his toes warm against my skin.

"Faith was okay coming to a Regional to find someone to initiate her wolf, but Alan doesn't have her confidence. He's also a man and it's more than a little humiliating for him. But if he could go as someone already initiated, at least initially, his confidence in himself would do all the heavy lifting. He's not a bad-looking guy and he'll have no problem attracting a bond mate, but only if he believes in himself and right now, he kinda doesn't. Does he?"

"No," I agreed.

"I'm sorry about what I said about your bond mate and your pack."
I held up a hand to stop his apology and he obediently shut his mouth.
"You want to call Alan or should I?" I asked.

Chapter 12

Faith, Scott and I were eating breakfast on the patio when Alan walked into the backyard. His wheat-colored hair gleamed in the June sunshine and he wore obviously new clothes—jeans that still smelled like the store and a sky-blue plaid button-down shirt with the sleeves carefully rolled to just below the bend of his elbow.

The shirt was unbuttoned enough to show his silver bond pendant chain. Gray lace-up sneakers so new the soles were clean. He radiated excitement, as well as nervous tension that made the blood pump beneath his skin so hard I could sense its movement.

In the chair beside me, Scott hid his grin behind his napkin and gave me a surreptitious kick in the ankle.

Faith smiled and gestured to the fourth chair at the table.

"Just in time for breakfast," she said as Alan's hand closed over the back of the chair and he debated whether to sit.

"I can't eat," he confessed then blushed. He wouldn't look straight at me, but I could tell by his posture and scent he was acutely aware of my presence. I hadn't had this effect on a man in a long time—if ever. A sort of helpless, desperate puppy love. Eager to please me, scared shitless, excited out of his mind.

His mood was infectious.

"Want to help me clear the table then, Scott?" Faith rose to her feet, lovely and graceful in a short denim mini skirt and raspberry chiffon blouse with a gathered scoop neck and short sleeves.

"Hell, no," said Scott. A huge grin threatened to split his face. "I'm not finished."

"Yes, you are." Faith swiped his plate away from him and he grabbed for his coffee mug before she could take that too. He gave a yell of pain when she yanked his hair and wouldn't let go until he pushed back his chair.

"Goddamn," he complained as she loaded him up with dirty dishes and marched him across the patio to the back steps. "I want to talk to Alan, Faith."

"Yeah, right. You want to help me do the dishes is what you want to do."

"Faith, you have this really fucked-up sense of reality. There is no universe in which I ever want to do dishes." Scott followed her up the stairs and through the back door. He threw one look over his shoulder at us.

"Go for it, kid. Remember that women like foreplay, so as much as it might be a pain in the ass, just do it. And don't forget to cuddle her after so she'll feel special. You look a little scared. You want me to write that down? Or maybe you want to watch me and Faith and get a few pointer—ow, goddamn, that hurt."

Faith had pulled his hair again.

"Don't you listen to him, Alan," she called.

"Really? He shouldn't? You mean I don't have to bother with all the foreplay bullshit? For real? Because that's not what you said last—ow, fuck!" Scott yelped.

The screen door squeaked shut and then the back door for good measure. A moment later Scott's face appeared at the kitchen window until he was yanked backward and disappeared.

"Wow," said Alan, his face bright red. "That was really embarrassing. And you're laughing. Great."

I tried not to laugh but it was impossible. Alan shifted from foot to foot, his face anxious.

"God, I wish I could have a drink," he muttered.

"It's nine o'clock in the morning," I reminded him. "Are you going to sit down or hover?"

He took a deep breath.

"Relax," I said with a smile. "Honestly, Alan, you'll be fine."

He held his breath for a distressing amount of time. My lungs hurt just to look at him.

"How much water have you drunk today?" I asked and his breath escaped with a whoop.

"Water?" He stared at me.

"For shifting. You need to drink a lot of water. It lubricates your muscles or something and, believe me, Alan, you're going to be sore tomorrow. The first time's a bitch but after that it gets easier. The more water you drink now, the better later."

Alarm spread across his face and he made a hasty grab for my coffee mug.

"No, not caffeine." I snatched it before he did.

"You're drinking it," he pointed out. His voice was shrill and he grimaced at himself.

"I've been shifting for fifteen years. And I only had half a cup. Here." I handed him my water and watched him gulp it down. "We'll get you more inside."

Unease creased his forehead. "If I drink too much I'm going to have to take a piss, Stanzie, and with my luck I'll have to right in the...well, you know, right in the middle of—things." His voice climbed with each word and I bit the inside of my cheek to keep from giggling.

"Drink a bottle of water for me, Alan, and then go to the bathroom and I'll meet you in my room, okay? It'll be fine, I swear."

When I said *my room* his face went white.

"Tell you what," I said as I got to my feet and gathered up my dishes. "We'll get some water and go talk in my room for a while. We're not in any rush, we've got the whole day."

"Oh, God." He groaned, but followed me obediently.

* * * *

"Oh, God." Alan clutched at my hair as I ran my tongue across his belly and unzipped his jeans.

We were on my bed, empty water bottles on the nightstand, shades drawn and a stick of patchouli incense burning on top of the radiator. Enough sunlight filtered beneath the shades to fill the room with a dim light. I wanted Alan to see everything, but not be blinded by artificial light.

"Stanzie." His voice was full of dark excitement coupled with anxiety as I pushed his jeans down to his knees and he struggled to help me. He wouldn't let go of my hair and it made it hard to move, but I didn't try to get him to release me.

He wore no underwear and he'd shaved for me. He was a sweetheart, this guy.

I licked the tip of his cock and he gasped. His fingers tightened with an almost unbearable pressure on my hair.

I took him in my mouth and he groaned—a sound of raw longing that sent a thrill of desire through me.

Virgins were hard work. I wasn't used to taking the lead or at least doing most of the heavy lifting. Experienced partners knew how to toss control back and forth between them, but Alan knew nothing.

I was down to my bra and panties, and I reached one hand around to unhook my bra.

When it was off, I moved on top of Alan and let my nipples brush his chest. He let go of my hair when I kissed him and his arms went around me as we twined our tongues together.

My fat lip was still a little swollen and tender, so kissing hurt, but it was a good pain and the more I did it, the better it felt.

Alan liked to kiss and, with just a little practice he would be great at it. Already he made my breath come shorter and shorter as I got into it and, when he reached a tentative hand between my legs, I spread them wider to encourage him.

His fingers were warm as he worked against the silk barrier of my panties which prevented his full exploration.

His erection poked at my belly, the tip slick and wet.

As I kissed him, I shimmied out of my panties and moved his hand back between my legs.

His touch was feather light and tentative so I took one of his fingers and guided it inside me so he could feel how hot I was for him.

"Stanzie," he said again, and moved his hands to my hips. His cock probed between my legs but didn't penetrate. I shifted my weight to my knees and eased him into me inch by inch.

He cried out and gritted his teeth as he strained to hold himself back.

I moved up and down slowly, but it was still too fast.

"I...can't. Stanzie," he cried.

"Shh, hold still," I whispered. I froze in place, my mouth against his hot neck and he held onto me and shuddered. "Think about something else, baby. Anything."

"I...oh, God, this feels so fucking good. I..." His hands moved to my hair again and we rested together, perfectly still, for several heartbeats.

I kissed his neck then the smooth line of his jaw and began to move again. This time he moved too. He followed my lead and we established a rhythm. I kissed him, the kisses deeper and deeper until we both were breathless.

I sat up and let him watch me move on top of him, his hands on my hips. His eyes burned with unearthly silver and I felt his wolf awaken. Feral energy rippled across his body and cast out a heat that snared us within it.

He felt it too and shock spread across his face.

"What the fuck is that?" he whispered and his eyes turned to ice white with just a tint of blue silver. He came hard then and a wild shout of triumph and lust ripped from his throat. His fingers dug into my flesh. I moved on top of him as my knees sank into the mattress and I made him scream again before he gave a convulsive shudder and went limp beneath me.

I buried my face in his sweat-slicked shoulder and relaxed. For the first time, I became aware of my throbbing broken toe and when I shifted my foot, relief was immediate.

Alan held me tightly and laughed to himself in amazement.

"That was intense." His voice was raw and he kissed my shoulder gratefully. "But it was quick, wasn't it? Too quick, huh?"

"No," I lied. It didn't matter. It hadn't been about me.

He shifted us so he was on top of me, but he held his weight off me so I wasn't crushed.

"I love you," he said as he looked into my eyes, his face full of sincerity and gratitude. "Thank you for being my first, Stanzie. Susan was right. I did have wet dreams about you. Sometimes I picture your face on the centerfold models when I beat off. To this day even." He sounded proud of himself and I laughed.

"Just wait until the Regional, Alan. You'll have a lot more masturbatory material than you'll know what to do with. Maybe even a real girl to partner with."

His laugh was more of a growl.

"She won't be you though, will she?" He kissed me and I combed my fingers through his blond hair. He really was adorable.

* * * *

Alan and I held hands on the way to the forest. Faith and Scott walked ahead of us. Faith had a six-pack of cold water and Scott had a soft-sided cooler filled with sandwiches.

I had a bottle of water in my free hand that I shared with Alan as we walked.

His eyes were silver blue still and when he looked at me, a thrill of Pack power ran through me.

Faith looked at us over her shoulder. Her eyes glowed amber and her smile held a feral secret, known only to those who could shift and run with her through the forest.

"You're about to cross the last threshold," Scott said as we approached the gate. He braced one hand on the iron rail and boosted himself over it in one graceful movement that took my breath away.

Faith scrambled through the rails nimbly. Alan let go of my hand and vaulted over the gate using both hands like a gymnast on the parallel bars.

The three of them waited on the other side of the gate for me and I gathered myself to jump. For the entire walk, I'd waited to feel my wolf. She was awake, I could sense that, but my eyes did not burn blue silver or at least they hadn't when I'd looked in the mirror on the way out of the bedroom.

A twinge of unease winged through me, but I brushed it aside and darted between the rails as Faith had done. My hood snagged and, for a moment I thought I would choke, but I broke free.

Scott gathered us into a circle and we put our arms around each other's shoulders, heads bent close so we could stare into each other's eyes.

He was Alpha and we instinctively looked to him to lead us. Faith had a quiet power of her own, but she was content to let him take control.

"Alan, these are the last moments of your childhood. The final minutes which separate you from the Pack. You've been our child, our son, but today you become one of us. A brother. You will never be the same. As of today you will always be more than what you once were. Your shadow self comes to the surface in the shape of a wolf. Guard him well. Guide him. Protect and nurture him. Love him as you love yourself.

"Stanzie and Faith are your wolf's guardians today, the first to show you the path you'll travel for the rest of your life. You'll have many teachers, but I hope you'll honor Stanzie and Faith above them all. For what they share with you today will mold you into the wolf you've yet to become. Think gratefully of them in the future. Remember today and this moment between the four of us."

"I'll never forget," Alan vowed. His heart beat so hard we could all hear it.

We broke apart and Faith stepped forward so she could kiss Alan's forehead. She smoothed the back of her hand down his cheek and his eyes closed as he leaned into her.

With a smile, she danced away from him and with incredible grace, she shed her clothes until she stood before us all proudly naked.

Her blond hair shimmered in the late morning sunlight that slanted through the canopy of leaves above us.

As we admired her slim, pale body, it began to stutter in and out of focus. I blinked and in the space of that blink, Faith fell to her hands and knees and her body jerked in and out of this plane of existence into somewhere else and back again.

Silvery fur began to ripple up and down her arched spine. A tail sprouted, legs shortened, hands became paws, which developed claws.

The feral scent of wolf stung our nostrils and Scott tore off his clothes so he could fall to the forest floor and begin his own shift.

Alan looked at me and panic flooded his silver blue eyes.

"Stanzie." My name was a horrified plea. I could see the ghost of a wolf's muzzle beneath his mouth. He held out a hand and recoiled when he saw the dark fur on his palm.

"Take off your clothes, Alan," I urged, but he stood there, transfixed.

I hastily unbuttoned his plaid shirt and pushed it off his shoulders.

"Help me," I cried as I tugged at his sleeve.

"I don't know what's happening to me," he whispered. His body gave a bone crunching shudder and he stared at Faith and Scott's wolves, terror etched across his face. The wolves waited together, shoulder to shoulder.

It was a damn good thing I hadn't shifted myself. Poor Alan was clueless.

I fumbled with the button on his fly and then the zipper. His throat rippled and he threw back his head and howled. The noise nearly scared the shit out of me, but I somehow managed to get his zipper down and then I pushed him onto his ass so I could pull his jeans off. He was no help at all, caught in the throes of the first emergence of his wolf.

His body morphed in and out of focus. It was like trying to undress someone by strobe light and I had to shut my eyes so I wouldn't lose my concentration.

Alan whimpered and whined. Shifting was painful sometimes—especially when we fought it and he was. He didn't know how to relax into the chaos and let it flow. He still struggled for control, for a way to reason out the process, and that was impossible. Shifting did not make sense. It just happened.

"Let go. Alan, just go with it," I coached in a quiet voice as I sat as near as I could to him. He writhed on the pine needles and screamed as his bones shifted beneath his skin. "It hurts less if you just let go."

"Stanzie!" My name turned into an anguished howl and just when I had begun to get scared, it happened. Alan blinked out of this plane and when he blinked back in, he was shifted.

His wolf was gorgeous. Dusky black with ice-blue eyes. A touch of gray at the tips of each paw. Big too. Bigger than Scott's gray wolf.

He rolled to his feet and sprawled onto his face when he tried to walk. Two legs to four was a bitch for some people. It had never fazed me, but Grey told me it had taken him half an hour to figure out how the hell to walk the first time he'd shifted. I grinned to remember the story and reached out to pat Alan's wolf on the head.

He whined at me.

"Get up and walk. Four legs are fun," I told him. I was on my hands and knees now, so we could look eye to eye. If he got up, that is.

Faith's wolf pranced over and nudged him with her dainty muzzle. He whined again and she gave a coughing bark. In wolf speak she told him to get off his ass.

Scott's wolf approached me and stared at me so hard I knew he tried to tell me something, but I couldn't figure out what.

Then it hit me. Duh. I was still in human form.

I stood up so I could strip off my jeans and t-shirt. Scott's wolf waited impatiently. Alan's wolf had gained his wobbly feet but seemed stuck in one position. When Faith's wolf nudged his back end with her nose, he promptly fell over again and I snickered.

Alan's wolf gave me a reproachful look and I patted his head in apology. Scott's wolf moved behind me and bumped the back of my knees so hard I fell over.

Alan's wolf wheezed with lupine laughter.

"At least I can walk on all fours," I muttered. Naked, I crawled away a few feet to give myself space for shifting.

Only nothing happened. The more I reached inside for my wolf, the further she retreated within me until I couldn't even sense her anymore.

Up until I'd actively tried to contact her, she'd been there, close to the surface. Sex had awoken her from her slumber. The other wolves had excited her. I'd felt her leap within me, scratching like an itch beneath my skin.

But now, nothing.

Again and again I tried to find her, until I broke out in a cold sweat and pine needles stuck to my knees and fingers. The sharp scent of pine resin made me want to gag and when Scott's wolf nudged my ankle with his wet nose I whirled around, face hot with humiliation.

"Fuck off," I snarled at him.

Faith and Alan's wolves were gone thankfully, but Scott's still remained. His electric blue eyes were full of confusion and, when he moved closer to me, I scuttled backward on my ass. I kicked pine needles and dirt at him, my toe throbbed.

"Go away!" I screamed at him. Hate boiled in me that he would see my mortification. My wolf was broken and he had no right to witness this. I scooped up a rock and winged it at him. It glanced off his shoulder and he yipped in pain.

Shame turned me hot and then cold and I hung my head. "You stupid bastard, I'm not going to shift. I can't!" I screamed and when I went for another rock, Scott's wolf darted away into the trees before I could hurt him again.

* * * *

When Scott, back in human form, lowered himself to the ground beside me, I was prone on my stomach, my face buried in my arms. My tears were sticky hot and my stomach clenched sickly.

Scott braced himself against the trunk of a pine tree and put a warm hand on my shoulder. He rubbed my back while I cried myself out and when I finally stopped and lifted my head, his face was full of such guilt I couldn't breathe.

My clothes were on the ground beside him. He had on his jeans but no shirt and his feet were bare.

His chest and side were bruised as hell—dark purple splotches that disfigured his toned skin.

The bruises on his face were still livid as well and when he brushed the tears and pine needles from my cheeks, his fingers had puffy red abrasions along the knuckles.

"I'm sorry," he whispered as I reached over him for my t-shirt. He helped me put it on then handed me my jeans. My bra and panties were still on the bedroom floor back at the house. I hated going braless but underwear just got in the way when I shifted.

Tears threatened again and I hastily pulled up my jeans and zipped them as I avoided Scott's gaze.

"So when people's wolves get fucked up like mine, what do we do? Is there some sort of fucking Wolf Whisperer we can go talk to maybe?" I wondered.

"This isn't the first time this has happened is it?" He held out his hand and I let him pull me down beside him. When he put his arm around me, I snuggled against him and let my head drop onto his shoulder. He brushed his lips across the top of my head. Nothing sexual about any of the contact. Pure comfort. I needed it so damn much it hurt.

"It almost happened the last time I shifted. Today is the first time she's totally refused. For a long time she's been resentful when I called her. She hates me, Scott." My voice twisted and I started to cry again. "My wolf fucking hates me."

"*Shh,*" He rocked me. "She doesn't, Stanzie. We'll figure this out, okay."

"There's nothing to figure out. She hates me and she knows his wolf isn't here so there's no reason to come out. And his wolf is never going to be here so now what do I do?" I wailed.

"You mean your bond mate?" Scott sounded pissed. "He had a hell of a nerve leaving you in the middle of your wolf's initiation."

"Initiation," I scoffed. "I've been shifting for over a decade."

"Who initiated your wolf, Stanzie? Over a decade ago?"

I didn't want to answer him.

Scott blew out an impatient breath. "You shifted with an eighteen-year-old guy who couldn't even speak much English. You freaked out on him and Tony had to come and take care of you, but he never got the opportunity to work with you again, and you needed that. Afterward you didn't shift for three years and, when you did, you shifted with a twenty-year-old loner who spent his time drifting from pack to pack until he found someone who'd bond with him.

"Then you joined a small pack where you were all friends and lovers and nobody initiated your wolf because you wouldn't let them, and I don't blame you. You needed a real Alpha to convince you and none of them were capable of that.

"I don't fucking know much about Riverglow except that there couldn't have been an Alpha who'd had a decent initiation him or herself or they would have known how to get through to you."

"Don't bet on it." I snorted, astonished and pissed he would use what I'd told him in confidence against me not even two days after I'd spilled my guts and told him my fucking life story. "I'm stubborn as hell and I didn't want to work with my wolf."

"Of course you didn't. What changed your mind? A powerful Alpha." Scott's mind was made up and his version of things was the right one. I'd never in my life thought of Grey as a loner, a drifter, someone who had bonded with the first person who'd have him. He'd loved me. He'd fucking loved me.

"Liam Murphy is not Alpha of Mac Tire," I snapped. "And Grey loved me, you bastard. He wanted to bond with *me*, not just anybody."

"Oh, for Christ's sake," Scott swore. "Sure he loved you, because you loved him. You didn't see the loner, the drifter, the guy who couldn't figure out how to keep things together in his birth pack and left before they could kick him out. Of course he wanted to be with you."

"Do you know his story?" My voice was icy, but he ignored it. I drew away from him and he let me go. His gray eyes gleamed with frustration and compassion. It was the compassion that made me want to hit him. Or maybe cry. Again.

"The one other relationship I ever had was with a girl from Rainfury."

I winced. Rainfury was Grey's birth pack in Ontario.

"Did he lie to me?" My voice trembled and I thought if I found out one more lie someone I loved had told me, I would disintegrate.

"Oh, shit, no." Scott touched my face and moved so our foreheads touched. We breathed together for a moment.

"He said it was because the woman who initiated his wolf was made Alpha and she wanted to change their relationship, make it more like lovers, less initiatory. He didn't. And the woman's bond mate was pissed at them both." If he'd lied to me, I wanted to know. He was dead and I couldn't confront him, but his ghost was all over this town. All over the motel room where I'd nearly been raped and the memories that gripped me around every other corner since I'd come back to Willoughby.

The funny thing was Grey had never been a part of Mayflower. He'd been my ticket out, my ultimate act of rebellion against my father and my birth pack.

"Yeah, he eventually decided he didn't want to pursue things with her. But only after Rick kicked the shit out of him and told him he was pressing his luck."

A lie then. Of omission if nothing else.

"Rick thought Grey was angling for a triad so he could be Alpha. At fucking twenty years old. Miranda was an idiot. Grey was the first guy she'd ever initiated and sometimes it happens. You read something into the situation that isn't really there. I mean, it's a rush when someone looks up to you and thinks you're so damn smart and sexy and experienced.

"Usually it's the other way around—the one who's being initiated falls in love with the initiator, which is why we're encouraged to work outside our generation—with men and women we think of as uncles and aunts, not the ones we might actually bond with.

"Anyway, Stanzie, the point is you didn't have a real initiation. I know Paul didn't want you to work with Tony because he was technically your generation, but he's fourteen years older than you and bonded with Susan. It would have worked even if you did have a thing for him.

"Did you? It seemed like you did from what I picked up at dinner Friday night."

"Yeah," I admitted and for the first time felt shame about it. Paul had given me countless lectures about the proper way to be initiated but I hadn't heard a word past Wes Hanover. "Scott, I was supposed to bond with Wes as well as be initiated by him. That was the plan."

"Fucked up," said Scott. "You really shouldn't bond with the one who initiates you. Some people do, but I'm against it myself."

"Do you think Alan should have been initiated by Rachel or Susan?" I sat back against the trunk of the pine tree and contemplated the hazy sunshine that filtered down to the forest floor.

"They can be harpies, but yeah, I think Alan was being stubborn."

"He asked Dorothy but she turned him down."

Scott growled something beneath his breath and picked up a pine cone. He threw it across the clearing and it tumbled into the underbrush.

"This pack is fucked up," he said. "No doubt about it. Which is why I'm glad you're here, partner. Together we'll figure this shit out. Believe me?" He flashed me a gorgeous grin and I thought for about the hundredth time that he was probably the most stunning guy I'd ever met. Better looking than Vaughn and even Murphy, although he didn't make my heart skip the way Murphy did. Even with the disfiguring bruises on his face, he was stunning as hell.

The bruises on his torso and stomach looked nasty and painful. Without thinking, I reached to trace one of them with my finger and then another as if I could connect the dots between them and make sense of everything.

When I looked up into his eyes, I saw they'd darkened and for a suspended moment. I thought he would kiss me. A part of me wanted that. Fuck Murphy, fuck Grey. Fuck everything but this moment. But we were partners, not lovers even if it would be accepted Pack behavior if we did decide to fuck each other's brains out on the forest floor.

I valued our growing friendship and, even though I thought he could handle sex between us, I wasn't sure I could. I was way too vulnerable and broken, and the last thing I wanted was to destroy the good thing we did have.

"I really thought between the two of us we kicked the crap out of Darren, but look at us. You're covered in bad bruises, I've got a split lip and a broken toe and he's walking around barely bruised. Unreal, huh?"

The moment between us vanished and Scott's eyes returned to their normal light gray.

"What the hell are you talking about, you loser? We did mess him up. He could barely walk when you got through with your ninja kicking routine. Which, by the way, really turned me on. Sexy."

"I broke my damn toe," I said, but with a grin. He was such an ass.

"And one of his ribs. I heard it crack," said Scott.

"I think that was my toe."

"Bullshit. I know what a cracking rib sounds like. And you broke his rib. Also, I won the fight. Yeah, I may have a few goddamn bruises, but he was in bad shape, Stanzie."

"Did you see him standing outside your back door yesterday? He was walking pretty straight and confident for a guy with a broken rib. And his knuckles looked a hundred percent better than your sorry-ass ones."

"I punched Tony at the midsummer's barbecue, remember?"

"Okay, sure. But your face? Your chest and stomach? Tony only landed one hard punch, you told me. So most of this damage is from Darren. Your bruises are blue and purple. His were yellow and green. Mostly healed which means they weren't bad to begin with."

Scott frowned. "No. It just means he healed faster than me, not that his bruises were any less intense. The color doesn't indicate how bad a bruise was, just where it is in the healing process."

"Okay, Dr. Charest, fine, be that way. But I still say Darren came out of the fight better than both of us."

"And I say he's healing faster," Scott argued. Hard-headed bastard.

I rolled my eyes. "How can he do that? You're both Pack and should heal at the same rate, right? It's not like you're an Other. They heal really slow."

"Compared to us, but it's normal for them," Scott, the stickler for precision, said. I resisted the urge to hit him.

I found a pine cone and began to peel away the outer layer, one flake at a time while Scott sat in aggravated silence beside me and fumed.

"It can't be right. His bruises should be the same as mine," he muttered and I rolled my eyes again.

"You saw him standing there on your doorstep, didn't you? What color were his bruises?"

"Green and yellow." Scott's frustration was palpable—I could smell it. "He's healing faster than me, Stanzie, that's the only explanation."

"Which is ridiculous." I laughed. It wasn't nice to mock him, but I couldn't help it. Then, for some reason, a memory slipped into my head. I saw Paddy's face and Murphy's and remembered my own annoyance.

"We have the Councils to oversee us now," I heard myself argue although neither man who had been with me had said a word. *"We don't need some barbaric method of mind control from the Dark Ages."*

"No fucking way," I whispered, revolted. But it all made sense. It made perverted horrible sense. I turned to clutch at Scott's arm and he saw how horrified I was and his eyes narrowed. "Scott, what do you know about pack bonds?"

"Not much," he admitted. "We don't use them a lot in America, do we? They still have them in Europe where the packs are bigger. You can't use them with less than forty members, right?"

"I don't think it's a question of can't, more of a law because there wouldn't be enough people to flow the effect out. Most of the power would remain with the Alphas that forged it. They'd have unbelievable control over the minds of their pack." I said. "Conceivably, they could make them do anything, right?"

Scott's whole body went rigid.

"Like heal faster for instance? And rape?" He caught on fast. When I nodded, he swore. "Stanzie, I swear to God Faith and I don't have a pack bond forged with Mayflower. Please Jesus Christ, you can't think I'd do something to you like that. Look, I'm not healing fast. Darren's the one doing that, not me!"

He looked as if I'd gutted him and I cursed myself.

"No, Scott, not you. Not you and Faith. Not Alphas. At least not anymore. Come on, partner, think with me. Who has the most influence over this pack and has for the past thirty years. Ever since he was Alpha?" I took Scott by the shoulders and shook him to get rid of the horror in his eyes at what he thought I'd meant.

"Paul?" he whispered, aghast. "But even if he had forged a pack bond when he was Alpha, he would have broken it when he stepped down. That's how it's done."

"But what if he didn't?" I asked. Our gazes locked and we were frozen with the terrible possibility of it.

* * * *

Scott paced around the clearing as we reasoned everything out. I stayed on the ground, back against the pine tree. I needed the contact of something based in nature and earth, something that could not turn against me of its own free will.

"But why? Why would he attempt something like that? Who in their right minds would accept a pack bond when they knew there weren't enough people to keep it from giving absolute control to the Alpha?" Scott shook his head as he paced. "Sure, Paul's got a hell of a lot of influence over this pack, but if you're right and there's a pack bond, it would be due to that, not Paul's charisma. So why?"

I leaned my head against the tree trunk. Bark scraped the back of my neck and shoulders.

"There must be a reason," I said with a sigh.

"I think you're wrong, Stanzie. It's too wild to think about. How would he even know how to forge one? Do you know? I sure as hell don't. I know you use the Alphas' blood and some sort of herb, but I'm damned if I know which one or how much of either to mix together."

"Grandmother Elaine would know," I said. "She's got a recipe book for food and for herbal concoctions and I bet if I looked through it right now I'd find the recipe for the pack bond. It's knowledge that's been passed down for generations, Scott, even if it's never used."

"Grandmother Elaine is Paul's blood grandmother." Scott tried to reason his way through the maze of contradictions inherent in my theory and looked as if he had a headache. "So, okay, maybe he could convince her to share her secret knowledge, but hell if I understand how he'd convince everyone to take it."

"Couldn't he just slip it into their drinks or something?" A terrible thought struck me. "The water bottles, Scott. Maybe that's what was in them. So I'd drink it and Paul could control me too."

"It can't work that way, I know that much," Scott argued. "You're not thinking straight, partner, because if Paul could just slip anyone he wanted the proverbial mickey, why hasn't he done it to me and Faith yet? Or Alan? We sure as hell aren't under any fucking pack bond. I know I'm not. I don't answer to Paul Benedict. It has to be an Alpha's blood and he's not Alpha."

He was right, damn him. Maybe I was wrong, but it made too much awful sense. Didn't it?

"Well, there had to be a reason why the pack agreed to do it, Scott. We just haven't figured that part out yet."

"Well, don't look at me. I'm not even convinced there is a pack bond." He dragged his hands through his hair so it stood up on end as if he'd been electrocuted. Even so, he looked damn cute. "And you still haven't tied in why the hell Paul would tell Darren to rape you."

"Because I didn't sleep with anyone at the hunt," I responded.

"Why the hell does that even matter? It's not like sleeping with one of us would convince you to come back to Mayflower."

I shrugged. "No, and I'm not sure Paul even really wants that. Or he didn't until recently. He had a chance to bring me back after Grey and Elena died. I was so fucked up then and I called him and Lauren every month but they never once even answered the damn phone, let alone asked me to come back to the pack. He renounced me as his daughter in front of the tribunal and everything. He never wanted to see me again.

Yet when I come for a visit, he's suddenly the genial father figure and wants me to sever the bond with Murphy so I can rejoin Mayflower. And this time I don't have to bond with Wes Hanover. I don't have to bond with anyone he chooses. He told me to write my own ticket. So why the complete one-eighty?"

"Well, if it's true there's a pack bond, he doesn't want it discovered."

"Okay," I allowed. "I'll buy that. But what does me rejoining Mayflower have to do with it? If anything, my continued presence here would seriously interfere with what's going on. I'd notice something was wrong, just like you and Faith have. And Alan, which is why they want Alan gone and you two removed as Alphas. So why the increasingly hard sell to come back?"

"Not come back. Sleep with someone in the pack." Scott and his penchant for precision.

"What for? That's going to keep my mouth shut?" I said with a skeptical frown.

"What if it would?" Scott stopped his pacing to stare at me. I didn't like the speculation in his eyes—it made me nervous as if I were a bug on a pin under a microscope. "What activates the pack bond, Stanzie?"

"Drinking the blood and herbal mixture," I said, but doubtfully.

"No, that sets it up. What if it doesn't actually kick into effect until you shift?" Scott began to pace again, his eyes lit with curiosity and excitement.

I frowned. "I've shifted plenty of times and never activated any pack bond. Plus I didn't drink the herbal mixture. It's not given to the kids, just the adults."

"Are you sure? You were obviously a baby when Paul was Alpha. And it has to be an Alpha's blood not just anybody's. Would you even remember drinking it?"

"But I've shifted plenty of times since Paul was Alpha." I repeated.

"Never with anybody from Mayflower," said Scott.

Horrified, I whispered, "I just slept with Alan."

Scott made a dismissive face. "He wasn't even born when Paul was Alpha. He couldn't possibly have drunk the pack bond elixir. We've already established that Faith, Alan and I are not under Paul's control, presuming there is a pack bond. Everyone else is. Including those who were children at the time. The only thing different between them and you is that you've never slept with anyone in this pack who took the pack bond. You've never activated it."

He sounded so convinced. I wanted to believe in him because he was Alpha, but I needed more proof.

"This sounds plausible, but we need to find out more about pack bonds. Ask someone who knows more about them," I countered.

"What about Kathy?" Scott suggested. "She knows everything there is to know about packs or if she doesn't, she knows who to ask to find out. I'll bet you she can make sense out of this. Come on, let's go back to the house. My phone's there."

I glanced into the woods behind him as I obligingly got to my feet. My head reeled with more questions than answers and I didn't want to believe anything that we'd discussed was true. I wanted Kathy Manning to tell us both we were full of shit and try again.

I registered the movement, but before I could warn Scott, two male figures stepped from the shadows into the clearing. I saw Scott's eyes widen and realized he must have seen something too, just as two men came to stand beside me.

One of them was Darren and the other was Paul.

Tony and Mark grabbed Scott by the arms and, even though he swore and struggled, he couldn't break free.

Paul stepped past me and approached Scott.

"I knew allowing you and Faith to be Alphas was a mistake." He sounded more peeved than furious and I took a step toward him. Darren snatched hold of my upper arm with a firm grip and icy panic froze me in place. "But then, not allowing you to be Alpha after Mark and Rachel had the twins would have been just as bad. What I should have done is made sure that Rachel took her birth control every day. I assumed when I told her to take it that she'd understand I meant ongoing and not just the one pack of birth control pills I gave her."

He flashed Mark, Rachel's bond mate a feral smile. Mark flinched. "These people are ingenious, Scott, at figuring ways around my orders. They've learned to take them at extreme face value and they never, ever anticipate my wants. Annoying sometimes.

"I didn't have the heart to make her have an abortion and now look. You and Faith bring Constance into the picture. The two of you I might have handled, but Constance has a perfect genius for thwarting me. She always has."

"Paul." I couldn't believe what I heard. "Are you saying there *is* a pack bond? You've had Mayflower under a pack bond for thirty years?"

"I see no reason to deny it now that you've forced my hand." Paul turned back to face me and slowly shook his head as he stared at me. I had the absurd urge to cross my arms over my chest because I wasn't wearing a bra and he disapproved of women without the proper undergarments.

Scott's face was dark with fury. "You bastard," he snarled and tried again to get free.

Mark and Tony held on grimly and, when Scott managed to break free from Tony, Mark punched him in the gut. When Scott bent double in agony, Mark and Tony grabbed his arms again and forced him to straighten.

"I don't want to hurt you, damn it. Stop struggling," Mark ordered.

"Then let me go," Scott gritted out between clenched teeth.

"Sorry, man. I can't."

"You really take your orders from Paul? Seriously? Tell him to go fuck himself you don't need to do whatever he says!"

Mark snapped, "Do you think we want to do this, you stupid shit? No, we don't. We have no choice."

"What are you going to do, Paul? Have Mark and Tony guard Scott for the rest of your life?" I sneered. Darren's fingers dug into my arm and I tried to ignore him. I couldn't afford to panic and sure as hell wasn't going to lose it in front of Paul and give him that satisfaction. "And me too?"

"You?" Paul's laughter was polite and condescending. "Constance, I won't need to have you guarded. You and Darren are going to finish what he started yesterday and then you will obey me like they do."

My blood ran cold then I smiled. Finally something he couldn't control.

"No, I won't. I can't shift. My wolf won't come out. Scott and I would be hunting together right now if we could be. So fuck you, Paul Benedict, that won't work."

Paul winced at my language and I resisted the urge to scream *fuck* over and over until my throat burst.

"For the sake of the sixteenth generation of Mayflower, I will at least give you the opportunity to activate the pack bond, Constance. I'm very optimistic your wolf will emerge. The pack bond will draw her out. As for Scott, it's unfortunate, but accidents do happen."

My mind reeled. Die? Paul would kill an Alpha to protect his damn secret? How had it gone this far? How the fuck were we going to stop this?

"How will you cover up my death, you prick?" Scott snarled. "How are you going to manage that?"

"Rest assured I'll get away with it. Accidents happen. Especially around my daughter."

I seethed. "There will be an investigation, Paul. There's already one going on and if the Alpha dies in the middle of it, do you really think an accident is going to fly as an explanation? You're delusional. Obviously since you've perpetrated this travesty for thirty years. I knew you were a control freak, but this is completely insane. Paul, you've broken so many Pack laws by this point I've lost count and you can bet your ass I'll nail you to the wall for every one of them."

Paul waited for me to finish, an arrogant smile playing about his lips. Fury burned so hot within me I thought I would spontaneously combust.

"I am going to enjoy owning you."

I spat at him, but it fell short. Darren was coldly furious, but not at me. He stared at my father with such hatred I shuddered involuntarily.

"My wolf is screwed up, Paul. I wouldn't bet on her coming out."

"You do understand the reason why your wolf is abnormal, don't you?" The condescension in his voice was infuriating.

"No, why don't you tell me. You're enjoying this so damn much I'd hate to interrupt you."

"Were that only true," said Paul. "Constance, the pack bond has been preventing your wolf from developing normally. She's had to struggle against the barrier of it all her life but once it is activated and dissolved into her and you, she'll be as normal as anyone's wolf. She'll have some development to undergo, certainly, but you will be amazed at her transformation, I assure you."

I think I would have fallen if not for Darren's support. The world seemed to tilt and shift and spin out from beneath me. Somehow I found my voice. "That's a lie. Everybody knows how fucked up my wolf is and not one person has ever suspected it's because of an inactivated pack bond."

"Why would they, dear? Everybody knows we don't use pack bonds in most American packs. And you've always belonged to small packs which would never use one to begin with, haven't you?"

"Mac Tire uses one. What would have happened if I took their pack bond?" I demanded.

"I'm not sure. I suspect it would have driven you incurably insane. So you see, it is very fortuitous that you returned to us, isn't it?"

"You would have let her take another pack bond and not spoken up?" Scott was enraged, his hands clenched into fists. "You're the incurably insane one here, Paul."

"Careful," Paul directed him a malevolent look. "Don't test my patience."

"You sonofabitch, you're not going to get away with this!" Scott's eyes were almost black with rage and the scent of his fury was infecting us all. I breathed it in deeply and added it to my own.

"With every word out of your mouth, you condemn your unborn child. At the moment I'm feeling generous and will allow Faith to bond with Mark and Rachel after your tragic death. But if you're not silent, I'll drive her out of Mayflower. She'll have to have an abortion and she'll be forced into another pack. You know how much she wants this baby. Is that really what you want to happen to her?" Paul asked.

All the blood drained from Scott's face and he sagged so that Mark and Tony had to hold him up. The hatred in Darren's eyes was nothing compared to the hatred in Scott's as he glared at Paul.

"So can we wrap this dramatic little scene up please? Scott, you're going to go for a drive with Mark and Tony, while Stanzie, Darren and I go to Darren's house. They have some business to attend to. I'll have you know it was very inconvenient to discover no one home when we stopped by.

"Luckily, by the stench of sex that permeated the bedrooms it was easy to figure where you were and track you here."

"Faith and Alan," Scott whispered and, in that moment, I knew he was broken. Paul knew it too by the triumphant smile that lit his handsome face.

"Alan is planning to leave the pack, isn't he? I suggest we all reinforce that idea. And Faith can live in blissful ignorance. She has for years and I see no reason to change that. She's as weak and gullible as her mother. Also, her new bond mates and her cousin will downplay all her fears and if they can't, ignore them. We only have a few months to go before she gives birth and then Constance, Wes and Maddie will be Alphas of Mayflower, and Constance will pass on the legacy and produce the sixteenth generation."

"And when he comes of age, you'll have to drive him out of Mayflower like you did Alan. He won't have the pack bond," I spat.

"Constance, I'll dissolve the pack bond when my Mayflower grandson or granddaughter is born. So you see, the end of this travesty as you called it, is in your hands. You determine the length and continuation of it."

"Tell you what, Paul," said Scott. He struggled to stay civil. "Here's an alternative. You dissolve the pack bond right now and Stanzie and I will forget any of this shit ever happened. It'll be over and you'll be safe in Mayflower. We'll call off the investigation and you'll get away with everything."

"I won't have a Mayflower grandchild," said Paul.

I swallowed the bile that spurted into my throat. The hope and the horror combined in Scott's face made me want to weep. I thought of Faith wanting her baby and Scott dying. I thought of all of Mayflower under Paul's tyranny for thirty years and how I'd escaped and done things they never would. Maybe it was time to pay back the time I'd stolen. But, oh, it wasn't what I wanted.

"I'll stay." The words killed me. Little bits and pieces of me disintegrated with each one. "Paul, I'll break my bond with Liam Murphy and I'll bond with someone in Mayflower. I'll give you your grandchild. You don't need to make me do it through the pack bond. Only please, not Wes Hanover. Anybody else, but please not him. Let Scott live. We'll all agree, right now, we'll never tell what you've done with the pack bond. Ever."

Tears pricked my eyes but I blinked them away. Scott's eyes glittered too and we stared at each other across the clearing, two trapped souls with no way out.

Paul pretended to think about it, but I could tell by his eyes he already knew what he would do.

"You could renege," he said at length, as if it pained him to even contemplate such a thing.

"I give you my word," I cried hopelessly.

He laughed. "Your word? Constance, you have no honor. You haven't done a single thing in your life that has required any sort of responsibility at all. You've run screaming from the very thought. Your word means nothing."

That was rich coming from him, but I bit back my angry retort.

Instead I said, "I still don't understand why everyone agreed to this pack bond in the first place."

"I never agreed to a fucking thing," Mark snarled, his eyes flat. "None of the kids did, Stanzie."

"Giving the elixir to the children was a desperate gamble, and ironically, most of the reason we decided to forge a pack bond," explained Paul with a benevolent smile. "We weren't sure it would take with children because, of course, you couldn't shift, and none of you seemed affected at all after you drank the elixir. Although you recovered from the red virus, Constance, you had a very light case. Wes and Maddie's daughter, Camille, drank the elixir and died anyway, even if all the adults that drank it got better. They shifted, of course. Giving it to the children was a long shot.

"To tell the truth I wasn't sure what would happen when Tony's wolf was first initiated two years later. Imagine my surprise when the pack bond activated. Imagine my dismay when yours didn't after you shifted with that fool of a German boy. It was then I realized the children who drank the elixir had to shift with someone in the pack who'd taken the pack bond.

"It does make perfect sense doesn't it? Especially when you think it took shifting for the bond to activate with everyone in the first place. Getting sick people to make love and then shift was the most difficult aspect at the time. Well, the women could just lie there, the men had to work a bit harder. But then we usually do." Paul chuckled and I wanted to brain him but I couldn't reach him.

He turned to face me and I looked at him. I hated him so much I could barely think.

"The red virus? That's why you did this? To stop it?" The reason why everyone took the elixir willingly finally made sense to me now even though they knew the pack wasn't big enough and Paul would have absolute control over them. No doubt he hadn't included Lauren's blood in the elixir. Of course not.

"You really don't think I did this for personal gain do you?" Paul widened his eyes in shock and I gritted my teeth. "I did it for you, Constance. It was Grandmother Elaine's idea. She had the elixir recipe and, when people began to die, she came to me with the idea. People would heal, she told me. It was the only way to stop the deaths. Whole packs are wiped out by the virus, you know that. It's very rare, but when there's an outbreak, no one is immune and it sweeps through the pack in a killing frenzy.

"I wouldn't even contemplate it until the day you woke up screaming and covered with the red rash. I saw the end of my line if you died. I really understood that all of Mayflower might perish and the third-oldest pack in America would cease to be. All our history, all our legacy, gone. Because of a stupid, mindless virus.

"They begged me to do it. The man holding your arm right now, the one who very shortly will take you by force, if you don't give in willingly, came to me in tears after the death of both his parents. Dorothy was ill too and he pleaded with me to forge a pack bond to save her. To save all the sick ones. But it wasn't until you got sick that I agreed. So you see, this is all because of you. For you."

"Don't you fucking blame this on me!" I screamed and a frightened bird in one of the trees took wing and whirred away.

"He was supposed to break it when he passed on the mantle of Alpha." Rage coated Darren's voice and made it thick and feral. "Ask him why he didn't do that. Ask him if he did *that* for you."

Paul laughed again and Darren growled softly. Terror spiked through my veins, although I knew he didn't growl at me. I thought of how in a few moments he would be forced to rape me and I knew I wouldn't meekly submit. I would fight and it would be awful and painful, degrading and horrific. And when it was over I would belong to Paul Benedict. He would own me.

Everything I was screamed out in protest but I knew I wouldn't win a fight against Darren. The best I could hope for was that he killed me in the struggle. I didn't want to die any more than I wanted to be Paul Benedict's slave.

"Of course that part wasn't for you, Constance. Three years of being in control admittedly went to my head. Also, I knew Todd and Lily were weak, and they wanted to take Mayflower in a vastly different direction than I did. Naturally, I couldn't allow this to happen. Could I?" Paul smiled at me again and that's when I saw Faith step out from behind the concealing trunk of a pine tree. She had a flat rock in her hand the size of a baby's skull and was nearly incandescent with rage.

I gave a small jerk of surprise but Darren, who saw her as clearly as I, did not react at all except to give my arm an irritated yank as if I'd tried to wrench free. He and Faith made eye contact but still he did nothing.

Paul didn't see her and I knew it was imperative he didn't or he'd order her restrained and they'd do it. Scott might break free but maybe he wouldn't.

"You egomaniacal bastard," I said in my most offensive voice. "A different vision? What? One that didn't include complete subservience with Paul Benedict getting everything he wanted? Oh, damn, that's tragic."

"Constance, I've not run this pack like a despot." Paul was irritated at last and his eyes flashed. "In fact, unless the situation was dire, I hardly ever issued a direct order. I've given more of them in the past year than I have the other thirty combined."

Scott, Mark and Tony were aware of Faith now as well. She crept across the clearing, the rock hefted in her fist, her lips peeled back in a silent snarl. Mark and Tony did nothing to stop her.

I just had to keep Paul's attention for a few more seconds. If I could.

"Because that's when there was finally an Alpha pair that hadn't taken the pack bond," I said and Paul nodded.

"But even so I would have stayed as much in the background as I could if you hadn't shown up. Do you think I liked giving the order to have you raped? It was the last resort. I tried to give you a chance. I tried to be reasonable, but as always, you rebelled. You have never listened to me, Constance. But you will. I am going to relish this. I don't want you raped, so I wish you'd be reasonable and give in willingly."

"I think you would be disappointed as hell if I gave in willingly," I accused and he sighed. "I think you'd watch if your twisted code of ethics would permit such a thing."

"Who says it doesn't?" He asked and Faith smashed the back of his skull as hard she could. He'd sensed her in the last few seconds, but he hadn't been able to react in time. His eyes widened then blanked.

Blood splashed across Faith's face and my father crumpled to the ground.

* * * *

Darren, Mark and Tony threw back their heads and howled. It seemed as if they all started in unison, but when I pieced it together it was Darren who started it. Startled, Faith jumped and the rock tumbled from her grasp to hit the ground.

Darren let go of my arm and rushed Faith.

"No!" Scott screamed and lunged forward in desperation. Tony and Mark let him go and, overbalanced, Scott crashed to the forest floor. He scrambled up half a second later but by then Darren had already reached his objective.

Faith cowered but Darren ignored her. Instead he snatched up the bloody rock, brought it up over his head with both hands and prepared to smash it down on Paul's skull.

Paul was still alive—Faith's blow had only rendered him unconscious. His chest rose and fell with each shallow breath he took.

"*Darren!*" I shrieked.

Darren pulled his lethal blow and swung around to confront me, eyes ablaze.

"He's still alive, damn it," he growled at me. "If we let him regain consciousness he'll take us over again. The pack bond's not broken. I have to do this, Stanzie. I am not going to live like this anymore. He'll never give up the pack bond and he'll own us forever."

"Let him do it, Stanz." Mark's normally gentle brown eyes were hard and dangerous now as he glared at me. "If you don't, Darren will rape you and you'll end up just like us."

"Hurry up, he's coming around," Tony cried. Impatience made him jittery and unable to stand still. "Don't listen to her, Darren. Just do it."

"You'll be no better than him if you do," I said. "Pack law forbids murder and that's what it would be. He's in no condition to fight back."

"Pack law? Fuck Pack law, Stanzie," Mark raged. "Where has Pack law gotten us all our rotten lives? Paul's broken the law, I say we break it right back."

"Then you'll have to kill me too, won't you? Because I'll have to tell the Councils what I saw if you don't. And you'll be charged and sent in front of a tribunal. They'll put Darren to death and you and Tony will be punished too for standing by and encouraging him."

"Encouraging, hell," Tony snapped. "I'll do it myself if Darren doesn't."

"Let me bring him to the Councils. Let him face a tribunal for his crimes," I begged. A part of me wanted my bastard father dead, but I didn't want anything to do with bringing his killers to justice and I'd have to. I was an Advisor.

"Don't you get it? Once he wakes up, he'll tell us to stop you and we will." Anguish made Mark's voice rough.

"So don't be here," I suggested. "Run. Now. Scott, Faith and I can handle him. He needs a doctor. He may die anyway from the blow he took."

Darren had seriously contemplated walking away, I could see it in his eyes, but now he tightened his grip on the rock. "If that's true, let me kill him for sure and then I'll take the blame not my Alpha."

At his words, Faith stood a little straighter and surprise flitted across her face.

"I am loyal to you," Darren told her. "And to Scott as well. Or I've wanted to be."

"Is that why you showed up at our house yesterday and made sure we saw how rapidly you were healing?" Scott's voice was gentle.

Darren jerked his head in assent. "It was all I could think to do. I wanted to do more but I was forbidden to speak."

"I understand," said Scott. "Because of you Stanzie figured it out, Darren."

"Come on, come on," Mark whined. Paul groaned thickly and we all froze.

"Go," Scott commanded, but he kept his voice low, his gaze fixed on Paul.

Darren dropped the rock and he, Mark and Tony scattered.

"My head," Paul moaned as his eyes fluttered open and then shut again. When he finally could keep them open and focused, he looked around for support and found only me, Faith and Scott. None of us were inclined to be very supportive.

Chapter 13

Later that night most of Mayflower gathered at the Stonewall Tavern. Lauren was a no show. She was with the grandmothers and the children at Grandmother Elaine's. Darren was also missing, although a subdued Dorothy attended.

Paul was in the hospital but due for transfer to the Hartford safe house as soon as he was stabilized.

Councilors were already being chosen for his tribunal.

"What does he have to do to break the pack bond?" Susan sat beside Tony and clutched his arm. Her face was animated but we could all tell she was very close to a breakdown. Tony kept one hand on her knee and made sure his shoulder brushed hers.

Alan sat close beside me on one side while Faith sat on my other.

Everyone at the table made frequent contact as if to reassure ourselves that we were okay. But most of us weren't.

"We have to drink another elixir. His blood but some different herb." Karen Driscoll answered her daughter's question. She was a taller, stouter version of her daughter, with the same Cupid's bow mouth.

"How do you know these things, Karen?" Susan's face was suspicious. "You're the one who made me drink the first elixir. I remember. I was nine years old. I trusted you."

Karen flushed. "I was trying to protect you."

"I don't think we should cast blame tonight for what the pack decided to do thirty-two years ago," Tony spoke up. "We should all agree it was done for a good reason. Some of us are alive here tonight due to that decision. This whole pack might be here tonight *because* of that decision."

"Are you saying you think it was a good thing?" Rachel's dark eyes were bright with malice. "Who here thinks it was a good thing?"

"Until very recently Paul didn't make us do bad things." Wes Hanover's voice shook mournfully. He looked as if he'd just lost his best friend. He probably had. "Stanzie was the one he was most harsh with because she wouldn't listen to him. He never did anything bad unless it had to do with her.

"Dorothy, you used to smoke two packs of cigarettes a day until Paul told you to quit. There's a good thing. He looked after us. I'm not saying what he did was right—he should have broken the pack bond when he stepped down as Alpha, but we're making him out to be a monster when he was essentially a decent man who wanted the best for his pack."

"Oh, I don't want to hear any more of this Stockholm syndrome bullshit." I slammed my beer bottle down on the table and everyone froze. "None of you at this table had to live with him or watch firsthand what he did to Lauren."

"You're just upset about your wolf, Stanzie," said Wes.

"You're fucking A right I am, Wesley." Nobody called him Wesley. Not even Paul.

A slow flush suffused his cheeks.

"I said what he did was wrong. Didn't you hear that part?"

"Sure, in between a whole bunch of poetic crap about the good he's done for this pack. He didn't do shit for this pack except make all of you dance to his tune. And you liked it, Wesley, good for you. But I don't want to hear it. If you can't shut the fuck up, get out. You pathetic piece of shit."

"You never liked me," Wes accused in a shaky voice. "I was always nice to you, but you never liked me."

"Nice?" I thought the top of my skull would blow apart. "Is that what you call undressing me with your nasty, weasel eyes and always touching me when you knew I didn't like it? If that's nice, you can fucking shove it, Wesley."

"Stop calling me Wesley!" he shouted and the whole restaurant got very quiet.

Beneath the table, Alan put his hand on my thigh and I laced my fingers with his because we both needed the contact.

Wes looked around the table for support, his beady eyes moist. Nobody would meet his gaze.

"You *were* always touching her." Maddie put down a fistful of onion rings and stared at her bond mate. I'd never seen her talk without being spoken to. Ever. "Just like you were always touching me until I got too fat. Why do you think I ate myself into a size twenty-two? You are a letch, Wes. You always have been. And Paul's toady. I wanted to die when Cami did, but that darn elixir wouldn't let me. You told me it would save Cami.

It didn't. I tried to commit suicide but Paul found me and told me never to do that again.

"You think once the pack bond is broken, I'll be able to do it? He said never but does that still bind me if the pack bond's not there? Guess I'll find out."

"Maddie." Karen reached across the table to touch Maddie's hand. "Please don't do that. Mayflower's been through enough. We don't want to lose you too."

"Who would miss me?" Maddie was genuinely curious.

"I would!" The whole pack chorused more or less at the same time.

Tears clogged my sinuses and, for a terrible moment, I thought I would burst into sobs. Alan rested his forehead against the side of my face.

"Something's different about you, Alan," Susan said. Everyone fixed their attention on him and he slowly straightened in his chair.

"I shifted today." His voice was full of pride and, when he looked at me, his eyes glowed.

At first I thought Susan would berate him for not doing it with her, but she smiled, genuinely pleased. "Good for you." She reached across the table and patted his hand. "You know we want you to stay here with us in Mayflower, don't you?"

"No," he admitted hoarsely.

"We do, don't we, everyone?" Susan looked around the table for support and they all smiled and nodded with enthusiasm. Alan nearly crushed my hand but I squeezed back just as hard.

"What's the punishment for forging a pack bond in a pack smaller than forty?" Susan demanded.

I looked at Karen and Maddie who held hands across the expanse of the table and felt tears threaten.

"There is none if a pack is foolish enough to agree to it," I said and dismayed gasps went up around the table. "But the punishment for not breaking it when a new Alpha takes over is permanent exile from the Great Pack."

I knew this because I'd asked Jason Allerton earlier after he'd finished reaming me out for not reporting Darren's attempted rape.

"What if Paul won't break the bond?" Rachel, always the gore crow of doom, peered around at all of us, her dark eyes bright. "Seriously. What if he won't do it?"

"The Councils will force him." Mark sounded unsure and miserable. He looked at me. "Won't they?"

How the hell would I know? I didn't say that, but I wanted to.

"If all they need is his blood, they can damn well take it by force, can't they?"

"If that's all they need, why didn't you do it yourselves? Grandmother Elaine has the recipe," Scott pointed out.

"Paul has to want to break it. It can't be broken by force," Karen whispered. "Believe me, the grandmothers have tried to find a way to break the bond over the years. They never could."

"Fuck, if he needs to agree to it, what if he won't?" Now Mark was alarmed. "We'll never be free."

"But if he doesn't break it, what's to stop him from coming back? I won't be able to sleep ever again. I'll never be able to relax." Susan burst into shrill tears.

"This is a nightmare," whispered Rachel, and she, too, began to cry.

"I don't think coming out in public was such a hot idea," Faith murmured.

"I told you," Scott said.

"I don't think we should worry about shit that hasn't happened yet." I wasn't loud, but my voice carried. Everyone focused on me, even Rachel and Susan, although they didn't stop the waterworks. "Why don't you trust the Councils for now and see what happens?"

"Easy for you to say, Stanzie. It's not active inside you. What's Paul going to do to you?" Susan sniffled. I handed her my napkin so she could blow her damn nose.

"If I wanted to lose my mind and freak out, Susan, I could come up with six different scenarios right now. Like he could send one of the men after me. He could rape me himself. But I'm not going to lose fucking sleep over that man. He's had power enough over me. I'm not giving him any more. If he refuses to break the pack bond and the Councils exile him, I'm not going to live my life in constant fear of what he might do. Fuck that. And neither should you."

"I'm not as brave as you." Tears welled out of the corners of Susan's eyes and the waitress who had been aimed in our direction, veered away. So much for another beer. "You had the guts to stand up to Paul and refuse to let Wes initiate your wolf. I caved and let him. I didn't want Wes, I wanted Todd but I caved when Karen and Ralph told me to go with Wes. You got out. I got stuck here. I had dreams, you know? I met this boy from Liberty when I was fifteen and we both said we'd wait for each other until we turned twenty, only by then the pack bond was alive in me and I did what I was told and bonded with Tony."

Tony bowed his head and Susan bit her lip.

"Not that I haven't been happy with you, Tony. It's just that I had dreams. And so did you, I bet."

"It's going to be hard to think for ourselves after thirty years," admitted Maddie. We all looked at her in astonishment. Again, she spoke without being spoken to first. "Sure, Paul didn't make every decision for us, but he made all the important ones. Is anyone else scared of what it will be like without him telling us the right way? One minute I think I want to go with Cami and the next I don't, but without Paul to tell me which way, what will I do? Maybe I'll be paralyzed. You ever hear that phrase? Paralyzed with indecision? That's going to be me, I think."

"Oh, Maddie, I've missed you." Tears poured down Karen's face until she wiped them away with the back of her hand. "You kids don't remember how Maddie was before Cami died, before the red virus, but we do."

"I used to be pretty," Maddie said with a wistful smile. "Remember that green dress, Karen, we used to share when we went out dancing? You'd wear it the first half of the night, I'd wear it the second? Fun times."

Karen burst into laughter, tears forgotten.

"You're still pretty," said Susan. "Okay, you could stand to lose a few pounds, but so could I. Want to go on a diet together? And maybe walks at night for exercise?"

"I still have that green dress in storage in the attic." Karen smiled and Maddie's face lit up.

"Oh, I would like to wear that dress again."

"It's back in style too. Retro is in," Karen said.

"The day you can fit back in that dress, Maddie, I'll bring you out shoe shopping," I offered and was bombarded with wadded-up napkins launched at me by nearly every member of Mayflower.

Later, as we walked to our cars, some of us steadier on our feet than others, I cornered Dorothy. She had her fingers around the handle of the driver's side door of a small Jetta.

"Where's Darren? Why didn't he come?" I demanded, aware of Scott, Faith and Alan nearby. Faith as designated driver had the Prelude's keys in hand, but she didn't get behind the wheel so she could hear what I said to Dorothy.

Dorothy hesitated. "He didn't think you'd want him here, Stanzie."

"I know he wasn't responsible for what happened."

Dorothy shook her head. "You may know it here." She tapped her forehead with her index finger. "But you probably don't know it here."

She put her hand over her heart and smiled sadly. "Good night, Stanz. Thank you."

She opened the car door and slid behind the wheel. I watched her for a moment then backtracked to the Prelude.

She was right, of course.

* * * *

Faith brushed her hair in front of the full-length mirror bolted to the closet door. I was already in bed, the covers drawn up to my chin. Scott was half-asleep beside me.

Scott, Alan and I were pretty drunk. After the Stonewall, we'd come back to the house and had managed to consume all the beer in the mini fridge behind Scott's wet bar.

Alan was passed out on the sofa in the cellar but I wondered if he'd wake in the middle of the night and make his way to my bed. If he could walk. Drinking copious amounts of alcohol before or after shifting was a sure fire way to muscle cramps the day after. Combined with this being his first shift, he was in for a hell of a bad time. I'd taken away half his beers, but he'd still managed to get drunk. Perhaps massive pain was an acceptable price to pay to blot out Paul's betrayal. Hell if I knew.

I'd tried to brush my hair but the damn brush kept whacking me in the nose or dropping on the floor so I'd given up and crawled into bed.

"Would you have really done it?" Faith asked as she pulled the brush through her golden blond hair. She turned her head away from the mirror so she could see me. "Broken your bond with Liam Murphy and joined Mayflower. To save Scott and my baby?"

"Even if I wasn't already going to break the bond with him, I would have," I told her.

"Why are you going to do that? You're really hung up on him."

"Yeah, but he's not hung up on me. You're blood family, Faith. That baby will be my blood too."

"You would have bonded with Wes Hanover for us?" Faith's eyes filled with tears. "At first I was going to run and call Kathy Manning, but when I heard you swear to come back to Mayflower to save Scott and the baby, and you begged him not to make you bond with Wes I got so mad I thought I would melt. I sent Alan instead."

"I always thought I had the Benedict temper but I think maybe it's a Newcastle thing. I just never saw Lauren mad before. In my whole life I've never seen her mad." In my drunken haze this fact seemed huge.

"Me either," Faith said, eyes wide. "God, Stanzie, you would have had Wes Hanover's baby to save mine? That's fucking love, isn't it?"

"Ah, I might have bonded with that pig, but nobody said I had to sleep with him. An Alpha female can have anybody's baby she wants, remember?"

Faith's lips twitched, but whatever she said next I missed, because I passed out.

* * * *

Deja vu. When someone rapped on the screen door the next morning, I was busily mixing pancake batter. I'd just dumped a cup of fresh Maine blueberries into the mix and when I whirled at the sound I knew who would be there and I was right.

Darren Drake was alone today and there were only two cups of Dunkin' Donuts coffee in the carryout carton, but the look in his eyes was the same as it had been two days earlier.

"French vanilla?" I pointed at the coffee and a hopeful smile lit up his dark face. He nodded.

I realized I was still in my nightgown. "Let me go put on my jeans."

Halfway into the dining room I turned back. His hopeful smile had died and he stood locked out behind the screen door, his shoulders slumped in dejection.

"Come in. I'll just be a minute." When I unlocked the door, his smile returned.

We sat at the white wrought iron umbrella table on the patio and sipped our coffees.

Darren made sure to keep his distance—no stray brushes of our fingers, arms or feet.

His gaze was watchful, as if he expected any minute I would pull a knife or a gun or maybe just launch myself at him using my teeth and fingers as weapons.

"I came because Dorothy said you asked about me last night."

We were halfway through with the coffee and I could smell blueberry pancakes. Faith had taken over breakfast preparation.

Scott was in the kitchen with her. Every so often he'd deliberately walk past the kitchen window to let me and Darren know he was only a few feet away. Other than that, he left us alone.

Alan was still dead to the world, sleeping in the basement. The smell of blueberry pancakes might rouse him, I supposed.

"I trusted you. I understand how pack bonds bind people and can be used to make them act against their will, but you enjoyed doing it." I hadn't been sure what I'd say until I said it.

Amy Lee Burgess

To his credit he listened to everything I said and didn't flinch or defend himself.

"I like rough sex," he admitted. "And to do what I had to do, I pretended that's what it was."

"I hated it," I said and took another sip of coffee. The taste of it made me think of the real estate office and how he'd sit on the edge of the reception desk and listen to all my teenage angst.

More silence. Scott walked past the kitchen window again and briefly glanced out before he disappeared from view. The sizzle of pancakes on the stove competed with the breeze which rustled through the leaves of the oak trees on the empty lot next door.

"What I don't understand is why Paul didn't force me into sex so I'd shift with someone in Mayflower before I took off with Grey."

"He didn't know the extent of your involvement with him." Darren played with the lid of his cup and focused on that instead of my face.

"Bullshit," I said. "I knew you were there. You followed us all over the place. I smelled you, Darren. Sometimes I even saw you. Grey did too. We kept waiting for a confrontation but you just stayed in the shadows. I stopped showing up for work at the agency so I could be with Grey, but told Paul I was still going. I never thought he bought the story because I had no money to contribute to the pack fund and he always made me donate most of my pay. Paul sent you, didn't he? To spy on us?"

"Paul told me to watch over you. And I did. I told him I saw you drinking beer and playing pool with Grey at the Stonewall Tavern. I told him I saw you riding on the back of his motorcycle. I told him what movies you went to together and how you liked to eat ice cream at Rummel's."

"You didn't tell him how we spent eighty percent of our time screwing our brains out in his motel room at the Wishing Well?" My voice oozed derision.

"You always pulled the curtains," said Darren with a shrug. "I couldn't tell him what I didn't see. It was always during the day and we were supposedly working during the day, right?

"You went home at night and I let Paul think you were still working at the agency. I made sure your contribution got into the pack fund. When Paul went over the accounts, he always saw your money in there.

"And when I overheard you planning to go the Regional in Vermont, I developed a splitting headache and had to retreat to my bed for a day and a half. By the time I told him, you were already bonded."

I digested this for a while.

"And back then, Stanzie, he didn't force us to do hurtful things. Sometimes uncomfortable things, sure, especially where you were involved. He had a stubborn streak when it came to you. You'd be bonded with Wes right now if he'd let Tony initiate your wolf the way you and Tony wanted. But Paul needed to control you. Because your pack bond wasn't active, I think his need for dominance and control was, let's just say, obsessive. And you were family. Look at the way he treated Lauren. She was under the pack bond, but he took it miles deeper with her than he did with any of us. She wasn't allowed to make any decision on her own. Not what to wear, what to eat, what to think. You and Lauren were always Paul's pet projects."

"Our bad luck." My voice was flat. "So I'm supposed to be grateful to you, Darren, because you managed to let me escape Mayflower? You always told me I ought to listen to Paul and let Wes initiate my wolf."

"I know. Paul told us all to encourage you in that direction. What do want from me, Stanzie? I did what I could for you and, no, I don't expect your gratitude. I don't expect anything."

"Then why are you here?"

"For old time's sake, I suppose. To make sure you're all right."

"I don't need you or anyone to look after me." My chin jutted angrily and he smiled at me.

"Okay, cards on the table. I came here to thank you. I would have killed him yesterday and you talked me out of it."

"Scott did that. He told you to leave. He's your Alpha."

"Always an argument, that's you, Stanzie. Good to see time and hard knocks haven't beaten that out of you. I wouldn't have listened to Scott if you hadn't paved the way. I listened to him because I heard what you said and it made sense. I'm finally about to be free and I almost threw away the second half of my life for a moment of revenge. The best revenge is to take my freedom back. Simple. Dreadfully obvious but hard to reason out when you're blinded with rage.

"So thank you, Stanzie." He pushed back his chair and got to his feet.

Halfway to his car, I stopped him by calling his name. He turned back so he could look at me.

I wanted to tell him I knew why Paul had chosen him to be the one who raped me and it wasn't because he liked rough sex. It was punishment for allowing me to escape with Grey. But some things are better left unsaid. At least with words.

Instead I walked over to him and gave him a hug.

He hugged me back and when he moved away, his eyes were suspiciously bright. I was outright in tears, as usual.

He wiped them off my cheeks with his thumbs and gave me one of his dark and dangerous smiles.

Then he walked away.

* * * *

Susan's fears proved unfounded. Two days later Paul was transferred to the safe house in Hartford to await his tribunal. Before he left the hospital, he willingly gave up some of his blood and, with Grandmother's Elaine's help, prepared the elixir that would break the pack bond. He'd also done whatever esoteric things he'd needed to do in order to make the elixir viable.

At least that was the theory and the hope.

Scott, Faith and I had spent most of the two days recounting our stories to the Councils in preparation for the tribunal. Jason Allerton and Kathy Manning were both present and completely civil and professional with each other to the point where it made my heart hurt. Kathy's smiles were devoid of all sentiment and she did not bake a single thing.

Jason watched her wistfully when he knew she couldn't see him do it, but although there were several opportunities for him to talk to her alone, he didn't take advantage of any of them.

By the time I descended the staircase to the basement that evening just after dark, my head was reeling with everything I'd shared and the combined pressure of what I'd seen and done. I felt as if I'd been turned inside out and, as a consequence didn't quite know how to fit myself back together again.

All of Mayflower gathered in Scott's basement retreat to take the elixir.

As Alphas, Scott and Faith would oversee. Alan would bear witness as well.

Before I even stepped off the last riser, I saw Lauren. Her head was bowed and golden blond hair spilled over her shoulders in messy snarls.

She wore a pair of light blue linen pants and a blue-and-white blouse. The combination did not pair well. The blues clashed and the blouse was more casual than the pants.

Black loafers for shoes. Autumn shoes, not summer shoes. No makeup. She still wore her bond pendant and that irked the shit out of me.

My expression must have been angry because Susan burst out, "I didn't have time, Stanzie, to pick out a nicer outfit. When I realized she wasn't dressed I just grabbed the first things that came to hand. I told her to get dressed two hours before we needed to leave the house but when I went to check on her, she had all her clothes spread out on the bed and the chair and was wandering around in her underwear in a bewildered panic."

"Paul always tells me what to wear," Lauren said in a defeated voice.

"Does he brush your damn hair too?" Susan snapped, aggrieved. She knew she'd fucked up. They'd sent her to take care of Lauren and she'd done a half-assed job.

But where had I been? She was my mother. I knew better than anyone how dependent she was on Paul.

"I was trying to figure out what to wear," Lauren whispered. She'd locked her fingers together in her lap and squeezed so tight they were bloodless. "But I had too many clothes."

"It's all right, Wren," I soothed. I knelt down in front of her and brushed some of her hair behind her ear. No earrings. Lauren always wore earrings.

Without makeup she was every bit as gorgeous as with it, only not as polished. Her smooth skin was very pale and I could see the faintest dusting of freckles across her ivory cheeks.

She fixed her hyacinth blue gaze upon my face and murmured my name as if she'd just realized I was there.

It was Thursday. I'd been in Willoughby almost a full week and the only time I'd seen my mother was briefly at the midsummer's barbecue. What was worse—I hadn't even thought of her with everything that had gone on. So Darren had nearly raped me, and I'd introduced Alan to sex and shifting. I'd discovered my wolf was more broken than I'd suspected, and, okay, I'd been in on unmasking my father and his goddamned pack bond, but hadn't there been one single second I might have spared to check on my own mother?

Especially after Paul had been taken away from her and she'd been stranded alone?

I couldn't get away with rationalizing that someone from Mayflower would have looked after her. Yes, they should have and apparently they had. But not the way I would have cared for her.

What a shitty daughter I was.

"We're going to drink the elixir and you'll be better after that," I promised. I hoped not rashly.

Jason and Kathy had assured me my wolf would be normal after I drank the concoction and I wasn't sure I believed them. So how could I be sure that just because there was no pack bond binding Wren that she'd be able to make up her own mind again after thirty years of being told what to do?

Would it be like a light switch? One second dark without any way to know what to do, the next bright and the way clear? Or would it still be dark but instead of someone to blindly follow there'd be nothing and nobody except herself and, after thirty years, she probably didn't know who that was anymore.

Just like my wolf. So the barrier would be gone and my wolf would know most of the things I knew, like names. It wouldn't take her hours to figure out three words, it would take a few moments. But she would never be the same unfettered, joyful creature she'd once been. How could she be when she was my shadow self and I was anything but?

"Is Paul going to be here soon?" Lauren looked around the room hopefully. No one would meet her gaze. They all appeared uncomfortable— some of them downright impatient.

"She wasn't the most forceful personality around even before the pack bond," Susan remarked and I bristled.

"How would you remember? You were nine years old when you took the pack bond."

Susan gave me a very insincere smile. "Nine is old enough to remember my mother talking about how exasperating it was to go anywhere with Lauren Newcastle because she was afraid to buy anything without Paul's approval. So even back then she let him rule her."

Karen flushed. "Susan, honey, that was just shopping. She never liked to spend money. That's called being frugal."

"That's called being whipped," Susan snapped.

"I think we should focus on why we're here," Faith declared in a loud voice. She and Scott stood behind the wet bar. A rack of glass tubes with cork tops sat on top of the bar. The glass tubes were full of a dark red liquid with floating bits in it.

My stomach churned to look at them. Disgusting. We had to drink that shit?

"You'd better be prepared to move Lauren in here with you, Faith. As Alpha she's your responsibility. She can't hack it on her own." Susan's voice burned in my ears like a wasp sting.

"I will do whatever is necessary for her. She's Mayflower and we'll take care of her," Faith vowed. She spoke to Susan, but she looked at me.

I opened my mouth to say something, but Scott picked up the rack of glass tubes and gestured for us all to gather.

In silence he handed them out. When he gave me one, he leaned his forehead against mine and we rested together like that for a few heartbeats. Enough to calm me down. He knew I was agitated. Scared, pissed, guilty.

When we all held one of the glass tubes, Rachel looked at hers with extreme doubt. "Do we just drink this? Is there anything else we need to do? Something we need to say?"

The room was filled with tension and uncertainty. We looked to Grandmother Elaine as the oldest person in the room.

"It's all been said and done. This is the unbinding elixir. We just need to drink it."

"Will we need to shift for it to take effect?" Tony asked. He looked specifically at me when he said it and his expression was not lustful, it was apprehensive.

I gulped. I did not want to sleep with anyone in Mayflower. At least anyone who had taken the pack bond. I most certainly did not want to shift even if my wolf would be normal. What if she wasn't? I didn't want them see my humiliation.

Sometimes they felt like family, but other times, like now, they were strangers. And I didn't even like most of them much.

"No. There's no need to shift. It's all been said and done. You are being released, not bound," Grandmother Elaine clarified. "And good thing too, because these old bones are too brittle for shifting these days."

Chuckles filled the air as she'd meant them to. I even cracked a smile despite myself. Some of the tension drained away from the room.

"Well, damn it, here goes nothing." Mark plucked the cork from his glass tube and tossed back the contents with a terrible grimace.

Everyone watched him intently to make sure he didn't drop dead or blow up, but all he did was gag.

"That shit is nasty," he informed us, but a huge grin threatened to split his face and something indefinable left his eyes. I could believe he was free of the pack bond. I couldn't put my finger on the reason why, but he just looked different.

Rachel went next. She was never far behind her bond mate in anything.

"It worked. I can feel it inside me. It's like something's dissolving!" Her face was radiant.

More people guzzled the elixir and joyous laughter bounced off the walls. They hugged and kissed each other and, after Susan drank hers, she burst into tears.

Wes Hanover cried too, but I think he wept more because he didn't want to lose the pack bond than anything else. He put down his glass tube and escaped up the stairs as the tears leaked out of his pale blue eyes.

Lauren sat still as a stone and made no move to drink hers. I put the stopper back in mine and went to her.

"You need to drink that," I whispered as I knelt in front of her again.

She blinked at me piteously for a second then struggled to take the cork out. She lifted the tube to her mouth and swallowed obediently. Everyone else had grimaced or gagged but she didn't. She did as she was told.

I watched her intently and waited for her to smile and acknowledge she was free, but she only sat there as if in a trance.

"Lauren?" I touched her cheek and she started, but then smiled at me. All around us people laughed and celebrated. Scott and Faith passed out bottles of beer to chase away the nasty taste of the elixir. Susan had Tony up against the wall. She was on tip toe so she could reach his mouth with hers and they were involved in a passionate kiss.

As I watched, she undid the clasp to his belt buckle and I knew there would be an orgy and they would shift anyway, even if they didn't have to.

Darren and Dorothy were on the sofa and her shirt was unbuttoned so he could bury his face between her pert breasts.

All I wanted to do was swallow my damn father's blood and get the hell out but I was worried about Lauren.

Faith and Scott talked at the bar with Maddie. Or rather Maddie talked and they listened. Her tongue seemed to travel a mile a minute and she was full of such joy there was an aura around her that rapidly sped to engulf Scott and Faith.

"I'm going to drink this and we're going to go upstairs. Maybe sit out on the patio, okay?" I turned back to my mother. She smiled and nodded agreeably. I could have told her we were going upstairs so I could shoot her in the head and she would have had that same damn smile on her face. She would have let me shoot her too.

With a muttered oath, I wrenched the cork out of my glass tube and gulped down the contents.

The blood mixed with herbs tasted putrid. Thick, viscous, gooey. And the bits of herbs stuck to the back of my throat on the way down. Vile.

I gagged and waited to puke my guts out. The bond wouldn't break if I did that so I tried to think of sunshine and meadows instead of blowing chunks.

"Motherfucker," I croaked when I decided the disgusting shit would stay down.

Rachel said she'd felt something dissolve inside her. I felt nothing but sick to my stomach.

"Here, you might want one of these." Scott's voice was excruciatingly loud in my suddenly sensitive ears. Yet the rest of the room seemed muted as if muffled in cotton and then submerged fathoms deep in the ocean.

The words he spoke hurt and ran together so they sound more like *Heeereyoumightwaaantonnneoftheeese*.

When I looked at him, his face was distorted. His wolf seemed to lurk just beneath the skin. Instead of a hand, he held the beer with his paw. Then it was just a hand again.

Everyone in the room seemed to morph back and forth between wolf and human. Darren and Dorothy on the sofa were the most wolf. She was on all fours and he was behind her as they did it doggy style. Or more accurately—like wolves because that's what they were most of the time to my eyes.

"Oh, fuck," I said and lost all control of my limbs. My bladder let go and hot urine splashed down both my legs. My body jack knifed on the carpet as synapses between nerve endings misfired over and over again. Was this how it felt to be tasered?

"Isn't there pain, though?" That was my last coherent thought. Agony ripped through me. My wolf was fucking pissed. Her claws shredded me from the inside out. All the parts of shifting that took place on the other plane happened in this one. And they fucking hurt.

Scott stared at me in horror. Everyone did. Sudden pandemonium gripped the room. Lauren screamed. Over and over again. Shrill and hopeless until Darren hauled her away from me. His pants were around his ankles but he didn't trip. Dorothy clutched her unbuttoned blouse together and shrank into the back of the sofa, her eyes huge as she stared at me.

Faces blurred above me. Scott called to me then Faith. My Grandmother Elaine tried to get me to drink something but she couldn't make my jaw unclench.

It was a good thing for her too because my wolf's teeth were razor sharp.

* * * *

The smell of my own piss was nauseating. I turned my head in the other direction so I didn't have to breathe it in so directly and a bolt of agony ripped down my spine. Fuck. That wasn't good.

"Stanzie?" Jason Allerton's hand was cool on my bare shoulder and I flinched because the pressure of his skin against mine hurt. He pulled his hand away quickly.

Bare skin. So I was human. I could have sworn I'd shifted.

"I shifted, didn't I?" My voice was ghastly, my vocal cords shredded. I must have been screaming although I didn't remember doing it.

"Yes, briefly." Jason's tone was matter of fact and I felt marginally comforted. He had the nicest voice. Soothing. He always knew what to do. "But you're fully shifted back now."

The way he said *fully* made me wince. No doubt I'd been in some fugly half-and-half state. I had to have been if my impression of what had happened was anywhere close to true.

"Everybody else felt a lovely dissolving feeling and I went Frankenwolf. Figures. Jesus," I muttered and Faith laughed, but then it turned into a sob. "Oh, goddamn, Faith, don't cry. I'll cry too and I think that would really hurt right now."

"Oh, Stanzie." She gulped. "God, what happened?"

"You're asking me?" I knew I sounded sarcastic, but honestly. How the fuck would I know?

"Apparently, the unbinding elixir has some rather unpleasant side effects on those who have never activated the pack bond," Jason said dryly. Way to understate something.

"I feel like shit and I need a bath. I also probably need to buy you a new carpet, Scott."

"Oh for Christ's sake," Scott said and he sounded perilously close to losing it.

"It also probably was not the wisest idea to take this elixir within forty-eight hours of sexual activity," said Jason.

"Oh, great. Now he tells me." I groaned. "This is what happens when I try to do a good deed for someone. I get kicked in the ass. Can somebody please help me to the bathroom? I so need a bath."

Jason lifted me into his arms and that's when I realized I was naked. Naturally my clothes had shredded as I'd experienced the unpleasant byproducts of the unbinding elixir.

"I meant my cousin," I protested, but he ignored me.

Everyone else had thankfully left, so the only ones who saw my undignified exit in the arms of a prestigious Councilor were Scott and Faith. I wished I knew where Lauren was, but I remembered her screams and apparently someone had had the common sense to get her the hell out of the house.

Once in the bathroom Jason made me sit on the toilet while he filled the tub with warm water and lavender-scented bath salts. Then he helped me into the tub and, instead of giving me some damn privacy, he took my vacated seat on the toilet and settled in to wait for me to bathe.

Nudity was not a thing with Pack but a member of the Great Council perched on a toilet watching me take a bath was a whole other story.

If only he'd leaned against the counter or maybe just stood, it might have been more dignified for both of us, but he seemed quite comfortable on the toilet in his Armani pants and Italian silk shirt. Damn bath salts. Why didn't they have bubbles?

Since he didn't appear to have the slightest notion of leaving and I didn't want to splash around in an embarrassed silence, I said, "How much of it did you see?"

He gathered his thoughts for a moment. His black hair was disheveled and there was a rip in the right sleeve of his silk shirt. A long, thin tear. As if made by the swipe of a flailing claw. Damn it.

"I owe you a shirt," I added before he'd had a chance to answer me. He looked down at the rip and half smiled. His blue eyes were full of affection when he looked back up at me.

"I have six others of the exact same brand. No need, but thank you." He leaned forward and clasped his hands together. His pack ring, a band of beveled yellow gold gleamed around his ring finger. His shoes were brown suede—Ferragamo. When he leaned forward, his bond pendant shifted around his neck. The top two buttons of his shirt were open and I could see the gold chain as it descended to his chest but I couldn't see the actual pendant. Would there be one stone or two mounted on it?

"You have a bond mate yet?" He didn't seem inclined to rush to answer any of my questions, so I figured I'd pepper him with a hundred of them and maybe he'd answer one by default.

He laughed and I thought again how handsome he was. Not male model gorgeous like Scott or an Irish charmer like Murphy, but a solid and dependable handsome. Like chairman of the board or president of the United States if he were in his thirties handsome. Like an ideal father.

"No, but thank you for asking." Wow. An actual answer.

"I'll need a bond mate in two months. We ought to hook up, solve both our problems." I couldn't fucking believe I'd said that. I blamed lack of oxygen during my attack. And my own idiocy.

"I'll take that under advisement. I'm flattered," he said with a diplomat's blinding smile.

"Yeah, right." I snorted and he laughed again. I liked it when I made him laugh. I don't think he allowed very many people to do that.

"Really. I don't receive many proposals from beautiful naked women in bath tubs." Jason Allerton was actually teasing me. My cheeks felt hot and I hoped he'd think my red face was due to the warm bath water.

"Many? You mean I'm not your first? The swinging life of a Great Councilor." I said and was rewarded with more of his laughter.

"You relieve my mind, Stanzie. You scared the hell out of me tonight." His laughter gradually faded as he became serious. "To answer your question, I saw most of it. I was just upstairs and when I heard Lauren's scream, I ran down to investigate. I have to admit I had no idea what to do. You shifted totally in this plane."

Aha, my impressions had been correct.

"It hurts like hell," I told him and he winced sympathetically.

"The process, while alarming, was fascinating to watch. The Council has often speculated on what precisely occurs as we shift and now that conversation can be taken out of the realm of the theoretical thanks to you."

"You're welcome," I said. "Bet you'll get invited to lots of fancy parties and expensive dinners on the strength of this story alone, won't you?"

"No doubt," he agreed with his special brand of dry humor. "Seriously, Stanzie, I'm very glad you're all right." His voice was so gentle my throat clogged with tears. I was suddenly so damn tired. "Now you'd probably better go to bed. We leave first thing tomorrow morning for Hartford and the tribunal. I'd like to ride with you if you don't mind."

"Will you drive? I'm not up to passengers yet," I confessed.

"I'd planned on it. You've been through a lot, Stanzie. I'd prefer it if you'd rest."

"That works for me." I pulled the plug on the drain and stood. He handed me a bath towel and let me lean on his arm for balance when I stepped out of the tub. My legs were like rubber.

My clothes had been ruined, so I wrapped the towel around me. I took a tentative step for the door and, if he hadn't been there to catch me, I would have fallen on my ass.

Once again he swept me up in his strong arms and, this time, he took me upstairs to my room.

Faith and Scott were already in bed. She was asleep, he read a book. When he saw us, he pulled aside the covers and Jason put me down on the mattress. Scott threw my towel onto the floor and gathered me up into his arms so I could sleep with my head on his shoulder.

I was too damn tired to care about being naked. Besides, we were Pack.

"Good night," Jason said after Scott told him there were fresh sheets on the bed in the master bedroom and he'd be sure to wake everyone before nine.

Jason gave us all a last smile and closed the door on his way out.

"Boy, he must think we're been having torrid threesomes ever since I got here," I murmured. "You smell nice, Scott." My nose was nearly buried in his neck. He had on a light cologne. Sexy.

"Would you rather I told him you have nightmares every night?" Scott asked. "You smell like Faith's lavender bath salts. I guess that's nice."

"Jesus." I groaned. "Lavender is for relaxation, not supposed to be seductive. Not every scent we use is meant to turn you guys on, you know."

"Well, good, because lavender does nothing for me. However, your very naked body on the other hand..."

"Good night, Scott, you asshole."

He laughed. "Night, partner. No nightmares tonight, okay?"

Before I could say something sarcastic, I fell asleep.

Chapter 14

Paul Benedict's tribunal convened at noon the next day. The tribunal consisted of the entire New England Regional Council and three members of the Great Council, including Rosemary Young, since she was familiar with Mayflower and other New England packs.

This time I sat in the back to watch. Jason and I had placed Lauren between us. All of Mayflower was present except for the children. Olivia and the twins were in the front room reading books and playing with a Lego set.

Faith sat on my other side, her face grim.

Paul looked awful. The doctors at the hospital had shaved the back of his head so they could stitch the six-inch gash Faith had inflicted with the rock. The skin on his skull was raw and pink, the stitches made an ugly zig-zag pattern that was painful to look at.

He wore his best suit—navy blue pinstripe and its severity only emphasized the stitches and made him look vulnerable and weak.

He sat at the foot of the conference table, erect and stiff. He answered their questions with uncharacteristic brevity and never once looked at any of his pack.

Two and a half hours later the tribunal pronounced judgment.

Guilty. Permanent exile from the Great Pack. All his belongings, money and property were deeded to Mayflower for Faith and Scott to do with as they deemed fit.

Paul was allowed the clothes on his back, five thousand dollars, and a plane ticket to the city of his choice as long as it was more than three hundred miles from Willoughby.

Paul chose Las Vegas. A decent choice. The climate was warm, casinos were open twenty-four seven and he could parlay his five thousand dollar seed money into more if he were lucky. I'd never known Paul to gamble, though.

He signed the necessary papers transferring his property and bank accounts to Faith and Scott, and the whole thing took less than twenty minutes after his sentence was pronounced.

When he rose to his feet to be escorted to the car which would take him to the airport, Lauren moved for the first time in three hours and got to her feet too.

"Lauren." I pitched my voice softly but she still jerked as if I'd struck her. Her hyacinth blue eyes were huge in her perfect face when she turned to look at me. "Where are you going?"

"With Paul," she whispered. The whole room went silent No one even so much as twitched.

"Why?" I asked.

Confusion knitted her brow. "He's my bond mate."

"Not anymore. The tribunal just stripped him of all his Pack rights. His bond with you was severed. You're not bonded anymore. You don't have to go with him." I wanted to grab her and rush her out of the room, away from his sphere of influence but I didn't.

"But where will I go then?" Her voice trembled and tears glistened on the edges of her thick lashes.

"Anywhere you like," I told her.

"Back to Willoughby?"

"Sure."

"But I could go with Paul if I wanted?" She darted a look in his direction and for once he looked at the room. His focus was on her. He said nothing, but he didn't have to, his influence over her was loud and clear. Still. Without the damn pack bond.

Jason Allerton fixed his gaze on my face as he waited for my response. This was a test for me as much as it was for Lauren. I sucked at tests, I always had. Jason wouldn't say anything, but I knew what he would counsel. Let her make her own decision. And, damn it, that's what I wanted too, but I wanted that decision to not be in Paul Benedict's favor.

"Yes," I had to tell her.

"What should I do, Stanzie?" The question I didn't want her to ask me. A derisive smile curled the corners of Paul's mouth. I'm sure he figured I'd use this opportunity to denounce him. Bastard.

"You have to make this choice, Lauren, not me." The words were dragged out of my mouth. Jason Allerton managed to radiate approval even though his expression did not change. I don't know how he did it. Maybe I imagined it.

"Could I...could I come with you? Wherever you go?" Lauren's voice was tentative as if she thought I would laugh at her or tell her no.

I tried not to scream in triumph. I could still lose her.

"Absolutely," I said with a small, but encouraging smile. Then I shut the fuck up, which was probably one of the hardest things I'd ever done in my whole life.

"Well," said Lauren and she chewed on her perfect bottom lip. She looked around and seemed to realize for the first time that everyone was hanging on her words. She gulped.

"I think," she said. "I think I want to come with you, Stanzie. If that's okay?" She cringed and waited for me to say no. Across the room Paul sagged. His eyes grew bleak and I hoped he contemplated the rest of his sad, sorry, lonely life. No contact with anyone Pack. No bond mate, no pack, no Regionals or Great Gatherings. No help, no support, no relevance.

It was that last one that would be the real bitch for him and I hoped it ate him alive.

"Wait 'til you see my condo in Boston, Wren. You can have your own room and I just painted it this tangerine color, but we can repaint it any color you like. We're going to have a lot of fun together, you just wait and see." I stood and embraced her. She was like a fragile bird in my arms, not much substance at all.

Paul walked out of the conference room with his Advisor escort and I sincerely hoped I would never see his face again.

Epilogue

The lilacs were in bloom. The bushes in front of the small white cinderblock house were a riot of dark purple. The last fling before summer truly settled in and the shrubs stopped producing flowers. I could smell them from where I stood on the rutted dirt driveway and I thought maybe I would gather an armful on my way back to Jossie and Vaughn's farmhouse.

But first I needed to do something.

The shed door was unlocked and I held my breath as it squeaked open. The woodpile was still there but all the tools had been removed. Including the chainsaw.

The steel shelving unit was gone too so the trap door was plainly visible in the dirt floor.

Sweat trickled down the back of my neck. Outside it was a temperate seventy-five, but in the shed it was a good ten degrees hotter. Plus, I was nervous. Okay, I was scared shitless.

Right after the tribunal, Lauren and I had gone to my condo in Boston but only for clean clothes and new shoes. After a shopping trip to Macy's where I bought Lauren the beginnings of a new wardrobe, we headed straight for Vermont.

I'd gotten over my fear of driving with passengers. As long as the passenger was Lauren.

Vaughn and Jossie had welcomed us with open arms and it had been nearly a week since the tribunal.

At first Lauren had been silent and tearful, but as time wore on she got better. Heather had a lot to do with it. Lauren wouldn't talk to Jossie and Vaughn unless I was with her, but she opened up for the baby.

They spent hours together on a blanket in the grass beneath the spreading shade of a maple tree in the front yard.

The rest of Maplefair trickled in and out of the farmhouse to visit, trade recipes, bring homemade cookies and pies, freshly picked strawberries and gossip.

Jossie and Vaughn were radiant together and everyone wanted to bask in their newfound happiness. Me too. Sometimes. Other times I couldn't help think of Murphy and wish he were there with me so I'd have someone too. I wondered how long these feelings for him would persist and if I'd ever have peace.

After I opened the trap door, I took the aluminum ladder propped against the wall and lowered it into the root cellar. I climbed down and switched on my flashlight. The electricity had been shut off. No one lived in Grandmother Emma's house and there was no use paying for electricity. Jossie was too frugal for that.

The flashlight cast eerie circles of light around the gloom of the root cellar. It was empty, of course. The metal gurneys had been removed and all traces of Nate Carver's nefarious work had been cleaned away.

The dirt near the ladder was darker than the rest. Blood. I could still smell it.

I could smell Bethany too. Her blood and sweat had dripped on the dirt floor. A lot of it.

The whole place reeked still. Old blood, death, despair.

The flashlight turned strobe-like in my shaking hand until I steadied it.

It's just a place. It has no power but what you give it. And you give it none.

"Fuck you, Nathanial Carver." My voice was strong.

* * * *

Jossie waited on the dirt driveway. She helped me pick an armful of lilac blossoms as the late afternoon sunlight slanted across her tanned face and picked up dark red highlights in her glossy brown hair.

"Can I talk to you?" She tucked some of her waist-length hair behind her ears and looked solemn. I wondered if she would lecture me for revisiting the root cellar alone and I nodded as I continued to pick lilacs.

"Vaughn is going to ask you to bond with us," she said, and I closed my eyes for a moment. I pictured my life with them. A room in the farmhouse. Company at breakfast every morning. Vaughn's mouth on mine as we made love, and the winter snow drifted down to cover the tin roof. A baby of my own with Vaughn's smile and my eyes. Spare to the pair, yes, but a good spare. Bonded to my best friends.

I could give Lauren the condo when she was ready to live alone and visit her every weekend. She'd adore being a grandmother. I could stay on as Jason's Advisor. My life could begin yet again. No more waiting on hold.

"I don't want you to say yes." Jossie's voice threw cold water on my rosy visions and I opened my eyes to see her face. She looked sad but very determined. "You're my best friend next to him, but I want to be in a duo, not a triad."

"It's okay." I forced a smile and lied to her face. "I wouldn't have said yes. You're right. You two should be a duo."

"Really? You really don't want to bond with us?" Her brown eyes were dark with relief. Even if she doubted me, she wouldn't let it get to her. She wanted to believe me, so she would. "I thought when you came here, that was what you were angling for.'

"I came to lay some ghosts to rest," I said, which was true. "I came here to confront Grandmother Emma's root cellar. I'm leaving in the morning, actually. Lauren will miss the hell out of Heather, but I really want to get her settled in Boston. It's done her good to be here, Joss. Thank you for everything you've done."

Jossie stared at me for a moment.

"I didn't mean you had to rush away." But she wanted us to leave. I wondered how long she'd felt that way and cursed myself for my selfishness. "I think you ought to work things out with Liam, Stanzie. You're just hiding here. Running away."

My throat closed over and I couldn't breathe. I never, ever should have come here.

"We need to get these in water." I gestured at the lilac blossoms. "Come on."

* * * *

Vaughn stood by the Prelude the next morning and looked profoundly unhappy. He'd had the same look on his face since I'd gently turned down his offer to bond with him and Jossie.

"You'll call me, right?" He sounded suspicious, as if he believed once I drove out of his driveway I'd never bother with him again.

"All the time," I promised.

Jossie, with Heather in her arms, came down the porch steps and walked over to the car.

Lauren stared through the window at the baby, her eyes wistful.

"I'm thinking of trying to work it out with Murphy." A bald-faced lie but Vaughn bought it. His face lit up and he grinned at me.

"That's what you need. I don't want you to be alone, Stanz. I worry about you. I love you."

"She's not alone." Vaughn and I were startled by Lauren's voice. She so rarely spoke first. "She's got me."

"Of course she does." Vaughn gave her his most winning smile, the one that melted the hearts and panties of women all across New England. My mother giggled. What a wonderful sound.

I started the car and lifted my hand to wave goodbye. Jossie stood beside Vaughn, her hand on his arm. Heather goggled adoringly at her father. His girls loved him and I was so fucking happy for him.

Wren's golden hair glowed in the spring sunshine that streamed through the windshield. She craned her neck to watch Heather grow smaller and smaller as we bumped down the rutted dirt driveway to the road.

Her expression was wistful when she turned to face forward.

"You scared of it being just you and me alone, Wren?" I asked. I knew I was. Jossie, Vaughn and Heather—hell, the entire Maplefair pack—had been buffers between us ever since the end of Paul's tribunal.

We hadn't talked about him or the pack bond or anyone in Mayflower. We'd barely talked. I'd been so busy laying ghosts to rest, I hadn't focused on her. What else was new?

I came to the end of the driveway and turned left. Guilt stabbed at me and I shifted uncomfortably on the seat.

"I'm not, but you are." Wren fiddled with the strap of her seatbelt nervously. "I saw how you looked at me when I was with Heather. I know you think I am a terrible mother."

What the fuck?

"Never!" I chanced a look away from the empty, rural road ahead of us so I could focus on her. Another stab of guilt sliced into my gut. Terrible was not the word. "When I was a little girl, you were the best mother ever."

"But not so much as you got older." Wren's eyes glittered with unshed tears.

"It was the pack bond," I said.

"You think I don't know how weak I am? The pack bond didn't help, Stanzie, but I was always weak. Lily begged me not to bond with Paul. Did you know that?"

I hadn't.

"She and Todd were the last ones to take the pack bond. They didn't want to. If it hadn't been for me, they would have left the pack. Neither one of them were sick. But they stayed for me. Because I'm weak. I think even then they suspected what Paul would do and they were right. But it was too late to do anything by then.

"I should have gone with Paul. It's not too late. You could put me on a plane to Las Vegas. I could find him." Her voice wobbled and I abruptly pulled the car over and narrowly avoided going into the ditch. My heart slammed into my ribs and cold sweat popped out onto my forehead. God, I'd nearly driven us into a frigging *ditch*.

"Wren." I tried to hug her but the damn seatbelt got in the way and she shrank back. "I'm sorry. I didn't mean to make you feel like I didn't want you with me. You know I do."

"Everybody always apologizes to me for things that are my fault, not theirs," Wren whispered. "Everybody tiptoes around me because they expect me to crack and shatter like glass. I'm not glass, Stanzie. At least, I don't want to be." Tears poured down her beautiful face until she looked like a drowned Ophelia.

I managed to unhook my damn seatbelt and pulled her across the gear shaft into my arms. It was like hugging wet sunshine. She was so insubstantial I could barely hold on.

"Wren," I murmured in her ear. "It'll be all right. We both have gone through a lot of shit lately. We're not going to be all cheerful and perfect. You know? We don't have to hate ourselves for not being the people we think we should be. Okay?"

"You never call me mom anymore," wailed Wren. She nearly blasted my eardrum into pieces and I jerked in shock. "When was the last time you called me mom? You don't think of me as your mother. You don't, Stanzie! I'm that fluttery, bruised wraith you call Wren. You don't even call me by my real name."

"Pack don't call their parents mom and dad once they're not little kids anymore, Wr-Lauren. I mean, look at us! We look like sisters."

"We aren't sisters." Wren pulled away from me and huddled against the passenger door like a battered bird.

How hard would it have been to look at the woman and call her mom? Just open my frigging mouth and let the word out? Yet it stuck in my throat and festered.

A dark wave of resentment slammed into me. I wanted to take her by her shoulders and shake her until her fucking perfect gold hair fell out. Her teeth too. I mean, what the fuck? What the fuck did she want from me? She *wasn't* my mother. A mother would have been there for me when I'd gone up against the iron will of my father and resisted being initiated by fucking Wesley Hanover. Even if she'd just been a shoulder to cry on. Even if she'd just held me while I cried. But no. No. I had to be the one to hug her when she cried because she accidentally burned Paul's supper

Amy Lee Burgess

or she forgot to wash his favorite goddamn shirt and he wanted to wear it. I never got to be the daughter once I hit puberty. Ever. Our roles had reversed and I'd done my best for her, but apparently even that wasn't good enough. She wanted me to call her mom. Mom. As if. And it wasn't all the pack bond's fault. She was weak, just like she said.

"We have to go." I fastened my seatbelt and clenched the steering wheel so hard my knuckles ached. My face was hot and I wanted to hit something. So I made a fist and punched the dashboard. That fucking hurt. It scared Wren too. She had been sniffling, tears mostly gone, but that started the waterworks again.

"You're scaring me," she quavered.

"Fucking Jossie. I wasn't ready to leave. Fuck her for telling me she didn't want me to bond with her and Vaughn. As if I'd do that anyway. Who wants to belong to a fucking bullshit New England pack in the ass end of nowhere? I hate everybody. I hate *everybody*!" I slammed the steering wheel for good measure.

The car was stifling. I couldn't fucking breathe. I undid the seatbelt and flung open the door. Once out onto the blacktop, I slammed the door against Wren's pathetic wails and stalked into the field across the road.

Tall grass tickled the backs of my bare knees. My toes and sandals slimed with dew.

God, I wished I could shift. Be my wolf. I would run and run and leave everything behind.

Tears gushed down my cheeks and made it hard to see. Where the hell was I going anyway? I had nowhere to go.

I dropped down into the damp grass and sobbed wretchedly into my arms. I smelled Jossie's lavender body wash and my J'adore perfume. Both scents mixed with the aroma of wet spring grass and fertile earth. My tears made everything salty.

Even Wren's shadow was tentative.

"Stanzie?" she whispered.

"I'm tired of being the strong one." My sobs made the words sound choked and gaspy. "I've always got to be the strong one and I'm sick of it. Just once I'd like you to tell me it will be all right. Even if the fucking world was ending around us and we had seconds to live. Just once I'd like to hear you say it. You want me to call you mom? Well, then, *be* one. How's that?" I rolled over to glare at her. The early morning sunshine cast a halo around her golden head. God, could she *never* appear less than perfect? Did she even have a bad angle?

Wren knelt beside me, unmindful of her pink skirt and grass stains. Her lovely mouth trembled as she reached out to touch my cheek.

"When you left Mayflower, all the light went out of my life."

"Oh, my fucking God." I groaned and covered my eyes with one arm. "Do not lay a guilt trip on me now. I am already on the mother of all guilt trips as it is. I've killed people, Wren. Good people. Shitty people. I've driven away a man I love more than anything because I can't be who he wants. I've fucked up Jossie and Vaughn by coming here. I got my father exiled. I can't handle any more guilt. I'm sorry I left you behind, but I'm not sorry I left Mayflower. Get over it."

"You're so beautiful," Wren whispered. She stroked my cheek and I wanted to push her hand away but I couldn't move I was so balled up with guilt. "From the inside out. I'm proud of you. Of everything you've done with your life. What you're still doing with it. If that Irish bond mate of yours wants you to be different than what you are, he can go to hell."

I moved my arm so I could stare at her. Lauren Newcastle said hell? Whoa.

"I'm good with babies and little children. I'm terrible with teenagers. I'm worse with adult children. Can you give me another chance? I probably don't deserve one, but maybe you could try?" Wren bit her lip and I realized I'd been holding my breath when my lungs began to burn.

"I love you, Stanzie." Tears stuck to her long lashes.

"I love you too, Wren. I always have," I said. I was exasperated and yet protective. I always wanted Wren to be safe. "That will never change. You're my mother."

Her face glowed and she smiled at me the way I remembered her smiling at me when I was a little girl and we'd play dollhouse or tea party together. When Paul was at work and it was just us.

It would be just us in Boston. We wouldn't play dollhouse or tea party, but we would be mother and daughter. For the first time since Murphy left, maybe the condo wouldn't be a sucking, empty hole of bitter reproach for the things I'd done wrong. Maybe it would become a haven—a place where I would find my mother and myself.

"Come on." I took her hand and let her help me stand up. "Let's go home."

Meet the Author

When I wrote the first novel in The Wolf Within series, Beneath the Skin, I didn't realize Stanzie and Murphy had hijacked my muse for a series of novels. Nor did I fully comprehend Stanzie's story. I always knew Liam Murphy's back story, but Stanzie's has continued to surprise and excite me. Her journey of self-exploration has become my own. I can't shift into a wolf--unfortunately!--but I can imagine what it would be like to touch something inside that is wild and beautiful like her wolf. When I'm not writing Stanzie's adventures, I can be found watching True Blood, XIII, old horror movies and Ab Fab. I speak passable French and my favorite city in the world is, of course, Paris. I live with a half-dachshund half Chihuahua named Nixie in a modern apartment in Houston, Texas and ardently miss autumns in New England, where I was born. I always love to hear readers' thoughts about Stanzie and company, so please keep in touch!

Amy's Website:
http://amyleeburgess.blogspot.com/
Reader eMail:
Amyleeburgess99@gmail.com

Turn the page for a special excerpt of Amy Lee Burgess's

Scratch the Surface

Something's rotten in the Riverglow pack.

Still learning more about each other as bond mates and adjusting to their new roles as Advisors to a Councilor, Constance Newcastle and Liam Murphy must deal with the ghosts of their past.

A quiet weekend in Boston is anything but that, when Constance comes face to face with the betrayal of those she considered the closest to her. Everyone has secrets, and wherever Constance goes, she has a knack for uncovering them. The only problem is that some secrets are deadly.

On sale now!

Chapter 1

Wind in my face. I happy! Friend with me! We look at strange water. No move now. Stuck. Put paw on it. Cold! Want to walk on strange water. I scared! Strange water make noise—Crrrack! Paw wet and cold. Friend has tongue out, Friend laugh. Friend look at strange water. I not understand. Water moves. But strange water does not move . Why? Why? Want word for strange water. Want know why it not move. Think! Think hard. Strange water there when it very cold. Me seen it with Him and Her before they go away and not come back. Us run on it. Run, run, run. Me not want run now, me want word. I. I want word. I want word for strange water. Think. Think. Friend watch over me. Think. Think. I so mad. I want word! I want word! No. No get mad. Can't think for mad in head. Go away, mad. Stop. Think. Strange water not move. Cold. White. Water. Not water. Think. Think. Want word. Word for strange, cold water that not move. Word is...word is...ice! Yes! Ice, ice, ice, ice! I see ice! I see ice! Friend, I see ice! Friend, I happy! I see ice! I lick Friend's face. Friend lick me. I happy. I see ice!

* * * *

The shrill ring of the phone dragged me out of sleep. Murphy and I had shifted the night before and we'd exhausted ourselves in wolf form. By the time we'd shifted back, shivered into our clothes and driven home to Boston, it had nearly been dawn. The sky above my condo had been a pale shimmering pink as I'd fallen onto the bed, my hair still wet from the shower. I didn't even remember Murphy coming to bed but he was there with me. The ringing phone had roused him too. He was snuggled up against my back, his arm across my waist and he rolled over into a defensive ball, swearing colorfully in Irish under his breath while he tried to shield his ears with one of the fluffy down pillows.

"Goddamn it," I muttered. I could tell it was frigid outside. Well, naturally, it was January. Barely. "Happy fucking New Year, Murphy."

His only response was more Irish swearing. The phone stopped ringing and I let my eyes drift shut again but that's when the damn answering machine kicked on with an earsplitting beep.

"Fuck." Murphy's curse was muffled by the pillow.

"Constance," said someone familiar. We both scrambled up on our elbows, wildly shifted the covers and tried to get the phone before it disconnected.

Since the phone was closer to my side of the bed, I won the mad race and scooped it up, panting and out of breath.

"Hello, Councilor Allerton," I gasped into the phone while Murphy performed some sort of strange-looking war dance on the cold hardwood floors. I didn't feel much sympathy. I had told him to wear socks to bed and he had refused.

"Is there no frigging heat in his place?" He hopped from one foot to the other.

"Good morning, Constance, did I wake you?" Jason Allerton was a Councilor on the Great Pack's Council. The Council oversaw all of the packs spread out across the world. Murphy and I were his newest Advisors. He sent us on assignments to other packs to investigate accidents, murders and disputes that could not be worked out by the Regional Councils and other projects as he desired. So far, we'd only been on one assignment for him and that one had been unofficial, before we'd affiliated with Mac Tire—one of the largest, continuous packs in the world. They were based in Dublin, Ireland, but we had yet to go there. I'd only met two people from my new pack—Murphy and the Alpha male, Padraic O'Reilly. The rest were amorphous strangers I supposed I would eventually meet.

At the moment Murphy and I were in Boston, Massachusetts. I owned a condo and we were in the process of cleaning it, packing up the stuff I wanted to keep and getting it ready to act as rental property. When all this was accomplished, we would go to Belfast to clear out Murphy's cottage there before we went to Dublin to meet the rest of our pack.

After Councilor Allerton had asked us to be his Advisors, Murphy and I had been asked to join Mac Tire. In Murphy's case it was rejoin since he had been born into the pack and had left after the death of his bond mate, Sorcha, but it was a new pack for me.

Murphy had bought a car in Houston and we'd spent the past two months leisurely driving to the East Coast, stopping at all the major cities that interested us so we could sightsee. I'd seen more of my native country in the past two months than I had the previous thirty-two years of my life.

We'd arrived in Boston the day before New Year's Eve, so we'd barely even begun to tackle the condo. Murphy didn't want to be on a time table. He wanted us to go slowly and explore. I think he meant each other as well as the cities we visited. We'd been thrown together and bonded under extreme circumstances and now that the dust had settled and we were still standing, we had a lot of getting to know each other to do.

In the three months I'd known him, he'd rapidly become my best friend and confidante. My teacher and my guide.

After my first bond mates, Grey and Elena, had died in a car crash two and a half years ago, I'd been kicked out of my small pack in Connecticut. Although the Councils had cleared me, my pack had never stopped believing I had been drunk the night I drove that car over the embankment and my bond mates died.

It had been later proved that it was Grandfather Tobias, another member of my old pack, who had tampered with the brakes of my new Mustang. He was part of an underground movement made up of some of the oldest members of the Great Pack who resented the new ways we were adopting that brought us closer into interaction with the Others—those who were not Pack—and brought money and prestige into our packs by way of this involvement.

The new direction was integration, although not going as far as to reveal we were Pack and could shift into wolves. The old way was behind the scenes, on the fringes. Jobs in retail were common, but some of us were con artists or magicians as well. The trick was to avoid attention and interaction with the mainstream world as much as possible.

This movement saw to it that certain young Pack members, who flouted tradition, met with fatal accidents. It was meant to scare us, stop the flow of revenue and destroy the ones with the closest ties to the Others.

Murphy and I, with Councilor Allerton's assistance, had discovered and unmasked this movement. We had not stopped it because it could not be halted simply by announcing to the Pack it existed. That would have caused chaos and panic. They had to be stopped one and two at a time—quiet arrests and detainment.

We'd barely scratched the surface and I knew a lot of work was yet to be done, but after what we'd gone through in Paris and Houston, I wasn't sure I had the stomach for it.

This was the other reason for the long road trip—it was a chance to regroup and get myself together.

Allerton had checked in on us a few times along the way, but I wondered if this phone call heralded the end of the vacation and was a wake-up call in more than one sense of the word.

However, his next sentence blasted everything out of my mind.

"We've arrested Tobias Green and he's confessed."

Murphy stopped hopping and swearing when I pulled out the desk chair and fell into it. My legs felt hollow, as if all the bones had melted.

Tobias Green. I called him Grandfather Tobias. I'd loved and respected him. I'd looked after him more than anyone else in my pack and, although I'd had a sense of duty because he was old, I'd done it more out of genuine love. He was not my blood grandfather, but he might as well have been. I loved him that much.

Ever since that moment in Houston when I'd realized the grandmother in Paris had deliberately put a lethal overdose of narcotics in the homemade pill she'd given Murphy, it was an easy, yet devastating, intuitive jump to understand that Grandfather Tobias was guilty of killing my bond mates. Once we'd uncovered the grandmothers' and grandfathers' plot, it had been horrifyingly clear he'd done something to the car. I'd brought it to him that afternoon and he'd gone beneath it to inspect it because he was a mechanic and he told me he wanted to see for himself that his dear girl and her bond mates were in a safe, reliable vehicle. Yet he'd tampered with the brakes so they'd fail and I'd lose control.

Without being able to prevent it, I flashed back to the accident.

* * * *

"The Comet or Blue Moon, Grey? Which club do you want to go to?"

I see Grey laughing in the dashboard lights as he fiddles with the CD player. Depeche Mode's Strange Love morphs into Billy Idol's White Wedding. Grey has an addiction to eighties music. Sometimes I find it endearing. Sometimes I find it annoying as hell.

"I don't care. It's your birthday, Stanzie. You choose. The Comet or Blue Moon, it doesn't matter to me." He turns his head to smile at me. The love he feels for me is written all over his face. His shaggy, dark hair falls into his blue eyes. He's got the back part confined in a rubber band. When it's loose, his hair brushes his shoulders. Right now it's about two inches longer than mine. I'm experimenting with a bob. I'm not sure I like it.

He needs a haircut. He has an appointment on Monday. I wrote it on the erasable calendar stuck to our fridge. I made it for him yesterday.

"Elena?" I glance into the rearview mirror to see her beautiful face. She is putting on eyeliner and her bright red purse is open on the seat beside her—a compact in one hand, the eyeliner stick in the other. She frowns at her reflection, with concentration, not because she finds fault with her appearance.

"Oh, you know I don't care, I just want to dance with you, Birthday Girl."

The Comet is closer and I have a sudden desire to be out of the car. I want to feel the summer breeze and hear my new metallic gold stiletto heels click against the soft, warm pavement of the August night. I want to hear music from this decade. I want to dance, to feel Grey's hands on my hips as we move together beneath the strobe lights and Elena guards our drinks at the table.

I make a decision. I take the exit. The road climbs over a small crest then dips sharply. I brake because we've been traveling at seventy miles an hour and now we need to slow down. We'll still be above the legal speed limit, but this is a Mustang GT, metallic gold like my stiletto heels, with an ink-black leather interior. My dream car is a present from Elena who has just signed a lucrative contract with a company that develops PC games. Elena is a whiz at designing games. We have six different PCs and laptops set up in our house in New Britain and she is always perched in front of one of them, sucking absently on her bottom lip as she contemplates the scenarios in front of her on the screen.

Yesterday she made an important deliverable to the company and they extended her contract for another game, this one even more ambitious— about werewolves. It is slated for tentative release October of 2010, which is two years and two months into the future.

I put my foot on the brake, but it doesn't seem like we decelerate. Confused, I press harder then we hit the dip and I see a shadow or a bird or something that distracts me then the wheel is a traitor beneath my hands. Elena screams in the backseat as the guardrail looms closer.

I have time to think to myself, This is just a dream. This is not happening. This is not—

The Mustang's front end smashes into the guardrail with a terrific bang. It crumples with a metallic grinding and tearing. The engine screams in protest.

"Stanzie!" Elena shrieks. Grey is stiff and terrified beside me. The whole car reeks of our extreme fear. It pours out of our skins like invisible sweat and the mad stink of it paralyzes my muscles and vocal cords. I am a mute statue. I cannot even blink.

As Billy Idol sings the Mustang turns up and over. Wind rushes in when Grey's door flies open. I see a blur of movement when he falls out and my paralysis breaks. I reach out for him, but the airbag hits me in the face and something hard smashes the back of my seat. Elena stops screaming. She stops screaming because her neck breaks under the force of her body slamming into the back of my seat. She, like Grey, never wears a seatbelt.

* * * *

Pressure brought me out of my trance. Murphy squeezed my shoulder reassuringly.

Allerton said my name, probably not for the first time.

The car crash was so vivid in my head I could still hear Elena's screams and the jagged sound of tearing metal.

"I'm here." I swallowed an obstruction in my throat. It was two and a half years ago. It was time to let go and get over it.

I'd been doing a good job of that, thanks to Murphy, but one sentence made me realize that maybe I would never truly be free. It was not a pleasant thought.

"I'm sorry if I've upset you." Allerton's voice was rich with sympathy. I visualized his handsome, distinguished face and his dark black hair he wore as fashionably cut as his designer suits. "I thought you should know. There's something else as well."

My stomach sank even though I had no idea what the something else could be, only that it wouldn't be good.

"He wants to speak to you. Privately."

My mouth dropped open in protest. Sick bile burned my throat and I must have twisted in my seat because Murphy put both hands on my shoulders. I was absurdly grateful for his touch.

With his Pack-enhanced senses, he could hear what Allerton said, and he could smell my distress. I know I reeked of it.

"Do I have to?" Tears clogged my sinuses and, if not for Murphy, I would have been bawling like a baby, I knew it.

"Of course not," said Allerton at once, and there was just a tinge of disappointment in his voice that I strove to ignore, but it was impossible. Damn him. Damn me for wanting to please him because he was a Councilor.

"Where is he?"

"He's being held in the safe house in Hartford. I'm here with him, along with one of the Regional Councilors. Riverglow is not being told the whole story. Just that he confessed to doing it not why."

Riverglow was the name of my former pack—Jonathan, Nora, Callie, Vaughn and Peter.

"Aren't they even curious?" I couldn't disguise the bitterness in my voice.

"He's saying he accidentally put a hole in the brake lining, causing the brake fluid to leak out, and he realized it when he went over the car after the accident but was too ashamed to admit it."

"An accident? And do they believe it?" My voice shook with outrage. "They didn't believe me. Are they going to believe him?"

"Constance, he had to say something. We need to keep the knowledge that people in the Pack are murdering others under wraps. He can't tell them the truth." Allerton was sympathetic but firm. "And you can ask them yourself what they believe if you come to Connecticut. They want to see you too."

I wanted to throw the phone into the wall and stomp on it. I wanted to spit in Allerton's arrogant face. What I didn't want was to ever see any of my former pack again—especially Grandfather Tobias.

"How am I supposed to face them? How am I supposed to look Grandfather Tobias in the eye after what he did to Grey and Elena? To me!" It was disrespectful to say the least to shout at a Councilor, but I rarely paused to think before I reacted. Allerton took my tirade in patient silence which is what made me stop shouting. My cheeks burned with humiliation.

"I'm not telling you what to do, Constance. I'm giving you the opportunity to hear the man out. It might provide some closure." He didn't say it, but I knew damn well he thought I could use a huge, heaping dose of it.

I squeezed my eyes shut and heard Elena screaming in my head again.

"When do I have to be there?"

"As soon as you can make it." Allerton paused then said, "He's not going back to Riverglow. The Council will acknowledge his cover story and accept it, but he won't return to the pack. He's going to go to sleep one night very soon and he's not going to wake up. If you want, you can hand him a glass of warm milk or hot chocolate to help him go to sleep. If you want." Allerton's tone was deceptively nonchalant but what he offered was the chance to administer the fatal poison. That would be closure for sure.

I didn't answer because I couldn't. A part of me wanted to kill that old man, not with poison, but with my claws and fangs—in wolf form. I didn't know if I could be such a civilized murderer. Or maybe executioner was a better word.

"Can I speak to Liam, please?"

I thrust the phone at Murphy and he took it, but when I tried to get up, he frowned at me.

"I want to take a shower." I had to get out of the room and away from the phone and Allerton and the sound of Elena screaming.

His dark gaze searched my face for a moment before he let go of my shoulder. He watched me as I stumbled for the bathroom. He acknowledged Allerton then went grimly silent as he listened. I smelled the anger that escaped from his pores and clouded the air around him—protective anger.